A SOUND OF SWANS FLYING

by

Lucille and James Horner

ISBN: 9798866414932

All rights reserved. No part of this publication may be reproduced, stored in a retrieval system, or transmitted, in any form or by any means, electronic, mechanical, photocopying, recording or otherwise, without the prior permission of the publishers and the author.

This book is sold subject to the condition that it shall not, by way of trade or otherwise, be lent, re-sold, hired out or otherwise circulated without the publisher's and the author's prior consent in any form of binding or cover other than that in which it is published and without a similar condition including this condition being imposed on the subsequent purchaser.

SYNOPSIS

Historical novel. Two families, one English and one South African, encounter the enigma that is South Africa.

DISCLAIMER

This is a work of fiction. The story, the incidents described and the names of persons in the dramatis personae all originated in the writer's mind and are not based on actual people or events. Any resemblance of the fictional characters in this fiction to persons living or dead is purely coincidental. Opinions expressed by the fictional characters are the opinions of the fictitious characters, *not the opinions of the author.*

BOOK ONE

NO SUCH LAUREATE EARTH?

CHAPTERS

1. Vygie.

2. Monika.

3. One Half So Precious.

4. Nocturne For Those Never Born.

CHAPTER ONE

VYGIE

by

Lucille Horner

For

Oscar

DRAMATIS **PERSONAE**

BELT THE REVEREND	Missionary, acquaintance of Henry 'Graph' Middler
MIDDLER HENRY ('GRAPH') 1883 TO 1961	Father of Natalie. Nicknamed 'Graph' for his fascination with telegraphs and communications generally. Of Scottish descent.
MIDDLER HESTER (nee CALITZ) 1900 TO 1979	Mother of Natalie. Plattelander (i.e. a lady who spent her entire life on the veld or living in 'dorps') (villages). Ultra conservative without knowing it. Of Dutch descent.
MIDDLER ANASTASIA	Eldest daughter of Henry and Hester
MIDDLER BELINDA	Second daughter of Henry and Hester
MIDDLER CHARLENE	Third daughter of Henry and Hester
MIDDLER NATALIE	Fourth daughter of Henry and Hester
MIDDLERS, OTHER CHILDREN	Delaine, Yvette, Frederic, Gavin and Garth
VAN MIDDEL LEONARD (LEN) 1881 TO 1957	Slave descendant. Man-servant to the Middler family. Of mixed Malay, Bushman, Hottentot and European blood.
VAN MIDDEL NAANIE 1881 TO 1961	Wife of Len. Slave descendant. Maid-servant to the Middler family. Of mixed Malay, Hottentot and European blood.

1918 TO 1933 OUDTSHOORN, CAPE PROVINCE,

UNION OF SOUTH AFRICA

VYGIE (Afrikaans for Mesembryanthemum)

"Dis 'n mooi meisiekind, mies," ("It's a pretty girl-child, madam,") Naanie said as she placed the tiny being on the receiving blanket.

The night's labour had been long. But with first light supplementing the lantern's glimmer, Naanie, servant and midwife, made steady progress.

"Nie te lank nou nie," ("Not too long now,") she said over her shoulder to the newly-delivered mother.

Hester listened to her child's intense cries.

The midwife, no stranger to the exigencies of childbirth, remained engrossed in detail. Concentrating intently, she severed the umbilical cord. The minutes ticked by.

Hester longed to cradle her baby. In that haze of loveliness which attends the beginning of life, exhausted, damp-haired, she summoned energy and raised herself on the pillows.

Naanie, a smile of satisfaction on her prematurely-wrinkled Hottentot-

Malay face, gathered up the new-born and lowered her into her mistress's arms. "Baie mooi!" ("Very pretty,") she said.

"Hallo, Natalie," Hester said.

Natalie, the wild rose, quick in thought and limb, was the fourth daughter. She had five sisters and three brothers. By virtue, it seemed to her, of the order of their birth, her brothers and sisters always attracted more parental attention than herself.

To compensate for parental preoccupation, Natalie resorted, early in life, to grand gestures and shock tactics. But this response, instead of bringing the recognition she sought, earned the disapproval of her siblings.

"Agh, Natalie's such a show-off," Charlene, the third-eldest sister, would remark.

"She needs to be taught *manners*," Belinda, the second-eldest, agreed.

Yet, beyond her immediate family, Natalie, even in her very early years, had friends. Her protection of the underdog, her loyalty in adversity, her flashes of insight and merriment, all were qualities that earned trust, made her one in whom the worried and sad chose to confide. Those who knew her well were drawn to a part of her being seldom seen by her family, an attractive world of inner peace in which, away from sibling rivalry, she was able richly to give and richly receive.

Loving her as they did, Natalie's friends accepted her eccentricities and defended her from her deep anxieties. Profoundly aware, the mothers in the neighbourhood discussed her attributes.

"Die kind het 'n spesiale intelligensie," ("That child has a special intelligence,") one would say.

"Ander stel haar uit," ("Others defer to her,") another would agree.

"Maar ek kyk met ontsteltenis," ("But I watch with dismay,") a third would add, "Sy is so soet en kwesbaar dat sy soms gewond raak deur die spontaniteit van haar eie persoonlikheid." ("She is *so* sweet and vulnerable that she's sometimes wounded by the spontaneity of her own personality.")

"Ons mense het 'n plig om sterk te word in ons wereld," ("Our people have a duty to grow up strong in our world,") a fourth would comment disapprovingly. "Ons s'n is nie 'n wereld waarin swakheid geduld kan word nie." ("Ours is not a world in which weakness can be tolerated.")

Whatever parents and siblings might think, Natalie believed in the openness of her own heart. "I must always be kind to people, no matter what happens," she often said to herself. "I must be *the best*."

In her small home town of Oudtshoorn in The Cape Province, the name given at Union in 1910 to the country formerly known as The Cape of Good Hope Colony, Natalie Middler set about proving and improving herself.

"You're a thinker, aren't you Natalie," her father, Henry 'Graph' Middler, would sometimes say. He looked kindly on the struggles rather too deep for one so young. "My Vygie," he used his pet name for her, "is always on the lookout for fine things of the mind. And for greatness of the heart. Isn't she?"

Natalie longed to rise above the taunts of siblings, to demonstrate self-sufficiency. "I must be able not just to stand alone," she would say to herself, "but to do so in a *friendly* way that earns respect."

But her youthful efforts met with scant success. Busy parents left the child largely to her own devices. The world of the nineteen thirties, having great things on its mind, ignored her flamboyance. Natalie used the vacuum to further her quest.

"*Youth* is even briefer than *Life,*" she said to a school friend. "We *must* use every minute. We *must* find things we *really* want to do. We must *search*."

Music was part of this search. She went to the Norwegian, Mrs Haugen, for piano lessons.

"Agh, Natalie can't hear anything else when she's playing the piano," Belinda complained waspishly.

"You're right," Charlene agreed. "You think she's ignoring you. But she isn't really. She just doesn't answer you because her tiny skull is full of sound."

Natalie spent many hours at the piano in the lounge. And on Thursday afternoons at the neighbouring church, unobserved in the semi-darkness of the pews, she listened to the organist practising. If she happened to hear the servants rehearsing for their choral competitions, she wandered off to their quarters to listen. There were some Saturdays when their singing lasted all afternoon and half the night.

One evening, Graph was reading his newspaper while Natalie played his gramophone. "People," she said to her father, "have strong feelings about music."

"People hold surprisingly strong views about many things," Graph replied looking at her over the top of the page. "Music is an expression of culture."

For the most part Natalie kept her search for self-confidence to herself. Exploration was a painful loneliness but self-censorship brought dividends. Her father was her confidante.

"Listening to music is like reading a book, isn't it Daddy?" she asked. "You have to listen to each note like you have to understand each word of a book."

"Yes, I suppose you do," Graph looked at her, intrigued.

"People think about their feelings when they listen to music, don't they?"

"Yes, I suppose they do," Graph agreed once more.

"And, often when they listen to music they're longing for something to happen, aren't they, Daddy. Or they're feeling sad about the past."

"Yes. Thinking sadly about good things that happened in the past is called 'nostalgia'. Do you know that word, Vygie? Nostalgia. It's a good one to know."

"Oh, well, everyone has something to be sad about," Natalie said.

"Yes, I suppose they do," Graph agreed once more, wondering at the conversation.

"But it's not always good to talk about things you love, is it Daddy?"

"Well……," Graph replied slowly, "it's important always to think about the consequences of your words."

"Daddy, please may I have a gramophone for my birthday?" she asked.

"Whatever for?" Graph asked. "Isn't mine good enough for you? You use it often enough. You've been listening to my Mozart all afternoon."

"Yours needs a new needle," she said.

"Len," Naanie alerted her husband, "hier kom nou weer die meisietjie." ("Len, here comes the little girl again.") It was 1927. Leonard van Middel, in his forties, was of similar racial mix to his wife. Both had wizened faces and woolly hair.

It was unusual for any white person, let alone a nine year old girl, to enter the sparse world of the servants' quarters. But Natalie, with her flowing black hair, finely embroidered dresses and Roman nose, had been visiting for some time. The desert-yellow of the servants' dwellings contrasted sharply with the greenery of the master's well-appointed house. Natalie had grown up with the contrast. She did not notice it. Drawn to local music, she turned the corner once more into the servant world of dust and iron and searing heat. She had come to listen.

At the same moment, a few yards away in the lounge of the master's house, Graph found himself on the defensive in a political discussion with a missionary newly arrived from England. "No doubt," Graph said to The Reverend Belt, "social injustices exist in South Africa, as they do in every corner of the world. But in the household of Henry 'Graph' Middler unkindness is banned. Acceptance of racial differences isn't just second-nature to my family, it's ingrained. In fact we delight in these things. And the delight is reciprocated. Especially by our servants. But not only by our servants. In fact, all who know us are aware of our ways. Mind you, there is of course a limit to our mixing. And, as you may imagine, there are many amongst our own people who think us too friendly with the blacks. To put it mildly."

"Well, howsoever you make your case," The Reverend Belt said testily, "your family must be an exception that proves the rule."

"My family is *not* a rarity," Graph felt his patience tested. "There are countless families like us. Of course regrettable lapses *do* occur," he admitted, "but in our home, family and servants alike hold, for the most part, to the fair-minded example set by my forebears. There is seldom discord. Respect is under-written.........By me. In fact the mutual interest in our divergence is a dynamo. It lends us a kind of energy. I try to foresee trouble and take steps to prevent conflict. My wish is to make life pleasant. For everyone. Wherever possible."

"Compared to your good-humoured and long-suffering servants," said The Reverend Belt, "you're a rich man. You have education, land and money. In these things your servants can never hope to compete with you and the truth is that in the economic and political circumstances of South Africa they have little choice but to defer to you."

"South Africa is no different to other countries," Graph replied. "The servants are free to leave us if they don't like us. For generations, the forebears of my servants were slaves in the service of my family. When the British outlawed slavery, the slaves were bemused. They had nowhere to go with their new-found freedom, little to offer. Their skills were limited to the menial work of slaves. They'd been slaves for generations. There'd never been any contact with the Dutch East Indies from which some of their ancestors had been pressed into slavery. There'd been generations of racial inter-mixing and at times, complete social breakdown. In reality their origins were beyond their ken. My ancestor, Charles Middler, the head of the family at the time of emancipation was not an unkind man. When he told his slaves they were free to go and that he couldn't afford to pay them, they asked to be allowed to stay. And he agreed. And when life at The Cape improved, my family began to pay wages to their freed slaves. Generation followed generation. A natural order of existence stood and was understood. Lives were closely shared. Acknowledgement by Middlers and Van Middels of births, christenings, marriages and funerals ran parallel to a clear divide of race and status. The world set the parameters, the families conformed."

"Maybe," said The Reverend Belt. "But I *cannot* believe that what you describe is real freedom. I don't believe the black people of South Africa are free."

"May I ask?" Graph's ire rose and he became confrontational, "Do *you* give your Christian converts freedom to leave your flock? No! You threaten them with eternal damnation if they don't follow your Christian teachings. That's the freedom you espouse."

The Reverend Belt scoffed his outrage.

"In fact Van Middel, the family name of the servants, is simply an adoptive form of Middler," Graph added tenaciously.

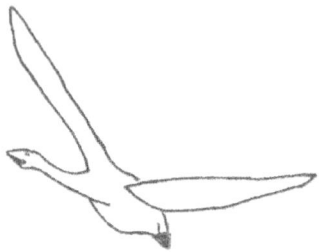

So, on that Saturday afternoon in 1927, Len Van Middel was seated in his usual Saturday afternoon place, on a rickety chair in a shady but bare-earthed corner of the quadrangle enclosed by the drab servants' quarters. And as usual, he was passing the time singing a song of his own composition on a lute of his own making.

"Hallo," Natalie said, greeting Naanie, her gathering of female friends and their pastorale of mixed-race children as she turned the corner into the quadrangle. Natalie was too young to understand that by visiting the servants she was once again breaching invisible divides. It never occurred to her to contrast her middle-class life with the relative penury of the servants. The racial divide did not alarm her. She had always known the disparities. But the bare-footed coloured children suspended their play for a few long moments and stood looking at her. Unconcerned, her polished black shoes shining in the sunlight, Natalie seated herself cross-legged before Len on the hard earth. She leaned her chin on her palms and watched attentively as Len sang and played. By her silent, attentive audience, the child often managed to strike an affinity with musicians, wherever the place, whatever the genre of music.

Len's status as a man-servant was no barrier to this special relationship.

Seeing the young mistress come innocently once more to listen to his songs, Len smiled at her but did not interrupt his playing. He was rewarded with a tiny smile in return. From his plain, clean family space, he now played for the sunlit child in the spotless white dress seated on the bare ground before him. Involuntarily his artistry took on fine precision. It was a long song.

Struck by Natalie's interest, Len briefly contemplated asking if the child could accompany Naanie and himself to choir practices at their church in the location. But the idea was instantly dismissed as unthinkable.

"Naanie, please may I have something to drink," Natalie asked when Len's song ended. Before Naanie could respond she continued, "Leonard, please sing us another song. Sing vir ons die een van '*die volstruis en haar eiers*'," ("Sing us the one about '*the ostrich and her eggs'"*). Natalie's unaffected directing of servants, even in their own quarters, was accepted without question. It was inoffensive, the more so since Natalie was so accustomed to their ways, so young, so natural with them. It was how things had always been. Were it not for generations of trust between the Middlers and the Van Middels, ugly connotations of suspicion might have arisen. The servants might have feared outrage. *"A white girl-child alone in the servants quarters?" "Nooit!" ("Never!")* But this was the Middler family. All present were at ease, a matter faultless and remarkable.

Political sparring between Graph and The Reverend Belt continued in the lounge of the big house. "In some ways," Graph said, "our families make better neighbours than do families living in the terraced rows of your English cities. We've the advantage of almost limitless space. England is so crowded. Yet, in a way, we're closer because we depend on one another rather than on institutions and the state. It's an impact of geography on the state of mind. For example, Naanie van Middel was midwife at the birth of all my children. Neither family," Graph continued "give thought to any other way of living. We're all happy. Trouble-makers are few. The racial divide is merely part of the order and decorum of it all. Native South Africans of every colour, up and down the country, recognise the pattern. Households of the Middler kind are not some ubiquitous imperial harmony. But, in South Africa, they're an everyday occurrence."

Down in the servants' quadrangle, Len began the song about the ostrich and her egg. Natalie listened with the solemnity of the very young. She was a child of many dreams. But at that moment in the refined long-gone peace of 1927 the sweetly brocaded nine-year old could not for a moment have imagined that eight decades hence she would still summon up Len's music of the desert. She would still hear his song from that long-gone afternoon, wonder at its loss, wonder at the complete overturning of the world into which they had all been born.

Naanie went momentarily into the dark interior of her house and re-emerged wearing servants cap and apron. "Ek gaan maar net a bietjie Webb's lemonade kry," ("I am going to fetch some Webb's lemonade,") she said to Len and her friends. "Wil jy 'n koekie hê Nattie?" ("Would you like a biscuit, Nattie?")

"Yes please, Naanie," Natalie replied in the matter-of-fact, ultra-polite manner of her upbringing and class.

Bidding farewell at the front gate, the conversation between Graph and The Reverend Belt had moved to languages. "We're all bilingual," Graph said. "Both families mix English and Afrikaans in everyday speech, as the subject and tenor require."

"Oh? I thought your wife spoke *Dutch*," said The Reverend Belt. "And that *Afrikaans* was for those Boer types who live in remote districts and are even *more* out of touch with civilisation."

"No, *we're* probably culturally more Afrikaans by nature, I think," said Graph sensing in The Reverend Belt the common English antipathy towards Boers. "Our family ancestry is English, Scottish, Dutch, German and French in more or less equal parts. But we hold the birth of our new language as a serious matter. We think Afrikaans should be an official language of the state."

"I see," The Reverend Belt replied. "I should think Dutch is a higher language and culture than Afrikaans though, shouldn't you?"

Graph bristled. But, he kept Hester in mind. She would be displeased if he fell out with any minister of religion. Moreover, Graph's experience made him shy away from conversations about Dutch and Afrikaans, colonist and republican. He knew such talk easily drifted into contentious matters such as demographics and The Boer War. He tried for a simple way out. "Well, there is Afrikaans and then there is Afrikaans," he said. "For example, the Afrikaans of the Van Middels is not quite the same as ours. When it comes to my family it happens that sometimes Afrikaans provides an idiom which serves the moment, sometimes English more nearly expresses a concept. This mixing of languages is, in our case, marital and geographic, not hierarchical. Variations in origin and education cause variations in vocabulary. Out of kindness, Hester usually speaks to me in English which is my home language and I usually speak to her in Afrikaans which is her home language. Mind you, perhaps she still thinks of her home language as Dutch, I'm not sure. But for the most part, the conversation will continue in the language in which it began. We think of our shared languages as a kind of wealth.

"Do you?" The Reverend Belt said looking at his pocket watch and not disguising an air of superior impatience. "I must be off."

"Drop in for coffee any time," Graph said. They shook hands. "You'll find dropping-in the norm in South Africa. We don't wait for invitations. As you do in England. We *expect* folk just to drop in. You'll see. You'll always be welcome. It's the frontier mentality. Born of insecurity."

Working on a Saturday afternoon?" Graph asked a few moments later when Naanie let herself into the kitchen. "Have you seen Nattie?" he continued without waiting for her answer. "The child's disappeared again."

"No, Baas (Boss)," Naanie replied in her deep Cape Coloured accent, "the child is safe. She is visiting us. So I've come to pour her a juice and fetch her a biscuit."

"Oh!" Graph said. He stopped in amused perplexity, his forehead wrinkling. "She's visiting you," he said kindly. "Of course." It was a revelation. Scratching his balding pate he exchanged a few thoughts with Naanie about the orchard, the egg-gathering and the biltong.

Graph allowed a good three quarters of an hour to pass before he went to the servants' area.

"Hallo Leonard. Just come to check on my daughter," he said as he approached.

The coloured children stopped their playing once more and stood staring.

Even the adults were silent now, listening, taking note.

"Afternoon Baas," Len said. "She is fine." He gestured at Natalie as he arose in greeting.

Natalie jumped up instantly and climbed into the adored and adoring arms of her father.

"And what're you up to, my child?" Graph asked lovingly but with a hint of concern.

Len was standing now.

"I'm listening to Leonard, Daddy. He plays *such* lovely songs. He makes them up *all* by himself, you know. And *he* made his guitar. Please stay and listen."

"Well……ummm," Graph began.

"*Please,* Daddy," the child implored.

"Well……….ummmm…………but ………. But maybe Leonard doesn't feel like singing to us……………," Graph countered. As he spoke, Naanie placed an old dining-room chair next to him. Graph recognised the chair as one long since discarded by Hester.

The chair was rickety. Graph seated himself gingerly. A line of laundry hung to one side. The courtyard gave off smells of wood-smoke, fresh and stale. Len took up his rough-hewn instrument. He tuned it for a moment or two before striking the opening notes of his next song. Natalie climbed onto her father's knee.

It was a long song in a vernacular of English and Afrikaans. Occasional Hottentot or Xhosa words and click sounds were interspersed. Graph roughly followed its ancient tale of Bushmen rustlers attacking Hottentot kraals (homesteads), committing murder and being driven off. In time the crimes were avenged when Bushmen died under the poisoned arrows of the Hottentots.

Coloured children stopped playing and came to sit on the ground around Graph and Natalie. Len felt his musical skill pushed to the limit. His audience had grown unexpectedly large and attentive. Even Naanie's friends, the mothers and fathers of the assembled children, stopped their conversations to watch.

Another song followed about a harvest damaged by fire and about the effect on the harvesters of 'burnt wine'. And then another about tribes and clans, about Xhosa, Sotho, Fingo, Pondo, Thembo, Griqua and white men, about the wildness of the desert and the unimaginable splendour of distant Cape Town which very few of those present had seen, and about the ocean which too was mere hearsay to most of that company. Lastly Len sang of wild animals attacking livestock. And of slaughtering for ceremonies and feasts.

From her seat on Graph's knee, Natalie followed Len's songs avidly, as did everyone else now "die baas" (the boss) had come to listen. It was the music of those in whose company Natalie had come to consciousness and whose conversation she had always known. To her the genre was not new. Her fresh mind, versed in the folklore, was open to it all.

But Graph, interested though he could not help being, secretly thought it all inferior. "Oh Lord," he said to himself, "there are so *many* things demanding my attention and I must sit here."

Concealing his longing to leave and wondering how he might extricate himself and his daughter in a way that seemed natural, Graph stayed on. He must humour his child and defer to 'the labour'. "What a primitive jingle-jangle this music is," he said to himself. He had lived much longer than his sweet daughter, seen more, knew the ropes and pitfalls. There was a status to maintain. He felt uncomfortable with this level of fraternisation, did not wish to set any precedent.

Soon enough, at exactly the right moment, Graph did leave. Taking great care that it was not too soon, he watched for a natural interval. When one came he arose, courteously thanked Len and Naanie for their hospitality, nodded to the gathering, and, daughter in hand, disappeared around that same corner by which he had arrived. A few steps and he was back home in his grand house.

After that day Natalie's visits to hear Len playing dwindled. But they did not altogether cease. And after a period of reflection, they became frequent once more. Yet as she returned to the music of the dusty courtyard, an awareness of social divides formed. Her father's attitudes continuously highlighted the loneliness of the white elite. She glimpsed complexities of birth. And there were her father's words. *"Never* forget, Vygie, you're a *white* girl. You *have* to *be* the better person you are. *All* white people must be. You can *never* allow standards to slip. *No* white person can."

This formidable insistence on obligations that came with being born white brought passages from her favourite book to Natalie's mind. The book, a birthday present from Graph, was Sir Percy Fitzpatrick's 'Jock of The Bushveld.'

"Like Sir Percy Fitzpatrick wrote," Natalie said.

"Yes. Just like Sir Percy wrote," Graph agreed.

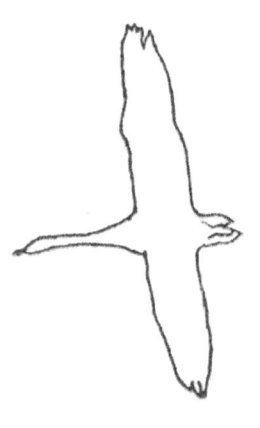

Natalie picked up her copy of 'Jock of The Bushveld', squeezed herself into Graph's armchair beside him and ran her finger lovingly over the marginal illustrations. "How many times have you read that book, Vygie?" Graph asked.

"Many times," she answered wistfully. "I almost know the first page off by heart."

"Ah yes!" Graph understood at once. "Those first pages go to the heart of loneliness. Such compelling writing."

"Daddy," she asked, touching a picture of a shield and assegai, "is Zululand a separate colony?"

"No," Graph answered, "it used to be, but it was annexed to Natal many years ago."

"What does annexed mean?" she asked.

"Sort of joined up and taken over," he replied.

"Why was it annexed?" she asked. Her concern was unmistakable.

"Who knows?" Graph answered. "Cost-saving, I expect. These things normally are. But why," he noted her disquiet, "does it trouble you?"

"Sir Percy liked the Zulus, don't you think, Daddy?" she asked by way of an answer.

"He certainly did," Graph answered with an uncertain smile. "Especially he liked his drunken savage of a manservant, one Jim Makokela, of whom you've no doubt been reading," Graph looked closely at his daughter.

"Oh, Jim was such a *funny* native," Natalie enthused. "I *especially* like the way Jim didn't like Sam because Sam read the bible. Don't you *love* him, Daddy?"

Graph laughed. "Jim didn't like any black man who wasn't a Zulu," he said. "Perhaps not being a Zulu was, to Jim's mind, Sam's major shortcoming."

"But isn't it terrible," Natalie lamented, "how Jim said he'd kill Sir Percy if the Zulu king ordered him to. And he said it at the very same time he said he knew Sir Percy had saved him and been a good boss."

"Oh yes," Graph agreed. "Jim Makokela *is* amusing. But he's also tangible evidence that the Zulu fighting spirit is very much alive. Even though we subdued the Zulus such a long time ago, they would, given half a chance, still be happy to kill every white man and every animal that we own, and burn down all our houses.

They're savages! Jim Makokela and his tribe are the epitome of everything that civilization'll always have to worry about. But……….."Graph pulled himself up, "you're too young to worry about all that." Looking at Natalie, he stroked her hair, reflecting with pleasure on the depth of her responses to the written word. Natalie's young mind had obviously been contemplating the enormity of the threat.

"So how can we be friends with the Zulus if they want to kill us?" she asked.

Graph stared at his daughter. "We must offer them friendship but be always on guard," he replied.

"Perhaps we should give them back Zululand as their own place?" she suggested. "Then they wouldn't need to kill everybody else because they'd have a place of their own?"

"Good heavens, Vygie! That book has really worried you, hasn't it?" Graph gathered her in for a hug. "I don't really have answers to your questions, my child. All I can say is if we all always do our very best, then that's all we can do. And," he embraced her, "*I'll* always look after you. So you needn't worry about it, my girl."

Graph thought for a moment. "And in a way, we *have* given them their own land, haven't we? That's what the tribal reserves are, aren't they?"

"Sir Percy Fitzpatrick loved the veld in a special way, didn't he daddy?" Natalie persevered.

"Well, yes," Graph hesitated. "In 'Jock of The Bushveld' he certainly loved the lands he passed through ………….. But in the other books he wrote, you see other things…….you see ….. a different Sir Percy."

"What other things?" Natalie asked.

"Well…. for instance," Graph suggested, "in his book 'The Transvaal From Within', you may, with hindsight, question his reasoning………. But……… you're still too young to read that. It's too political and difficult for you."

"Well," said Natalie, "Sir Percy thinks we all have to be very clever and very kind and very brave and very strong if we are to stay in charge. Except. He doesn't actually say that. But you know that's what he means."

Kindness was not the response when the older sisters learnt Natalie had again been a guest in the servants' quarters. Anastasia, Belinda and Charlene Middler seized on a moment when the adults were out shopping, to deride Natalie's non-conformity.

They cornered Natalie in her bedroom. "So," Anastasia began the amusement. "You've been visiting the servants again!"

"Even though we've told you *not* to," Belinda added forcefully.

"Don't you know your place?" Charlene smirked. The surprised Natalie, in silent terror, held close the cloth doll she had never really outgrown. Wide-eyed, she stared up at the towering aggressors.

"What colour are you?" Belinda demanded haughtily, pressing home the attack. Natalie puzzled over their words.

"What is the colour of your skin?" Belinda insisted.

Natalie stared at Belinda. "White," came an almost inaudible, uncomprehending reply.

"And what colour are the servants?" Belinda sneered.

"They are coloured," Natalie said in pale terror. She would have preferred to remain silent but she feared physical aggression if she said nothing.

"White people don't mix with coloureds or blacks, do you hear?" Belinda bent forwards. Face to face with Natalie, her eyes drilled menacingly into Natalie's eyes.

"Do you hear?" Belinda repeated, raising her voice.

"Yes," Natalie answered, overawed.

"*What* do you think you were doing there?" the intimidating Charlene demanded. "Who do you think you are? Who do you think *we* are that we'd allow a sister of ours to go *there*?"

"I was listening to Len's playing and singing," Natalie answered with a sudden lift in her voice as she became tearfully, fatalistically defiant. This was not the first time she had been subjected to sibling pressure. And yet it always came as a surprise. She would have to learn to be prepared for it.

"Well, you're *not* to go there, see," Belinda commanded as she took hold of Natalie's arm and began twisting. Natalie erupted in all-out resistance shouting, crying, kicking, biting and calling for help.

For some minutes, pinned down, she was roughly handled by Belinda and Charlene.

Anastasia's young brow furrowed. Her stomach muscles tightened. She suddenly re-evaluated the circumstances. Fearing parental disapproval she called a halt to the bullying. She doubted Belinda's motives and was shocked at Charlene's intensity. She had not meant an amusement to turn so nasty and wondered how she would reply if Graph learnt of the episode. As eldest, she had, after all, been in loco parentis.

"*Okay, stop this!*" she said in a loud voice.

"Belinda, that is *wreed! (cruel)!*" she insisted.

"Charlene, *hou op! (stop it!)*"

"Natalie needs to be taught a lesson," Belinda answered venomously.

 "Yes, she *definitely* does," Charlene agreed.

"Yes, But daddy left me in charge and now you've *hurt* her," Anastasia said determinedly. She looked apprehensively at Natalie huddled in the corner of her room, holding a bruised arm. "What am I going to say to daddy about this?"

Natalie, trembling violently and overwhelmed by tears, remained defiant. "I'm going to tell daddy everything. *Everything*," she sobbed and shouted at the same time.

Charlene raised a fist to pummel Natalie again but Anastasia caught the raised arm and screamed at her, *"Charlene, stop it! Now!"*

That night, in the lounge, Graph did notice the bruising on Natalie's arm.

"Goodness, what've you *done to your arm,* Vygie?" he asked. He walked over to her, lifted her arm and studied the blue and black patches.

Noticing Natalie was fearful and how she winced in pain, Graph persevered. "Tell me," he gently demanded, looking into her face, an eyebrow raised.

The full truth came out.

"Come with me, the four of you," he led the girls into the privacy of his office.

Belinda, Charlene and Natalie standing by, Graph rebuked Anastasia.

"I expected more from *you*, Anastasia," he said acidly. "You're old enough to understand. I trusted you, left you in charge. It was up to *you* to stop this happening."

"And as for you two, Belinda and Charlene, you also ought to know better. This home is a haven of peace. Do you understand? *Not one* of us can take tranquillity for granted. You girls have a good life. If you are to have any hope of maintaining your position you *must* be decent in everything you do. Most especially, you should care for one another. You're sisters after all. Are you not?"

"Now, all three of you apologise to Natalie and to me and do *not* let this happen again," Graph said sternly, hoping his stance sufficiently strong.

Anastasia and Charlene mumbled crestfallen apologies. But Belinda stood deeply sullen. She always competed with Natalie for paternal praise.

Keeping Belinda back, Graph dismissed the others.

Hester Middler, the girls' mother, played no part in this interlude. Her mind was fully engaged on another matter, a matter that had, for all too long, been a great worry.

Something destructive was making its way towards her. She felt an obligation to solve the problem, whatever the cost. And she knew the blessing of reasoned normality would be painfully tested. Graph's constancy would be tried as never before.

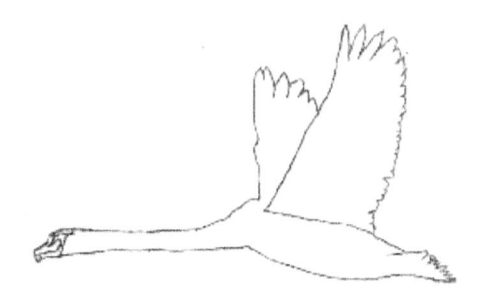

CHAPTER TWO

MONIKA

by

James Horner

For

Elizabeth

DRAMATIS PERSONAE

BELL MISS MONIKA
Wimbledon friend of Rosemary, Eric and John Carpenter in the 1920s. Godmother to John Carpenter.

CARPENTER MRS EILEEN, FORMERLY GREEN, NEE MANDELSONN
Neighbour to Eric and Rosemary Carpenter. Married Eric in later life.

CARPENTER ERIC 1879 TO 1952
Father of John Carpenter and Neil Carpenter. First wife Rosemary. Widower. Second wife Eileen.

CARPENTER JOHN 1910 TO 2002
Father of Colin Carpenter. Colonist. Elder son of Eric and Rosemary Carpenter. Attended Exeter College 1929 to 1932. Emigrated to South Africa 1937.

CARPENTER NEIL 1912 TO 2001
Younger son of Eric and Rosemary Carpenter.

CARPENTER MRS ROSEMARY 1880 TO 1926
Mother of John and Neil Carpenter. Wife of Eric Carpenter.

GREEN NEILL
Son of Eileen Green.

LEECH MRS
Wimbledon friend of Monika Bell and Rosemary Carpenter.

RICHARDS CANON
Wimbledon Anglican clergyman.

1927

WIMBLEDON

Rosemary Carpenter's Anglican funeral in Wimbledon in the autumn of 1926 drew a crowd. Unconsciously egalitarian and a good listener, Rosemary had many friends. Her mourners came from many walks of life.

For John the day of his mother's funeral passed in a blur of rain, tombstones and the mud of the churchyard. In a state of suspended animation, his thought was impressionistic. Some of his mother's words, however, still reverberated with clarity. "Remember this," she would say, "no matter how smart our clothes, how grand our buildings, how eloquent our words, we are *not* civilised if we do uncivilised things." Eric, John's father, stood tall at the graveside. Neil Carpenter, his brother, was present, but silent and inscrutable.

Also amongst those gathered at the grave, stood the small darkened figure of Eileen Green. She lived next door to Rosemary and Eric in an equally large house.

The soil lying neatly at the edge of the newly dug grave, brought eternity into focus. But eternity was, for the moment, too raw to ponder.

"Are we really," John, in silent disbelief, asked himself, "going to leave her lying there? Just lying there? In the rain and the sun and wind? For ever! Under winter's ice? In the mud? Mother? With no warmth or light? Let the leaves fall on her?"

Too soon they did just that. The mourners walked away.

Miss Monika Bell, Rosemary's close friend and John's godmother, put her arm around John's shoulder. She coaxed him away along the churchyard path. They walked in terrible silence amongst the low conversations of mourners. Monika was definite. This day she would not leave John's side, not for half a minute. Her godmothering had long since ceased but her close friendship was part of the Carpenter family routine. She walked beside John the three-quarter-mile to the Carpenter home.

In Rosemary's drawing room, friends, relatives and neighbours conversed over tea. "It would," Mrs Leech, a neighbour, nudged Monika and whispered, "require considerable latitude with the truth to describe *her* as a mourner."

"I suppose," Monika whispered back, "*she* might be thought of as an *investor*?"

Monika, whose house stood at the other end of the village, added. "That lady knows what she wants."

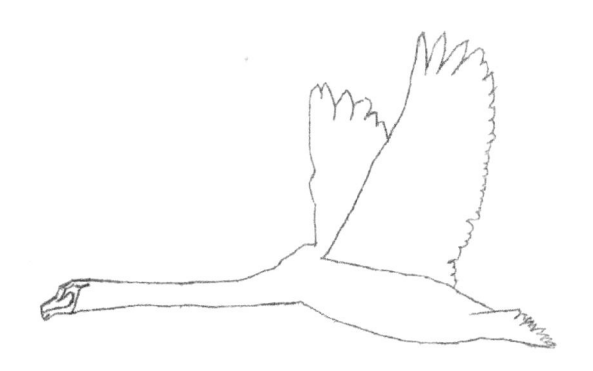

Soon after his wife died, Eric Carpenter changed his domestic arrangements. One evening in the spring of 1927, over dinner, he broke the silence which, since her death, had grown to smother the joie de vivre of Rosemary's home. "Six weeks from today I shall marry Eileen Green," he announced. This was all the warning he gave of his intention.

The boys, unversed in the ways of the world, reacted differently.

"That's nice," Neil said blandly.

To John the surprise was as unwelcome as it is was alien. What?" he asked looking from Neil to Eric and back again.

Eric found it tedious to explain. "Eileen is going to move in with us, look after us," he said with dour impatience.

"But what about mother?" John asked.

"What about her?" Neil asked. Neil Carpenter was a close friend of Neill Green, Eileen's son.

"*Mrs Green?*" John asked again.

Eileen Green, assisted by her son Neill, engaged in changes natural enough to them.

"*Mother*, this won't do," Neill Green asserted the day after he and his mother moved into the Carpenter house.

He stood hands on hips in the centre of the lounge, surveying everything. "This is *your* home now. You must make the place your own, replace all this dross with modern things, things to your taste. Everything here," he added, "is *so* third-estate."

"Damned nerve," John said and left the lounge.

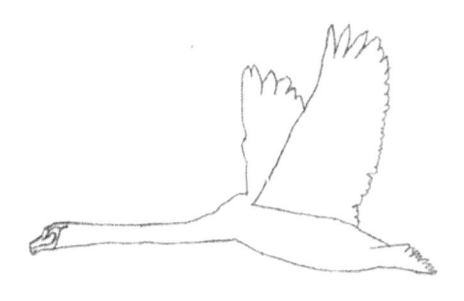

Miss Monika Bell turned up again. She had promised the dying Rosemary she would visit regularly.

Entering the garden through a spanking new gate which, in contrast to its reluctant predecessor, moved silently on black hinges, she leaned her bicycle against the hedge. As she had always done. Straightening her hair and brushing off her blouse, she looked down at her soon-to-be middle-aged form and then up at the house. She was not altogether unhappy about the slim trim of childlessness. But like anyone, she regretted the passage of the years.

Hoping it would be John who answered, she knocked on the door.

She was in luck. She had a keen affection for the elder son of her dead friend. But now that Eileen was lady of the house, Rosemary's invariable warmth had been replaced by awkwardness. Monika would not, however, allow a small adversity to interfere with protective instinct. Certain of John's need and mindful of Rosemary's wish, she kept the routine.

"Oh! Miss Bell!" John welcomed her. "I've been thinking about you and hoping you'd come."

"Just stopped by to see how you are," Monika studied John as he opened the door. Not only was the youth similar in appearance to Rosemary, but he embodied regeneration and continuity.

John loved Monika Bell. Childhood playmate, frequent companion, muse and mentor, Miss Bell never shied away from his questions, even the awkward ones, always gave her time. She detected needs. When he reflected upon their discrete conversations he felt surprise. Sometimes, when she volunteered information, he realised she must have noticed his anxiety before he spoke of it. There was no-one else like her. Except his mother. But Miss Bell was more independent than his mother.

"I'm very glad to see you, my dearest," she said, kissing him on the forehead. "You may kiss me here," she indicated her cheek. "And now you're seventeen, I think it time you called me 'Monika', don't you? Let's forget Miss Bell."

"O.K……..Monika," John sounded her name tentatively, kissed her where indicated and processed the strangeness of using her first name.

In the altered kitchen Monika looked about at the newness everywhere. But she worked as usual with John at making scones. "The smell of fresh paint disturbs me," she said. "It doesn't feel like your mother's kitchen any more. I no longer know where things are kept. It feels a bit as if I should ask permission."

"Presumably it's still *my* kitchen, though," John answered. "So you needn't feel that way."

Over tea in the lounge, Monika commented again. "New wallpaper, new carpets, new furniture, new ornaments, new paintings, new everything, and all florid," she observed.

"My mother is swept away," John deplored. "Most of the things she called her 'precious things' have gone. When Eileen and Neill moved in, the day after the marriage, my father insisted they make whatever changes they like. And since that day change has been constant."

"I know dear," Monika's forehead wrinkled. "So do the village gossips."

Seeing John downcast, she took his hand. "*We'll* not forget how precious your mother was."

"My father accepts everything they do. He no longer cares about things that *were*. How could he change so much?"

"I know dear," Monika repeated solemnly.

"When I tell him I want to keep something because it was mother's, he always sides with Eileen. He says his first duty now is to make Eileen feel at home."

"Hello Monika," Eileen spoke deliberately loudly, as she entered the room.

"Hallo, Eileen," Monika responded neutrally.

John and Monika imagined they might have been overheard. Tension filled the room.

"Can I make you a cup of tea, Eileen?" John asked rising from his chair.

"No thank you," Eileen replied. "I must straightway go speak to the carpenter about the new floorboards. Good-bye for now," she frowned at Monika and busily left the room.

"Your mother'd be proud," Monika praised John. "You were mature and well-mannered then."

"For all their sakes", Monika attempted to conceal her mistrust of Eileen. "I must *not*," she demanded of herself, "say anything to make visiting more awkward than already it is." But nevertheless, Monika's visits put Eileen on edge. Delicate about being *the newcomer* Eileen was especially sensitive to Monika's conversations with Eric. Monika and Eric had been childhood friends. In marrying Rosemary, Eric had married Monika's closest friend. It was a contorted history giving much in common and making for easy conversation between Monika and the Carpenters. But it left Eileen an outsider.

"Eileen," Monika told herself, "knows I see through her, envies my knowledge of the family."

A fortnight passed. Monika noticed John had grown more solitary and desolate than ever. She returned to the subject. "How are things with Eileen?"

"Poor," he answered.

"Are you talking to her," Monika persevered, "much?"

"There were, and probably still are, reasons for trying to be sociable," John broadened out. "Deplorably, Eileen *is* now the lady of the house and …… incredibly ……. my father's wife…… So I probably should make an effort. Actually, there's no alternative. I must live with her …. but when I try to share thoughts she makes me feel alien. My words seem….. futile and misdirected. So……… I've more or less stopped trying," he admitted.

"Don't give up!" Monika urged.

"Well……..." John's voice fell, "I suppose it's obvious I *cannot* accept her. Anyhow, whatever the cause, we walk over one-another's graves. I sometimes literally shudder when I think of her. And she doesn't like young people much, I think."

"I must say, boy," Monika's brow furrowed, "Life has forced you into rapid exchange of youth for maturity. The fact is, Eileen's *not* your mother. No-one can listen and laugh with you as Rosemary did."

"Eileen can't wait for the day I leave home," John surmised. "Whatever my needs, they're always opposite to hers."

"She's as hard as nails," Monika agreed. "To her normal conversation's a waste of time."

"Perhaps she doesn't have any 'conversation'?" John said. "Perhaps she thinks only of *power*. And how to better her position"

"Oh, she has conversation enough when she needs it," Monika said grimly.

John noted Monika's definite stance. "Her listening, from what I see of it, is confined to one purpose and one purpose only. She wants information about other peoples' circumstances. Sometimes she seems to be deliberately gathering information to use against *me*. But actually, in *her* scale of things, I can't be important. Unless it's something to do with the house...... I suppose it could be that. But it's *business* information she craves. It's never your normal old gossips' information. I grant she shuns *that*. No. Her interests are personal finances, business plans and investments."

"Yes," Monika shook her head. "She never *gives* of herself, never speaks her heart. But! She *does* speak her mind. And goodness! Does she have a mind to speak! Many in the village have felt it."

"Her policy is clear," John confirmed unenthusiastically. "Anyone she doesn't need is a minion. She shuts down my attempts at humour with a blank response and withdraws. Doesn't want to know spontaneity, prefers cold informed silence. As if all around her are idiots. I've come to expect nothing from her. *Nothing*."

"Hmmmmm……." Monika said.

"She and my father argue a lot," John said. "One of their repetitive rows is about the sale of her house next door. He's aggrieved because she put the money into her own bank account and didn't share it with him."

There was silence for a few moments while each contemplated the matter.

"And what about your father?" Monika asked. "How is he……. *within* himself?"

"He said something yesterday about my bedroom being needed for other purposes."

"What other purposes?" Monika asked.

"I don't really know. Something to do with Eileen's son. I did question it but Eileen called him away so we didn't finish the conversation."

"Hmmm…….." Monika said, "…….. perhaps you should find out more?"

"Yes," John agreed, "I should. But I wonder whether it'll make any difference. My father's loyalty has switched to his new family. It hasn't made him happy. The rows with Eileen are terribly loud. I think all Wimbledon must hear them arguing. Before mother died I thought Eileen's house was unwelcoming. Now ours is. My mother's presence has gone out of it. A hard-driving Jewish form has replaced our tranquillity."

John returned from school to a fait accompli. He had been moved.

Entering his room as usual, he stopped in the doorway, gaping in disbelief.

His bedroom was not his bedroom. Bed, cupboards, bookshelves, chairs, Rosemary's oil paintings, everything assembled for him over the years, everything except his big desk, all were gone. In their place, new and geometric, stood Neill Green's belongings and furniture. A bright smooth carpet smelt of newness.

Unschooled in domestic strife, John stalked to the lounge where Eric and Eileen sat in heated disagreement over money.

"My room?" he interrupted angrily.

The newlyweds, already irate, reacted furiously to the extraneous challenge.

"What do you mean?" Eric asked rising swiftly. Obviously fractious, he was expecting more trouble.

"Where are all my things?" John demanded.

"My Neill needs space to study," Eileen's voice filled with venom.

"Is that so?" John stared at Eileen. "Well, *I* need my room for *my* studies. It's *my* room. It's been *my* room since I was born. I want it back and I want it back *now*."

He ran to 'his' room, began overturning the new furniture, throwing things at the wall and doing as much damage as he could.

In response to the commotion, Eric, Neill Green and Neil Carpenter ran in. They overpowered John. In a minute Eric held John in an arm-lock on the floor. The step-brothers, Neil Carpenter and Neill Green, stood back. Side by side they looked on.

Eileen appeared. Dismayed at the damage, she instantly understood. "The boy is rude," she raged. "He has led too sheltered a life." She shook her fist in anger at the damage, looking from Eric and John to the two Neills and back again.

"Now that mum's dead," John, still pinioned, upbraided his father, "you care only about your new woman and her son. You've forgotten your real family."

"Remember you're a child," Eric stormed. "You do as you're told and are thankful for food and shelter."

"Since taking up with this woman," John spluttered, "you've supported her and her son in every way and neglected your real family."

A brutal expression passed across Neil Carpenter's face. He clenched his fist, stepped forward, thought better, stepped back again.

Still on the floor, John stared up at his blood brother in disbelief.

"Marrying so soon after mum died," John continued, "and," he nodded at Eileen, "bringing *her* to mother's bedroom, it's disloyal. It's disgusting. By comparison my wrong-doings are *nothing*. Mere peccadilloes."

"Peccadilloes?" Neil Carpenter sneered. "You grandiloquent twit."

"You are insubordinate and offensive," the incandescent Eric insisted. "I *told* you the other day, except, as usual, you weren't listening, Neill needs the big desk for rolling out his engineering drawings. This room is the only room large enough to accommodate a desk that size. That's the *only* reason for the exchange of rooms." Eric still pinned John to the ground but even as he did so he recalled recent comments concerning his choice of second wife and the transfer of attention to his new family. He wavered between attempting reconciliation and continuing his confident stance.

"I'm expendable now, aren't I?" John asked sourly. "No longer your 'first-born'? Or, only technically so? Now you've a new family?"

"Of course you aren't," Eric said releasing his son and standing back. The two Neills involuntarily stepped up their readiness for more trouble.

"Goodness, you've a perfectly good room all to yourself," Eileen put in, her voice going up an octave. "Many a child in London would count itself lucky to have what you have. Why can't you get on with my Neill just as your brother does?"

"Itself!" John echoed icily. "From a room with a view to the box room!" Rising, he dusted himself off vigorously, although there was no speck of dust on the new carpet. "Nice carpet," he said sarcastically.

"Your son," John addressed Eileen, "isn't even going to *be* here most of the time. Because he'll be away at Oxford. So his room, which is really *my* room, will be *empty* for long periods."

"Yes," Eileen replied, "but for the times he *is* home, my son's time is more valuable than yours. He's more advanced, more senior."

"Is that so?" John looked at Eileen with disgust.

He looked at his father. "And you, father? Will you not change your mind? Is your stepson's claim more valid than your son's?"

He waited for a moment.

"Your silence tells me my question's unanswerable. Are you afraid of your new wife?"

There being no response, John walked out.

Going to his new small room, he squeezed around the edge of the bed and then sat on its end, resting his chin on his palms. His mind drifted. Somehow he could not focus on his predicament.

The incident brought one clarity. Always unsure what name to use for

Eileen, from that day on he called her "Mrs Carpenter" with politeness amounting to derision.

Neill Green he simply ignored wherever possible.

Leaving an oppressive dinner table, John excused himself. "He'll come round in his own time," Eric, aware of the tension, suggested to Eileen.

John overheard. He turned in the doorway. "You two are completely self-engrossed," he said and made to leave.

"Come back here!" Eric roared, incensed at another challenge to his authority.

John returned and stood facing his father. Eileen, her mouth working, glared angrily through large smeared lenses at the slight figure before them.

"You'd better apologise to Eileen and to me young man, or there'll be hell to pay." Eric's voice, curtly disciplinarian was not brutish.

"Hell *has* been paid. You wouldn't want Hell paid twice, would you? This *was* my mother's house. Now it's Mrs Carpenter's."

Eric contained apoplexy. One of Eileen's feet swung furiously back and forth causing her body to rock and her head to nod. "Eric! This is bad! Speak to him!" she demanded.

Eric was out of his depth. His son accused him of immoral haste. His wife required him to quash rebellion. He proceeded carefully, searching for a harmless way to discharge a range of frustrations. "The nub of the matter is sensitivity," he said and instantly suspected it better to downplay, if not to scoff at, soft sentiment. Eileen, he knew, was not disposed towards lenience.

"If he can't like us, he'll jolly well have to lump us," Eileen said fiercely.

John looked knowingly at his father, "If you don't mind, I'll leave you now," he paused, "with your new happiness." This time his departure went unchallenged.

Eric stared straight ahead for a moment. "It's only a matter of time," he said.

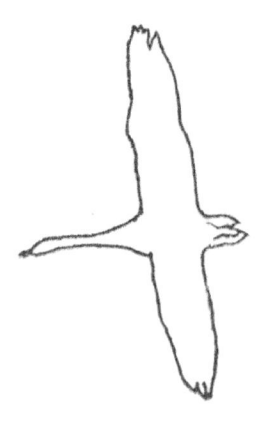

Monika's house became John's home.

"You see, my friend," Monika said after listening to his description of the latest incident, "Eric and Eileen are *consumed* by marital strife. They've no energy left for your needs."

"Oh I'm *glad* you also think that" John said. "I often wonder whether *my* ignorance and self-centredness is to blame for the velocity of the ridiculosity. But you're experienced and have an arms-length view. Sometimes when you speak, I listen not so much to *what* you say as the *way* you say it. You're from that same vein of gold from which my mother was forged."

"My boy," Monika counselled, "when you're troubled by their ways, remember *this*. Love is often exclusive. Difficult relationships can make people *incapable* of looking beyond themselves. Much."

Monika gave John a key. His presence was natural. He came and went as he pleased. As spring advanced he took to arriving early on Saturdays, staying the night in Monika's guest room and leaving after dark on Sundays.

Eric and Eileen knew. And were relieved to be free of him.

"Our days aren't long enough," Monika said one Sunday morning. "Maybe I should stay again tonight?" he asked. "No. It's school tomorrow. I'll change quickly. Would you like elder-flower water again? Before breakfast? On the garden table?" "But I love your dressing gown." "And what do you feel like for supper?" "Don't mind. You're good with food and things. You decide. Let's picnic in the orchard. And read again. If it's fine. Maybe more 'Rubaiyat', *and* start 'Klingsor's Last Summer.' *Or* 'Trekking On.' Isn't there a lot to read?" "Reading aloud," she sighed, "is a meeting of souls."

Returning, she set down the elderflower water and drew her chair to a secluded spot. "Bring your chair." He carried the table and returned for his chair.

"This garden is my favourite labour."

"Gardening is a balm. But *this year*, spring brought new blessings. Picnicking and reading."

"I *need* the digging in the sun, weeding, pruning. *Sweating*. When we rest I can't stop admiring the work we've done. We've come to *know* this piece of land. The insects and the worms."

"Gardening's a *medium*. A small piece of land produces *so much*."

"Physical work is pure."

"Labour transforms and absorbs."

They sipped elder-flower water.

"Now," she said, "I *am* going to change before I bring out breakfast."

Soon back, she came and went with trowels, seed packets and breakfast trays. "There are primroses, hyacinths and poppy seeds to plant. Mow the lawn and edge that bed while I'm out."

John pondered the routine. "Why does she worry?" he asked himself. "What difference would it make?"

When it rained they played chess. Or sat reading on the couch. "If Rosemary is looking down," Monika asked herself, "is she pleased with me? *What* does she *want* me to teach her son? *How* safeguard him? Or, is she *far* beyond such cares? After all, I'm her son's *godmother*, am I not? She would've done everything a mother could. Her death made John and I *companions.* Godmother. *That's* my answer. Godmother!"

The spring progressed. In the shade of the orchard, they rested often from planting and tending, cooling down with her lemonade. The garden, burgeoning and blossoming, reflected human complexities. Monika had patience for this youth.

"You're skilful and kind," John recognised their state of being. "You read my thoughts and know what's happening inside. You respond before I've even seen there's a problem."

"I *am* ….. experienced," Monika agreed. Secretly, however, she acknowledged vulnerability. "My God," she thought, "I don't feel as confident as I sound."

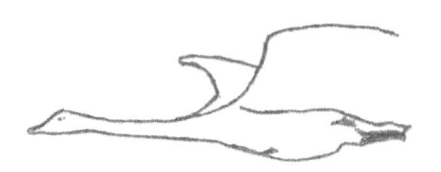

"And………………," Monika began one day. When thinking deeply, she often started conversation with the word, 'And' followed by a pause. "And…….. I knew your father of old …. even if he and Eileen weren't completely taken up by their own disputes, they're both "too selfish and too proud." They think only of practical benefits. Love isn't an easy subject for them. I imagine they don't speak of love in any form. Not of what exists between them, nor of the worlds of their children, nor of other wondrous things within and without."

"They avoid the subject like the plague,'" John agreed. "Just thinking about it makes them cringe."

"I know that kind of marriage," Monika continued. "Everything in their personal lives is 'an arrangement' 'taken to be understood' or 'not to be harped on'. They prefer to leave things unspoken. All nuances and subtleties, all the spires, domes and towers of the many cities of love, all the numberless forests and dales, canyons, deserts, flowers and thorns ...."

"Numberless dales and canyons!" John echoed.

"…..canyons and deserts," Monika would not be interrupted, "love's daring, its droughts and oases, its countries, tribes, cultures, customs, harbours and havens. …. *All* its *colours* are, so far as Eric and Eileen are concerned, the dreams of silly romantics."

"Yes, I know," John responded slowly. "They think it's too private for words. To them poetry is guff. They silence any drift in conversation from science to art. And …. in their case 'science' means 'money.' They dread any thought or word which might reveal inner worlds or start uninvited exploration."

"Theirs is a practical, mechanical life."

"My father," John said, "does sometimes, on Sunday afternoons, pick up a volume of George Meredith or an essay. But he thinks it heady stuff, semi-valuable, possibly profound, but best left in obscurity. If it doesn't offer mathematical proof, it's mere light entertainment. When he puts such a book down he almost always says 'great wits are sure to madness near allied.' And Eileen complains 'You're not reading vapid nonsense again, are you?'"

"What does Eileen read?" Monika asked.

"Oh," John dismissed the idea, "she doesn't read. We have fewer and fewer interesting books. She throws them out. And arranges what's left on the bookshelf by shape, rather than by subject. But she *does* study balance sheets and profit and loss accounts. Is that reading? And ponders clauses in leases. And draws up tables of foreign exchange rates. And interest rates. And compares them. That's her 'reading'. She wouldn't waste time on anything else. The place has become her office. To her, financial statements have *meaning*. She's constantly on the look-out for threats to her assets and talks to dad about manipulation of statistics. Literature doesn't come into it. Mind you, she *is* impressed by authors who've made a lot of money."

"Well……….," Monika reflected, "Eileen's opinions and her single-mindedness undermine the opinion others have of *her*. But………," she sighed, "*most* people are snobs about *something*. Aristocrats are proud of their status. Liberals are snobbish about intellect. Even proletarians who say they hate snobs are snobs about their *own* ideas. But," she paused, "Eric and Eileen must know that *big* consequences will flow from their decisions. It's just," she concluded, "they can't help themselves and *cannot* look beyond their own priorities. They're actually *incapable* of grappling with their *real* problems. Those two *have* to be the ostriches they are and *have* to work with things they think will enhance their power. Their kind of power. They dismiss other things."

"It seems to me," John continued one day to Monika, "I now have two step-parents. Even though one isn't. My father has diminished. His stature echoes the changed view from my bedroom window. Do you remember my view before the arrival of a step-brother? Leafy Wimbledon in summer and snowscape in winter. Now, from the box room, I look at the brick wall of Eileen's former house. Summer and winter. It's dreary."

He nestled against Monika. She drew his arm around her shoulder. "Dismal loneliness and isolated old age will be the result of their choices. Glad fulfilment will not be theirs."

"And ………" John mimicked Monika's mannerism. "And ………. something else is happening. I may have lost the view from my window and ….. many personal spaces, but what we have here is steadily overtaking that which is lost."

Monika nodded.

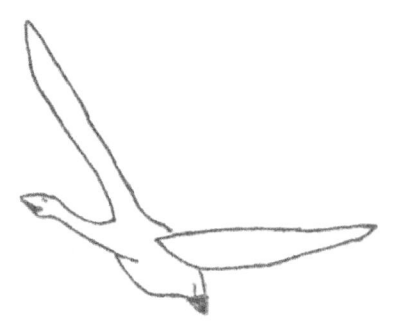

At the house of Eric and Eileen, the distribution of post became another source of friction.

"Mrs Carpenter, why do you hold my mail up to the light, when it arrives?" John asked tersely when he caught Eileen in the act. "Why do you study the handwriting and squint at the postmark?"

"It's the habit of a lifetime," Eileen replied, pricked into anger by what she regarded as insolence. "It's the result of having always been a businesswoman. Does it bother you?"

"Do it for your own post," he said, "not for mine."

"I did *not* intentionally single out *your* letter," Eileen walked off aggrieved.

Whether or not a result of this incident, the next day Eileen kept back an official-looking letter addressed to 'Mr John Carpenter' and marked 'CONFIDENTIAL.' Eric found it waiting for him when he took his place for the evening meal. He opened the envelope and read the contents before handing it to Eileen, who also read it. As Eileen focussed on the writing, she grew intent. She pushed back her chair, her mouth worked and a foot swung swiftly back and forth. Only when, without a word, she passed the letter to John, did he realise it had been addressed to himself.

John stared at the letter. "Are you both *blind?*" he surged in anger. "*Why* are you reading my confidential mail? Did you not see this letter is headed 'CONFIDENTIAL' in *capital letters.* The capital letters are double-underlined. *Double underlined.* Also, the word 'CONFIDENTIAL' is on the envelope in *large* capitals. This is a letter *from my doctor addressed to me.* It is *absolutely not* the business of *either of you.*" He looked in turn at Eileen, at John and at both the Neills. "Don't you *know* the meaning of the word, *'CONFIDENTIAL?'*"

"Everything under my roof is my business," Eric's eyes narrowed in reply.

"And you gave it to *her* to read!"

The two Neills looked at one another and prepared for another confrontation.

John waved the letter at Eric. He stared at his father. "You gave *this* to *her* to read! To *her* of *all* people. When you know she's *the last person* on earth with whom I'd discuss such a matter."

"Just as well it confirms there's nothing wrong with you then, isn't it?" Eileen glowered at John, her foot swinging.

"This is no ordinary trespass," John stormed. "It's *uncivilised*. Thank God, Mrs Carpenter, you'll 'lead these graces to the grave and leave the world' only one 'copy'"

"What?" Eileen demanded.

Neill Green guffawed.

"Nothing," John answered. Taking the letter, he left without touching his food. No-one thought of persuading him to return.

"My father *might*, as my parent, have *some* claim to the letter's contents," John protested to Monika the next day. "But *Eileen* certainly did *not*."

"And yet," Monika said as mildly as she could, "you told me all about it. Even before you went to the doctor." Partly she questioned. Partly it was self-analysis.

"Yes, because *you've* become my next of kin," John averred. "Nowadays those two *both* rank *only* as stepparents. There is less and less I can speak to them about. In contrast, I could ask you anything, trust you with anything, *absolutely* anything, physical, philosophical or poetic, and be unembarrassed. Thanks be to God … whoever *He* is."

"I'm not a good person," Monika was soft and subdued.

"You don't value yourself above a farthing but you're *gold-dust*," John's certainty erupted vividly.

Monika relaxed. "I'm glad you feel that way. Very glad. But," she became gentle and serious, "you need to detach from your deep anger about them."

"More than detach," John asserted. "I need to leave, go away, get as far from Wimbledon as possible." He leaned against Monika, absorbing her warmth. In so doing he missed the glimmer of pain on her face.

"Would you like," she asked, "to go to see "This Year of Grace?" It's on at The Pavilion. *Or* ….. there's something new at the picture-houses. It's called 'Wings'. We could go to that."

His voice lifted, "I wouldn't just *like* to. I'd *love* to. By the way, what *exactly is* detachment?"

"Oh ….. ummmm …. detachment is the absolute leaving of something or someone you love …. When you can't live with them and you can't live without them. It is *itself* a kind of love."

"Like death?" he asked.

"Like death in life. It …. replaces presence with absence….. *But* ……. It needn't be geographical. It can be, and often is, metaphysical. The detached person is often physically present. It's the process of replacing intimacy with love at a distance. Absolutely and for ever. I sometimes think it entails reaching a state in which you're happy to die. *And* happy to live."

"A cousin of 'courtly love'?"

"A distant cousin."

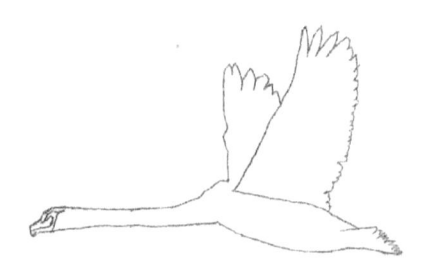

Further disputes arose. The Carpenters lived in disagreement. Yet the two Neills were unaffected. Their lives took them along diverging paths. But they continued the friendship begun in schooldays. Flying fascinated them. They went to aircraft exhibitions together, discussed Handley Page and visited Croydon to study the comings and goings from London's skies.

One day Neil Carpenter, too, was caught up in Eileen's re-ordering of the house. He found himself moved to what was little more than a pantry adjoining the kitchen when his bedroom was taken over by Eileen as office and library.

"Aren't you angry at being turned out of your room?" John asked, surprised at the absence of complaint or comment. "It doesn't bother me," Neil replied. "The old man wants his piece of fluff. So we must accept her ways."

John stared in amazement. "We've never really understood one another, you and I, have we?" he said.

"Well….. I won't be living at home much longer anyway," Neil grudgingly explained.

"He really *doesn't* seem to mind about his room," John said to Monika a few days later when he described his increasing estrangement from his brother.

"The strains of living affect people differently," Monika said levelly. "It's a difficult time for you all. Neil has his own way of coping."

"I heard the housemaid," John confided, "telling Eileen he needs *yet* more white shirts. Because he's been cutting them up again. He dyes the pieces different colours and stitches them into miniature replicas of flags. National flags. And flags of steamship lines. I hope we're not all going mad. He spends most of his time in his room reading. In semi-darkness. To be fair he does go out sometimes. With friends. But, like me he's taken to leaving the table as soon as possible at meal times."

"Oh, you Carpenters don't know how lucky you are!" Eileen protested when John asked Eric if he thought Neil Carpenter had become insecure. "You know *nothing* of *real* hardship. If you knew what it is to *really* suffer, you wouldn't complain so much."

John let the matter drop. But he stored away a question in his mind. What was the 'real hardship', to which Eileen referred? Had she herself known what it was to '*really* suffer?'

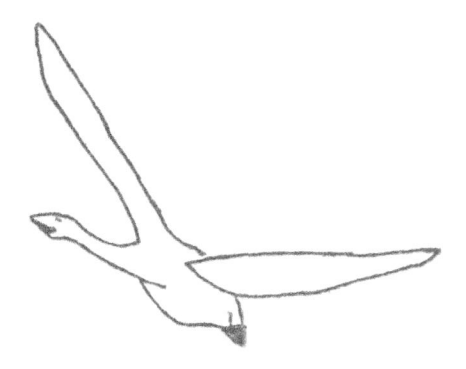

Monika asked Eric over 'to discuss matters'. Eric accepted. "After all." he reasoned, "We've known one-another most of our lives."

John sat on the couch next to Monika. Eric took the chair once used by Rosemary. "Our home," John began at Monika's instance, "has been wrecked. Physically and mentally *wrecked*. It's become a place of manipulation and plotting. The step-mother removes anything she doesn't want, without asking if it's important to anyone else. She calls it progress. I call it vandalism. Her only humanity is to her son. It's only money and power that are of any interest to *Mrs Eileen Carpenter*. I mean to say," John asked, "do these women who take on the role of step-mother even *begin* to think what they do when they marry into an existing family? How could *you* ... *think* of marrying such a person? It seems thoughtless to me."

"John ...." Monika glanced at Eric. She took John's hand, "men often find the solitary life just *too* lonely. They *need* marriage. I know your feelings. But ... your father has always provided. You've never known hunger. There's always been a roof over your heads."

"He's unable to see beyond his own needs," John answered.

Eric remained silent.

"Your father," Monika continued, "*needs* to be head of his house. Your mother played to his strengths. She smoothed troubled waters. Rosemary was a listener." Monika struggled with grief for a moment. "But, since she died, her essential gift, *to us all*, of understanding, has been lost." She turned to Eric. "John and Neil are *your sons*. Remember to acknowledge *them* ... as well as giving Eileen the attention she deserves."

"Do you think Monika," John asked, "that my father's mother ever *even attempted* to teach him to consider others?"

Eric straightened up. He looked at his son with a constrained frown but said nothing.

"No, John," Monika remonstrated, "that's *too* hard. Your father is *also* a human-being. *No* mother can guarantee her child's decisions. We don't know your grandmother's trials and distractions. It's difficult enough understanding the living without trying to reach back into the minds of the dead. I knew her when I was little. She was good, if rather silent. Perhaps you *can* try to know *yourself*. Look sometimes into the mirror and say, 'I am John Carpenter, son of Eric Carpenter and Rosemary Carpenter.'"

When Eric left, Monika accompanied him to the door. "*Eric*, we knew one another long before we knew Rosemary. Now, your son spends time with me. Rosemary made me *promise* to look after him. I promised *gladly*. I plan to give him other interests. Because you and Eileen don't have time for diversions. Does this bother you?"

"Not in the *slightest!*" he said. "Jolly good thing! Not a bother at all. I'm *glad* of it. Couldn't be better. It's a weight off my mind. Thank you," he clasped her hand with both his hands, remembering their shared childhood.

"*Mother!*" Neill Green expressed pent-up concern, "*how* are you going to keep control of the money?"

"Son! Don't take me for an *idiot*," Eileen countered. "An antenuptial contract is *in place*. I wasn't born yesterday. We live in the twentieth century, you know. I'll control the *combined* finances *in the same way* I've always done."

"With an *iron* hand?"

"Of *course*," Eileen affirmed, "an *iron* hand. Eric's signature's *on* the contract. He'll forfeit *this house* and *half his investments* if we divorce. He's not sophisticated. It wasn't difficult to arrange. I told him, 'No signature, no marriage.' *Simple.* Naturally he'd keep his children. By accepting my terms he'll have an affluent retirement. Fair's fair. I'll manage *that* for him. It won't cost much for servants to look after him when he's old. I have him thinking of me as house-keeper and insurance."

"And by the way, we've also signed new irrevocable back-to-back wills. If I die before Eric you'll have ninety per cent of the Carpenter net worth. Of course, if I die after Eric you'll have it all."

"Why would Eric agree to that?" Neill asked.

"Because he trusts me to do *all* the work from now onwards. He never has to work again."

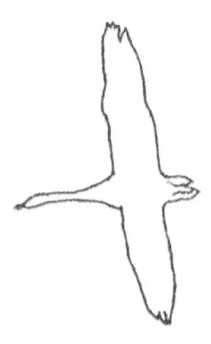

"Your father is largely oblivious," Monika explained. "He's not alone. Many of us can't see our own faults. If we could, there'd be fewer of them. However, some important people have told him things aren't right. But nothing changes ……… because to his mind, the decision of the man of the family, right or wrong, is final. We've always known that about him. All of us. I accepted his lead when we were kids. I was young and the world was new. Perhaps I still accept *the idea*. Circumspectly. It's ………………. easier."

"He *was* head of the house when mother was alive," John stressed, "but now it's all posturing. Spends his time bumbling around. He's not head of anything! He's *so ..... pushed* around. Everything's different. Mother was kind, *never* screamed at him the way Eileen does. I must go away. I long to belong once more, whether to a woman or an organisation. Or just to a group of friends."

"Your mother created happiness," Monika lingered over the memory, "in us all, but especially in Eric. I saw your father grow happier with her... Paradoxically," she mused, "he can be charming, free-thinking, an intellectual. He engenders respect. But his liberalism vanishes when threatened or scrutinised." Monika checked herself and frowned, "I *mustn't* criticise. We *all* struggle to live up to our ideals. I'm no better."

"Family bonds have been damaged," John muttered.

"I often ponder solutions," Monika said slowly. "because your family means *much* to me. ….. There are various paths ….. And ……. regarding *belonging* ….. you're too *young* to cleave to a woman yet. And …. I think I know, my boy, the kind of organisation you've in mind. *Fascist membership* holds real dangers! You must *not* fall for *that*, my dearest." She stroked his hair. "Don't be swayed by *fashion* or *trends*. You've a *good* brain. Use it in constructive work rather than politics. *Independence* brings greater reward than 'belonging' or 'membership.' Just *be* yourself. Individuality is *key* to success. *Self-reliance* is a way of life."

"Yes, well," John elaborated, "my father and Eileen *often* talk about Neill Green's future. Almost never about mine or my brother's. They think work a beatitude. My beatitudes lie elsewhere. My brother simply doesn't care. Mind you," he grinned, "he wouldn't know a beatitude if he collided with one."

"You have me to talk to. Talk to *me*," Monika said.

"So …………….." John acknowledged this closeness, "*Why* are you negative about the need to belong?"

"I fear mesalliance, dear," Monika answered serenely.

"I suppose you're right," John imagined things beyond his experience.

Monika stirred. "We need to talk about something," she said.

"Of course," he said, wondering what was coming.

"It's the parent's task to tell the young certain things. But, your mother's not here. And your father won't. So would you accept it if *I* tell you those things?"

"Of course," John said again.

"You're young," she said forthrightly. "It would be natural for you to think of women. Am I right?" she asked.

Taken aback, "You're right," he replied.

"Don't be embarrassed. 'The nakedness of women is the work of God.' For the sake of happiness and for your protection, you must know things."

Monika went into detail.

"A woman's trust is no small gift," she concluded. "In fact it's *the big* gift. Unfortunately, sooner or later, most people take love for granted. And by so doing lose the greatest thing in Creation. *Tend* your love. *Never* neglect it. Nuances and subtleties will be noticed."

At first light he began to write.

Of Monika

Nuances and Subtleties

The peace of
spires, domes, towers,
forests, dales, canyons,
deserts, oases, palms,
droughts, storms, snowfields,
lands, tribes, tents,
maps, rails, roads,
cultures, customs, verse,
harbours, havens, scents,
flowers, thorns, buds,
colours, contours, valleys,
tragedies, intrigues, grace,
labyrinths' insight,
Eden to end.

In black cassock and white collar, Canon Richards knocked at the door. Strong, well-built, white hair, his massive sense of purpose made Wimbledon too small for him. He longed for the imperial spaces and distances of his youth.

"Come in, sir," John showed the clergyman to the lounge where his father was reading.

Canon Richards wasted no effort on pleasantries. "How's your new family?" He glared at Eric. Rosemary's death meant to the canon not only the loss of a hard-working church member and a personal friend but also the loss of a whole family from his congregation. "I think the new Mrs Carpenter is of the Jewish faith? Which explains your family's absence from church?"

"Perhaps," Eric, remaining seated, replied neutrally.

Canon Richards declined the chair John offered.

"Even if you allow your family to cease religious observance, I hope you notice how your son, here," he indicated John with a wave of his arm, "is entangled in youth's web of self-discovery. The change in circumstances means he must, unaided, extricate himself from the dreary mystery of a world grown cold. Grown cold at your instance."

"Extricate himself from a world grown cold?" Eric turned the words into a question. "At my instance?" Unaccustomed to disapproval from Canon Richards, he soured rapidly.

"He feels dispossessed and looks to progress without his family. Who knows *what* might come of it?"

"How do you know this?" Eric asked.

John remained silent.

"It's common knowledge," Canon Richards replied.

The conversation faltered. With a searching glare, Canon Richards left.

Monika listened carefully. "'Dispossessed' is a powerful word," she commented. "But perhaps it's the right word. Although," she hesitated, "assuming the worst could be a mistake. And yet …… a priest must watch over his flock."

Eric's encounter with the family doctor was another negative.

"Blinking cheek!" he protested to Eileen. "He said I pay too much attention to you and neglect my children. Who does he think he is? Does he forget I pay his blinking quack-fees? How dare he! It's not professional. And it's none of his business. Damn nerve! Upstart!"

"Oh, it's time to change physician! *Immediately!*" Eileen responded. "We can't have that! And as for the church! The church is a racket!"

"Surely Unconditional Love is unchangeable?" John lamented. "Just like The Deity from which it came is immutable? It *cannot* be harmed and must continue in the ether after its time on Earth?"

"What makes you ask, love?" Monika touched his cheek.

"I heard them *again* last night," John lowered his voice.

"On earth, everything's fleeting," Monika said. "But we must hope our *best* things live on somewhere. In some perfect eternity."

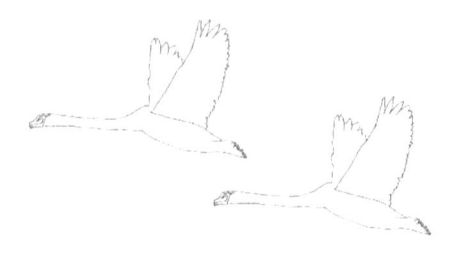

"As Life would have it," he thrust a sheet of paper into Monika's hand, "we discussed Hamlet's mother in English today."

Monika read the words John had neatly copied.

"Have you eyes?
Could you on this fair mountain leave to feed,
And batten on this moor? ha! have you eyes?
You cannot call it love, for at your age
The hey-day in the blood is tame, it's humble,
And waits upon the judgement, and what judgement
Would step from this to this?"

"I know the passage," Monika held her hand to her cheek.

"It's exactly my situation, isn't it?"

"No! It's not *at all* like your situation," Monika remained calm. "In your case no-one was *murdered*. And your circumstances are nothing like as bad as Hamlet's. You must avoid using literature as a weapon."

"I suppose you're right," John agreed, subdued. "But didn't Shakespeare himself use literature as a weapon?"

"Shakespeare was just embellishing a bit of history as a way of earning his living."

John contemplated this.

"*You*," Monika continued, "for your own good must *create* a healthy way out of adversity. I'll help you."

"How?" John asked.

"I think," Monika suggested, "sometimes, you should sit at your desk and write down your thoughts in detail. It's a way of purging feelings. When it's done, read it over. Then burn it, so no-one else ever reads it."

"I don't have a desk any more."

"You can use mine."

"And now," Monika said, determined to change the subject, "we're going out. We're taking the train to Waterloo and going for a ride on an open-top omnibus if it's still light. Better still if it isn't. We'll have supper somewhere. Come on. 'Wings' is on at the picture-house."

John awoke again in the early hours. He turned over. Reaching to the floor, he found the note-book, pencil and flashlight given him by Monika. On the front cover he had written,

"MY TABLES."

Opening the note-book he began to write by flashlight.

"PREFACE"

"It is meet that I set it down in my tables."

And then he wrote a heading.

"Unconditional Love."

He underlined the heading.

"Profanities," he wrote, "occur in the world of man……."

The words flowed. Writer's cramp made his hand ache.

After several pages he wrote a new heading.

'Paternal Matters.'

This too he underlined.

"Daily disbelief," he wrote, "continues to expand. Why does he countenance such change? Is he blind? Is it fear of loneliness?"

More pages followed on this subject.

There came further headings, each with its own essay.

"<u>A Fair Solution</u>"

"<u>Step-Mothers And Property.</u>"

"<u>Children Whose Parents Remarry.</u>"

"<u>Failures Of The Law.</u>"

"<u>Desecration and Reconsecration</u>"

"It falls to me to keep reason alive."

"I've written down some thoughts," John showed the pages to Monika. Like Hamlet I've called it 'MY TABLES'. May I keep my writing in your desk?"

"You do appreciate, John, don't you" Eric said in a conciliatory moment, "that Eileen and I keep a fond memory of your mother?"

"But!" John was aghast, "you've left no tiny shrine to her. You've altered every inch of her house."

"Moving with the times isn't a failure to mourn," Eric answered.

"Always think young, John," Eileen coaxed.

"Good night," John said and left. As he went he thought, "Hollow, all hollow, worse than hollow. Stepfamilies! Duplicitous sophisticates who sacrifice truth in attempts to convince themselves. They cast about *anywhere* rather than look within. They *fear* simplicity and *must* have their own way, abhor any *hint* of guilt and seek absolution."

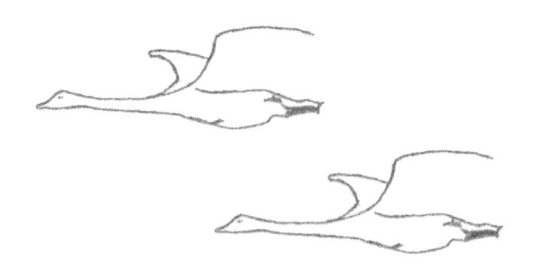

They sat on a bench to the side of the tennis courts. Monika drew breath. "That was one *strenuous* match," she said. "It's 9.30. Enough light for another match?"

"You're better than me," John said sipping her home-made lemonade.

"Monika?" he asked, looking at the Art Deco embellishments on her midi-pleated tennis dress, white tennis shoes side by side. "Do thoughts ever come *unbidden* into your head?" She towelled away perspiration. "*Such thoughts* as to make you think, 'But, I'm *not* to *think* these thoughts!" She stopped towelling. "*Where* do they come from and *how* do I stop them?'"

"Yes dear," Monika resumed towelling, "That's your reverie. My reverie," she said, "I'll never silence. But in silence lies my peace of mind.

Why? What were you thinking?" She leant forward to brush away an ant.

John noticed the shimmering neatness. Exertion had produced high colour. He tried not to gaze. Breathlessness had subsided. She was fit, finely built, attentive.

"After *so* many changes," he said, "in my family …. I find *myself* …….. profoundly changed."

"Tell me more."

"I think ……..." he hesitated. "I think ……I….. love you."

Silent for a split-second, eyes dancing, reaching over to touch his knee, she put her head back to laugh a long, comradely laugh. "I'd be sad indeed if I thought you *didn't*," she said. Her eyes fixed on his. "By the way, half the village too, thinks you do."

"What?" John gasped.

"Oh! don't worry," she continued. "No need for concern. The gossips see me as the stand-in for your mother.......They know my man died on The Somme *and* class me a spinster. Friends see how I find happiness in tennis. Grow flowers. Admire Helen Wills. Go with me to theatres, picture-houses, restaurants, tea-rooms. And ride open-top buses. I'm pigeon-holed an independent." She thought a moment. "Of the love between thee and me, I'll say little. But take comfort. I love you too. *Platonically.* And of it neither of us should speak. Because for some things there *are* no words. Silence is better."

"What does 'platonically' mean?" he asked.

Days passed.

In the evening of a day spent gardening, they lay on the grass of the orchard.

"I think we should give this house a name," he said. "We should call it 'Clear Sky'. Because here we found loveliness."

"Okay," Monika agreed. "We shall call it 'Clear Sky' and the name will remind me of you. Long after you've gone."

"Gone?" John was startled. "I'm not going anywhere."

"No. Not now, you aren't. But one day you will. A young girl will come and take you away. And I'll yield because that'll only be right."

"It'll take a great deal for any woman to separate me from you," he said. "A whole bevvy of nubile maidens couldn't do it."

"It helps," she said, "when you look back, to know you did your best."

"It's your eighteenth birthday soon," Monika said. "Would you like to invite a friend or three to dinner?"

"I'd love dinner," John replied, "but just you and I. My ruffian-friends are too immature for your house. I've already told my father I'll be out that day. And night."

"Your mother always thought you a 'home-bird'," Monika said, "but I notice you've been going out more…… and staying out…… which worries me, a bit. Of course I'm glad to see you becoming independent. And……. it's a delight to hear the warmth in your conversations with friends."

"Going out more?" John echoed.

"Yes, going out more," Monika repeated leaning languidly against a door-frame and examining him.

"Oh, you're always so careful not to be provocative," John said, seeing her friendship and returning her gaze. "*You* have *many* friends because you're free and ingenuous."

"Many acquaintances and just a *few* good friends," she said.

"In your case, they're almost the same," he asserted. "But, to answer your question, you're right, I *have* been going out more. It's a way to avoid the step-family when I'm not with you. In their solar system I'm a *remote* moon, they're seldom aware of my absence. Usually they don't comment. They're not *kind* like you, Monika. Anyway, I'm always glad to escape them and their bickering. I'm sorry, by the way, I wasn't here on Tuesday."

"Did you go somewhere nice?" she asked. "I was expecting you."

"Well ……… I was continuing my *life-search*. Do you remember that notice board at the library?"

"The one where we laughed because someone had pinned a naughty advertisement amongst all the notices of art exhibitions and town planning meetings?" she smiled.

"Yes, exactly." He faltered. "I didn't go to the talk about 'New Uses for Electricity.' I went to the political meeting you didn't want me to attend."

"Ah……. And? …. What did you learn?"

"It was as you said it would be," John answered. "Stormy and thuggish. Which suited my companions. You would *not* like them. Bucket-loads of wind. On several occasions the debate gave way to fisticuffs. *Blood* was spilled! People became heated about the French occupation of The Ruhr and the collapse of the mark. My struggle was for inner calm. The intended subject was *'The Versailles Treaty Will Cause Another War.'* But it deviated into argument about why The Great War started in the first place."

"When a thing is bad," he continued, "you *must* have the freedom to call it bad. .... The British, French and Americans could *not* have thought of a surer way than The Treaty of Versailles to start another Great War. Even if they'd *deliberately* set out to do *just that*. Enslaving all Germans with war reparations! As if ordinary Germans started The Great War! Reparations are *oppression!* A *massive* blunder! Even a *slave* wouldn't take *that* lying down! Not for long. Hitler's right. Better to die trying for freedom than submit. The Germans *will* break free."

"Oh," Monika said pensively, "if German airships return to drop bombs on us again, I'll know why. And ….. But ….. I want *no part in all that madness*. There's *not one* violent fibre in my body. I hope and pray you stop concerning yourself with all this political nothingness, my boy."

"Next time it won't be airships. It'll be aircraft. Highly engineered German aircraft."

"What a *nightmare!*" Monika said gloomily. "Hitler's popularity is waning now. Let's hope he *doesn't* win the next German election."

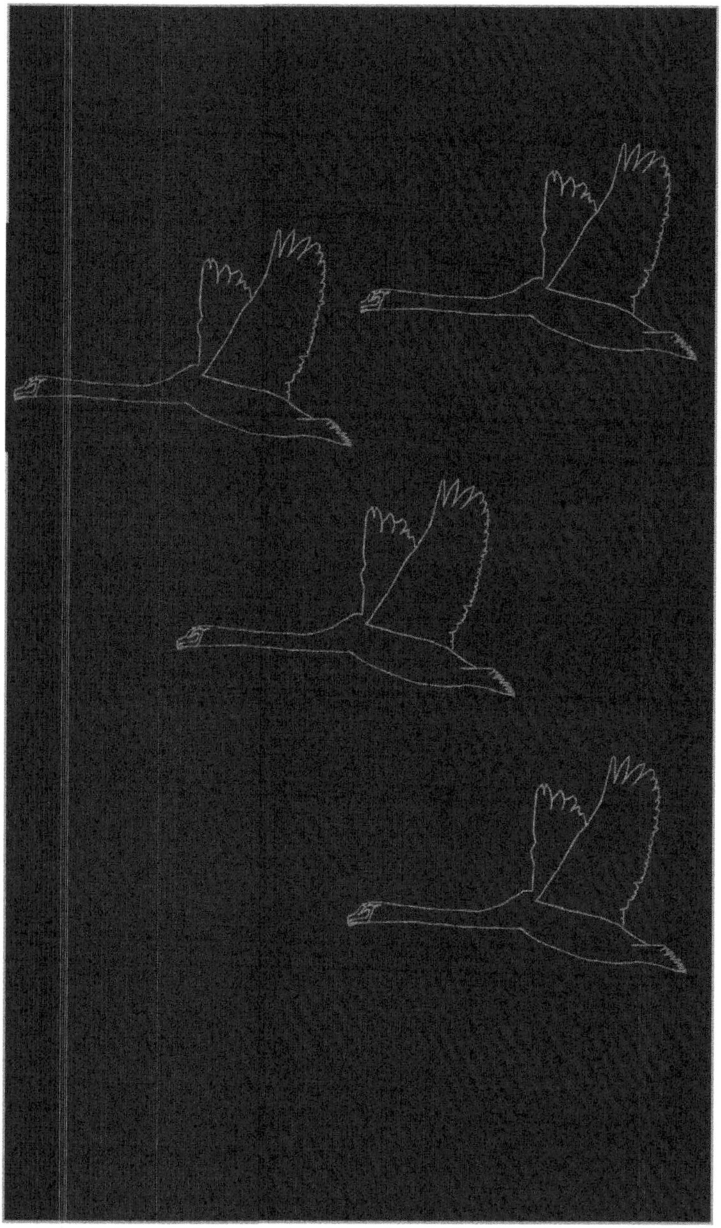

"I repeated my mistake," John said a few days later. "I attempted another conversation with my family. It seems fair to try now and again. You never know. They might respond. I told them about the political meeting and asked if they'd ever wondered what freedom *really* is."

"And? What did they say?"

"Absolutely nothing to the point. They have *no* interest in any exchange of ideas. But Eileen did say they'd been wondering where I go and asked unpleasantly whether you travel with me when I'm away for two or three nights."

"Oh," Monika responded.

"Of course I said you didn't. Isn't it absurd to feel uncomfortable about telling the truth? I mean to say, even if you did travel with me, it's not their business. They want to know about me but I'm not to know about them. Do you think it's because Eileen's Jewish?" John asked.

"Absurd ...." Monika echoed distantly. "Partly it's because you're young," she reflected.

"To change the subject," she said stoically, "I have the tickets for 'That's a Good Girl' tomorrow night. So bring overnight things. The trains out of Waterloo after the show are surprisingly frequent."

"I think," Eileen said, "there's a girl somewhere. Why else would he be away at night? I'd begun, like the rest of the village, to think he'd a liaison with Monika. But it's not Monika. I know because when he was in Birmingham I bumped into her in Elys. So it's *not* her. But it's *somebody*."

"Perhaps you're right," Eric replied. "Perhaps there's a girl somewhere. Or maybe he *is* just travelling to meetings and lectures. Either way, I'll let it go. Better to defer to notions of privacy. All things considered. Let's face it, John's no lotus-eater."

Eileen sniffed. "There are meetings and there are *meetings*," she said.

"I still argue with Eileen and my father about trivial domestic things, but I keep from them the enormity growing, day by day, in my mind."

"What enormity?" Monika asked. She turned away from the washing-up, dried her hands, and leaned against the kitchen wall.

"The bumptious nature of Eileen and her son, magnified by the ways of their race, drive me to seek revenge. I'm like a microcosm of the German nation. Everything's been taken from me. My family and my inheritance. My response is to remain active even though dented by defeat. *Defeat and dispossession* go, in *any* man, to produce the nothing-to-lose outlook."

"But *there's no comparison*, my boy," Monika said soberly. "You've *not* lost everything." She hugged him. "You have food to eat and a place to live and one day soon you'll go to a university. So by most standards you're fortunate. It's *up to you* to do your best and to use your education to better yourself. It'd be fair to say you're one of the lucky few." She stroked his hair. "Use your time for *work*, not *revenge*. Be *creative*, not destructive."

"And……….." Monika continued, "it's a mistake to assume disinheritance. You *may* have been disinherited. But you can't be certain. Making the assumption could actually increase the possibility if it makes the atmosphere at home any worse. That's how these things work. And………. nobody can be certain of inheriting. And……….. even if you *were* disinherited, you're not economically enslaved as the Germans are by war reparations." Monika drew him to the couch and sat down beside him. "*You* are a relatively free person," she insisted.

"At political meetings," he said, "when they talk of Jewish financiers and say the world's greatest problem is a de facto semi-secret Jewish state within and above states and spanning national boundaries, then I think of Eileen and her international dealings. She's Jewish."

"*No*, dearest, *no!*" Monika implored, "you *cannot* go down that road. We *all* want more money. For ourselves and for the country. What matters is how we go about making it."

"Exactly!" John responded. "You need look no further than Eileen."

"No, no, no, *no! Sweetheart,*" Monika pleaded, "*All* nations are avaricious. It's not just the Jews."

"You're not Jewish are you, Monika?"

"You know I'm not."

"Oh well," John sighed, "you're the exact opposite of Eileen. Within your fair mind there's *never* any greed. I think of you as my best friend."

"I'm *glad* to be your friend," she said. "I want to be your friend. *For ever. But*, I think one shouldn't rank friends as best, second best, third best and so on. Rather they're like portraits. A painting hangs on your wall for *years* without being studied. Friends are the same. They're with you, one way or another. In the background or in the foreground. Even after they're dead. Just as your mother is with me. I speak to her every day, even though she's been gone a while."

"The law of nature seems to be," he pondered, "that in return for the gift of children, a man must work all his life, often with minimal thanks. He has been a success if he leaves his children something of value when he dies. But!! *You* think I should be at ease with the ineffable matter of my father marrying a Jewess."

"Yes," Monika replied, "most *emphatically* I do. And you *must*. And ……… *peaceably*. Even if things are ……… not quite right ……. at the moment. Keep in mind that everyone has faults."

"I'm not just unappreciated," John said. "It goes further. I feel myself the object of their contempt."

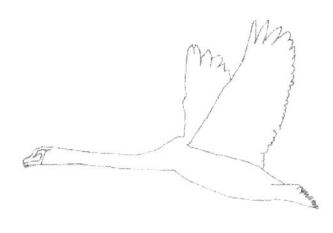

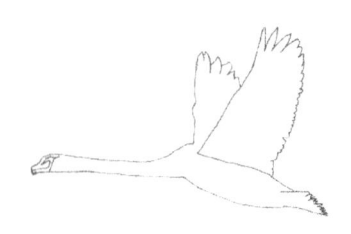

"Eric!" Eileen complained, "our lives are difficult *enough*, without having to put up with John's nonsense. So? He spends time away from home going you know not where? So! *Take* the initiative! *Fund* his exploration! Give him *money!* Give him the means to put up somewhere safe when he travels. Then you'll not worry so much. Think of it as money well spent because it'll buy us time and privacy to save *ourselves*."

Later that day Eric took John aside. "Here's money. Eileen and I've agreed to give you an allowance. Use it wisely. We expect you don't wish to tell us where you go when you're away. We won't intrude on your privacy by asking. It'll be a monthly allowance. I think it's generous. It could pay for reasonable accommodation when you're not at home. We hope it'll serve an educational purpose until the time comes to go to university."

"So, now I'm a 'remittance man'?" John studied his father. He took the money. "Compensation?" he asked.

"Well, I don't know," John reflected one cool autumn evening, as he and Monika read side by side on the couch, keeping one-another warm. "Why do we *still* labour through an age in which dictator and democrat despise one another? Why are class and culture at *such odds?* Why can't we just be *free?* Why can't we just live? *Fully!* And without interference!"

"No matter *how* bad or good things are," Monika suggested, "one might turn to poetry. As a way of staying sane. *Sanity's* more important than failure or success. *Except!*" she smiled, "*Love* is both sane and insane. And more important than anything."

John pondered this. "Better to withdraw into isolation," he mused, "leave for some faraway place where it's possible to stand alone. And not be caught up in mass consciousness."

"I've been reading," he continued, "about The Transvaal. We could buy a *huge* farm there, *cheaply!* And be individuals. The white population is British, Dutch and German. They've *learnt.* From The Boer Wars, from

German East Africa. *And* from the trenches ...... they've *learnt*. Astonishingly, they fought for Britain in The Great War. But they'll probably remain neutral if the *stupid* Europeans go to war again."

"I don't want to go *that* far away," Monika said sadly.

John searched on. For something. He knew not quite what. He kept changing his mind.

Monika watched. "I see," she said, "you're often deep in thought. I'd like to help. …… Somehow ……. But the best solutions are the ones we invent ourselves."

"I know. And……thank you……," John embraced her.

"But," John told himself, "I'm secretly at a crossroads. Monika's 'poetry' solution is attractive. Her 'existential independence' is logical. But neglecting Western culture in favour of 'poetry' is *abdication*. The doctrine for the future is National Socialism. Of course, Monika'd be *distraught* if she knew my thoughts. She's so gentle. But the very *name* rings with logic….. National Socialism …… It's like wind on reeds."

He thought of his rough translation written down in 'MY TABLES' after a visit to a library.

"The Gist of a Paragraph in 'Mein Kampf'

Translated From Memory a day or two after I visited the library.

'People dare not nowadays recall the high splendour of our past achievements, so magnificent then was our culture. For, in our time, by sharp contrast, the result of the wrongful capitulation of our erstwhile princes, all that is left us is our misery.'"

"And yet……." he thought, "I'm *not* yet ready to commit to National Socialism. Is it chaos? Or is it perfect order? Perhaps Machiavelli was right? Perhaps the state *is* more important than God! For me it's either National

Socialism or migration with Monika. Those are the choices. Perhaps," his thoughts drifted ………. "my hesitation comes from Monika. From her influence. She says women often teach men ……… *Why is everything so obscure?"* Anyway, perfection probably doesn't exist in this world."

Out loud, he said, "I want to use my allowance to search for a way to live. So far I've found false trails and unpalatable truths. I've insufficient hatred to go along with current ideologies ………….. I'll know the solution when I see it."

"Good," she said, "Good. Keep going."

"I've found, sacred or profane, actual lives differ from what the world sees. People are secretive. One man's freedom often leads to another's imprisonment. Battles of the mind are more interesting than gun battles."

"Yes," Monika agreed. "And …. the search is restricted by time. We're granted just 'threescore years and ten.'"

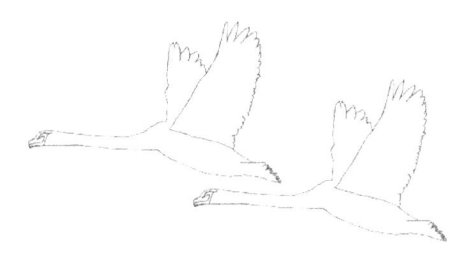

CHAPTER THREE

ONE HALF SO PRECIOUS

by

Lucille Horner

For

Jim Brazill

DRAMATIS PERSONAE

BARKER DONALD :
Owner of motor works in Oudtshoorn.

CALITZ ARTHUR
An habitual drunkard. Brother to Hester Middler.

CALITZ JANE
Wife of Arthur Calitz.

MIDDLER HENRY ('GRAPH')
1883 TO 1961
Father of Natalie. Nicknamed 'Graph' for his fascination with telegraphs and communications generally. Of Scottish descent.

MIDDLER HESTER (nee CALITZ)
1900 TO 1979
Mother of Natalie. Wife of Graph. Sister of Arthur Calitz. Plattelander (i.e. a lady who spent her entire life on the veld or living in 'dorps') Ultra conservative without knowing it. Of Dutch descent.

MIDDLER ANASTASIA
Eldest daughter of Henry and Hester.

MIDDLER BELINDA
Second daughter of Henry and Hester.

MIDDLER CHARLENE
Third daughter of Henry and Hester.

MIDDLER NATALIE ('VYGIE')
Fourth daughter of Henry and Hester.

MIDDLER, OTHER CHILDREN
Delaine, Yvette, Frederic, Gavin and Garth.

VAN DER WESTHUIZEN, DOMINEE JACOBUS
Oudtshoorn clergyman.

VAN DER WESTHUIZEN, MEVROU RITA
Clergyman's wife.

VAN NIEKERK, MRS
Natalie's landlady in Oudtshoorn.

VAN MIDDEL LEONARD (LEN)
1881 TO 1957
Slave descendant. Man-servant to the Middler family. Of mixed Malay, Bushman, Hottentot and European blood.

VAN MIDDEL NAANIE
1881 TO 1961
Wife of Leonard. Slave descendant. Maid-servant to the Middler family. Of mixed Malay, Hottentot and European blood.

VAN TONDER KITTY
Of Calitzdorp. Hester Middler's sister.

VAN TONDER PIETER
Of Calitzdorp. Kitty's husband.

WHELAN ROGER
Susan's husband. Father of Walter. Church organist.
Owner of haberdasher and general store.

WHELAN SUSAN
Mother of Walter. Book-keeper.

WHELAN WALTER
First husband of Anastasia Middler.

1918 TO 1935

MOSSEL BAY, OUDTSHOORN and PORT ELIZABETH

"I often wonder what the Vintners buy
One half so precious as the Goods they sell."

(Note : Two words, "mos" and "now", are frequently used in this chapter in a way that is curious to the non-South African reader.

"Mos" is, or was, a word without meaning inserted at haphazard intervals throughout conversations. More often used only in gentle conversation than in argumentative moments.

Sometimes the word "now" was used instead of "mos".

"Now" was considerably more assertive than "mos".)

"Weg is jy!" ("Get out!") Jane Calitz screamed at her husband. "En kom nooit weer terug nie!" ("And never come back!") She gave her inebriate a rough shove. Tottering backwards he fumbled to steady himself on the wall of the entrance hall. Before he regained his balance she opened the front door. It was then an easy matter to turn him by the shoulders, propel him over the threshold onto the stoep (porch) and watch as he tottered involuntarily down the stairs onto the garden path.

"You've been sacked from *how many* jobs, Arthur?" she raged. "And you keep *promising* and *promising* and *promising* that you're going to *stop*…….. But you *never, ever* even *try*…………. Never!

In the background, thoughtful, teenage children watched the final scene.

"*You never try!*" she stormed. "You *said* if we moved to Mossel Bay you'd *change*. You would *make* the effort. *For your sake* we moved. But it's been *all* for nothing. *Heeltemal niks! (Absolutely nothing!)*"

Jane advanced onto the stoep. She looked down on her husband. "All the *talk* and *persuasion!* The reasoning and the pleading! The promising! *Where* has it got us? It's made *absolutely no* difference! The drinking just goes *on and on!* Bottle after bottle after bottle after bottle *after bottle after bottle!* So! *Hier eindig dit! (Here*

180

it ends!) Niks meer nie! (No more!) *Go away!* Don't ever *even try* to come back! *This time* it *is* for *good! I really mean it!"*

Jane retreated indoors. In a demonstration of forceful decisiveness, she locked the door. "Hierdie keer *bedoel* ek dit! (This time I *mean* it!)" she repeated aloud to herself. So the children could hear.

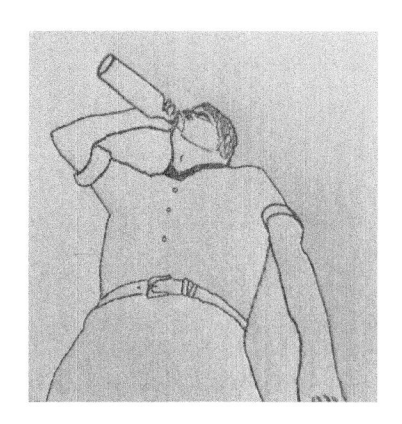

The next day Jane had the locks changed.

Expelled by his wife, feared by his children, Arthur Calitz, Hester Middler's derelict brother, still unable to suspend disbelief in his predicament, left Mossel Bay. Destitute and distorted, he found means to cross the Outeniqua Mountains and made for Oudtshoorn, where he burst upon the daily toil of the Middler family.

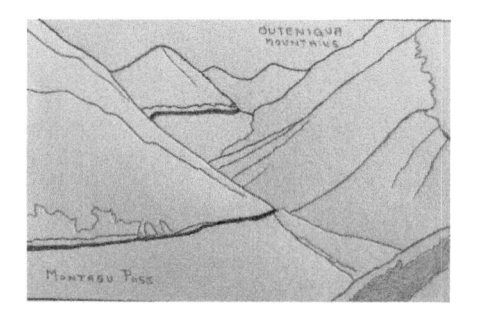

In his sister's smile there lived on, for Arthur, a remnant of a time when life had been good. Arthur and Hester were born in The Cape Of Good Hope Colony in the last decade of the nineteenth century. As close as brother and sister could be, they were innocents. There were no secrets in their laughter-filled childhood. They learned together, shared self-knowledge, found respect.

But childhood changed to youth. And peace changed to war. Arthur's service in The Boer War was brief and bloody. By 1903 he had recovered from a bullet wound in his right arm and another in his right calf. To his surprise he found himself fit and well. Edwardian empire, the thing he had fought against, now flourished. It even, so it turned out, flourished for a young veteran of a kommandotjie. (small Boer commando). The Edwardians seemed to repent their victory over The Boers. For a decade the world offered prosperous normality.

Then came 1910.

"Although Ma and Pa argue about it, a lot," Hester observed to Arthur one day in 1911, "to me, nothing seems to have changed in the year since we became part of The Union."

"Except we're now citizens of The Union of South Africa instead of the The Cape Of Good Hope," Arthur replied. "Our Cape Of Good Hope is now mos just one district of a very big state."

"Yes, and I suppose," Hester agreed thoughtfully, "a uniqueness *has* been lost. *And,* it's been *equally* lost by each of the colonies that joined together to make The Union. The individual character of the old republics and the old colonies has been blended and diluted. Gone forever. Actually, it's quite a *big* loss, now I think of it."

"Probably," Arthur enhanced his sister's thoughts, "such disappointments are felt mostly by the traveller and by the nationalist. And the farmer. And ……. I suppose …. old themes still run true. Bloemfontein is still Bloemfontein. Pretoria is still Pretoria. The platteland is still the platteland."

"Yes," Hester re-examined her perceptions, "but the old themes are not so individual any more. Not so quaint. They've all been submerged in one entity to serve the interests of commerce and politics. *Magtig!*

(God!), independence is *so* important."

"Agh, the financiers and the politicians believe Union means progress," Arthur was critical. "And ……… if it's a way to prevent more wars, then I'm forced by experience to accept it. But in 1901, when we lost the war, the biggest thing we lost was sovereignty. Cultural sovereignty. *That's* what made us truly great. In our republics. It gave us *life*. And *purpose*. Gave us *quality*. In our eyes, at least. And in the eyes of the Germanic world. Cultural individuality is what we *really* lost. Because this Dominion the British are so keen on ….. it's a British idea. Not a Boer idea. Let General Botha say what he will. This Union does nothing to restore Boer sovereignty. Things are back to what they were when The British abandoned us by withdrawing from Queen Adelaide Province. The things that made our people, *eighty* years ago, trek away from The British have now been, *everywhere,* reinstated. Our way of life has *again* been overthrown."

He thought for a moment.

"Actually, Hester," he looked into an unseen distance, "the desert is all that matters."

A few years later, for love of an English girl, Arthur went to Belgium, to northern France, to the trenches.

Still smarting from the loss of the Boer republics, still struggling with his thoughts, an event known as The Battle of Delville Wood destroyed any vestige of decency that might still, in Arthur's mind, have attached to human existence.

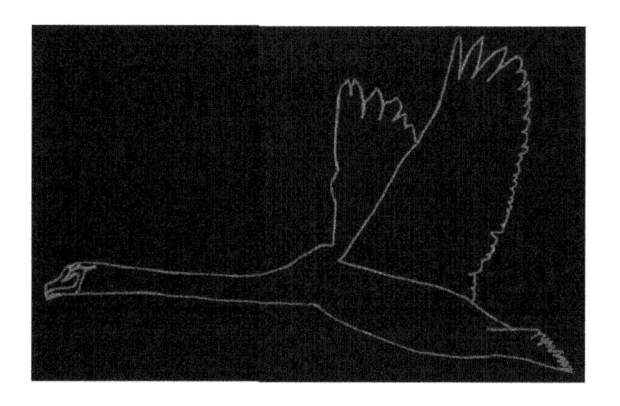

"Hester! Nobody doubts your brother's bravery," Graph protested to his wife, "nor his above-average intelligence. His service records say it all."

"But this invasion of our domesticity by a drunkard is a menace. The children suffer. They see his raucous behaviour every day. In *our lounge*. They dread his presence. They literally all come to me at night. The little ones get into bed with me when they hear his shouting and cursing. And the bigger ones huddle together on the foot of my bed. And it's all making our marriage more than a little……….uneasy."

"As I've said so many times before," Hester replied vehemently, "Arthur's troubles all come from shell-shock. Everybody was *very* happy to wave him goodbye when he was *made to feel* obliged to risk his life for a cause in which he *didn't* believe. That was quite okay! But now! Now that he's back and *shaking with shell-shock,* now *nobody* wants to know his troubles. He only went to France because *the English girl* said he must. Now, at best, he is shunned! And the English girl? *Where* was she when he came back? *Nowhere!* That's where she was! *No bleddy where!* So, now *I* think a little *plain humanity* might be in order! Actually, instead of criticising him and turning their backs on him, the community owes him *every respect* and sympathy for the sacrifices he made. They should *pay tribute* to him!"

"Okay, Hester," Graph replied steadily, "you've long been incensed by this. And I can see why. But at least admit that it was in youth that Arthur began drinking too much."

"So you *always* say," Hester was deeply aggrieved. "But you've *never* given *proper* thought to what he went through in The Boer War. He was *just sixteen* when he joined the commando. And The Boer War was *as bad* as The Great War. In its own way. Because war is war. Death is death. Injury is injury. And fear is fear. There's *never* a good time for *any* of it. It isn't made any less or more by the time or the place or the climate or the cause. By whether it happens in *desert* or in *mud*."

"He *drinks*, Hester, because he drinks, because he drinks, *because he drinks*," Graph replied wearily but softly. "It was *not* the wars that caused the problem. He's simply an alcoholic. Why do you deny that? Why can't you *see* that? Other people went through far worse than he did without turning to the bottle."

"*My God, man!*" Hester exploded. "You *undervalue* my brother *just like all the rest!* Can you *not* see that Arthur is *my own flesh and blood?* Just as my children are my own flesh and blood? I shall care for him, *no matter what*. Even if you choose to divorce me. So you had *better think carefully* about that."

Graph did not actually raise his voice. But he replied with the firm intensity that only emerged when he knew everything he held dear to be under threat. "So. You would sacrifice your marriage and the peaceful childhood of your children, to support a …….tramp?"

"*Don't you dare call my brother a tramp!*" Hester was verbally aflame. "Those tramp-clothes he wears, tattered and torn as they may be, are the uniform he *inherited* from wearing that other uniform in the trenches. For *three years*! His rags are as much the uniform of forced conformity as was that soldier's uniform which the English girl demanded he should wear. Do you think all those months in the mud watching men have their lives taken from them had no effect on him? All the blood and the pain and the shattered hopes? And the thought that at any moment it could be his turn? *Can't you see* it could drive *any man* to drink?"

Graph knew it pointless to continue. "The war was grotesque, Hester," he agreed. "I *do* understand your feelings."

"But," he thought, although he did not speak the words, "why *doesn't* she admit that his really heavy drinking began before wars took their toll?" Out loud he said, "Hester, do you not perhaps think you should ask Jane to make one last attempt?"

"You're so clever with words, Graph," Hester, still grimly angry, countered, "it's your idea. You go and speak to Jane."

Graph and Hester took the train together to Mossel Bay, to discuss Arthur's alcoholism with his wife.

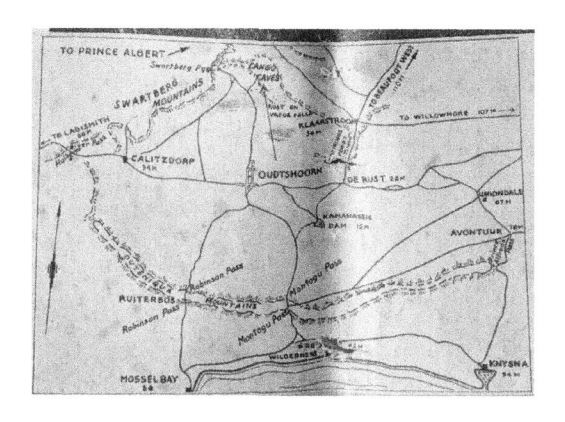

"Agh, ja, Hester," Jane, on hearing the request that she make yet another attempt to rehabilitate her husband, chose her words carefully and deliberately, "Arthur is mos *very* sick. *Too* sick for me or anyone else to cure."

"But, *Jane!*" Hester appealed, "Arthur's not only my brother. He's *also* your husband *and* the father of your children."

"That he is the father of mos my children, I own," Jane replied. "*But my husband?! No! Nie meer nie.*" *("Not any more.")*

"Agh, nee Jane," ("Oh, no Jane,") Hester could not accept the reality.

"Agh, ja Hester, di's 'n feit." ("Oh, yes Hester, it's a fact.")

"Wat van, (what of) 'til death do us part?"

"Death *did* part us, Hester," Jane replied instantly. "Once I loved him. *Deeply*. But *the bottle*" she said severely, "*murdered* our marriage." Her face grim and drawn in despair,

Jane fell silent as spectres of the ruin visited upon her stalked across her memory.

Graph respected her silence. For a long while he sat resting his chin on one hand. But then he too tried. "Do you not perhaps see, Jane, that there may still be an obligation? Do you not, do not we all, *have* to keep trying?"

"And the children, Jane?" Hester persevered, "What of *the children?* Do they not mos *long* for their father?"

"Unfortunately, Hester, *the reverse is true*," a touch of defiance edged Jane's voice. She spoke with conviction. "They're *just so definitely* glad he's gone. No longer must they put up with a drunkard's madness. They don't, *any more*, have to hide from his violence. And they no longer lie awake at night, listening. In case they must rush to protect me from another attack. *Now*, they can mos fall asleep at night. Like other children. Now that he's gone."

There came another silence.

"And by the way," Jane asked with some disbelief, "have you *really* left your children in the same house as Arthur while you come all this way to plead with me? Natalie must mos be only *eleven*? And the others much now *younger?*"

"Leonard and Naanie will look after them," Graph replied in studied composure.

"But……….." Hester pleaded, "you and Arthur knew one another when you were children. Doesn't that count for anything?"

"Agh, Hester, that was two wars ago," Jane looked at her ex-sister-in-law with the certainty of a woman who has made an irrevocable decision. "That was *long* ago when we lived in a Garden of Eden. We had *hope and innocence* in the Cape colony days. Even though we found it dangerous and exciting to support the Boers. In any way we could. In a way we were too young."

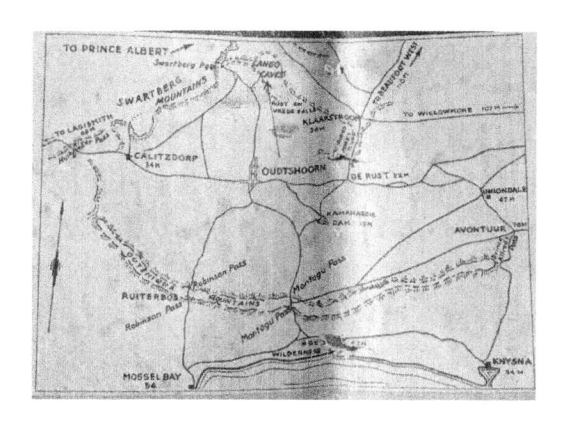

"You still live in that same place," Hester insisted, "just the name's changed. You're still the same. You can mos *regain* innocence. And re-kindle hope."

"Agh, Hester. You *were* my sister-in-law. And I *love* you. But you patently do *not* know *what* you're talking about. The Garden of Eden is now mos a desert. Drier than the mos Kalahari. Innocence has been *destroyed.* By *alcoholism* and *wife-beating.* It *cannot* be regained."

"Did The English girl turn you away from him?" Hester asked uneasily.

"Yes! Of course! But once I was sure of his contrition, I forgave him. Fully," Jane was completely frank. "It was a lot to forgive. But I did *forgive* him. And he *knew* it."

"It was a lot to forgive," Graph agreed. "Forgiveness is a grace."

Hester looked askance at her husband.

"Arthur *still* dreams of being a *proper* settler," Hester persisted. A pioneer. He *still* has both the colonist *and* the trekker vision of *hard work*. He *longs from the bottom of his heart* to support his wife and build a *good safe place* in which his children can live. In peace."

"Yes, Hester," Jane answered. "He *does* want the domestic charms and children and the hearth. And God *gave* him these. But he didn't have the strength to *keep* them. One by one he squandered *all* his opportunities of reaching that mos *idyll*. Alcohol is the mos *mendacious* antidote to all his mos *pain*. He always *tells* himself he'll give up drinking *tomorrow*. But that tomorrow, Hester? *That tomorrow??* That tomorrow mos *never* comes. He *cannot* say 'Good Bye' to the bottle. Years and years of chances have been *lost*. All lost. And he had more chances than most. It's all *mos irreversible*. Strong drink has a stranglehold over him. Drink has taken *everything we have* and all prospect of anything we mos hoped one day to have. If we worked hard. Which we promised one another to do. Now all we can do is survive as best we can. *Drink!* Drink *will* kill him, Hester. In the end. In the end drink will kill him."

There were moments of silence.

"So………." Jane continued, "the more he dreams, the more his sobriety diminishes and mos diminishes. He should mos *many* years ago have started the hard work needed to make our mos dream come true. But he always just mos said the world always treats him badly. He thinks the *world's* indebted to him. And he always says that same world refuses to pay its debt." Jane's anger intensified. "That's how he justifies the weakness of mos *procrastination*. As for the things a wife or a woman can give him, they count for mos nothing, Hester. *Nothing!* Those things! I would *even* have let him have another woman if that would've helped now anything. I *even told* him. I told him I would now share him with The English Woman if it made him happy. If he could find her again. If it stopped his drinking. If it gave us all a chance. *There.* Now I have mos told you about it. But he couldn't. Instead of now taking up his mos great responsibility, his now *anger* always tells him that the now barbarous world definitely owes him as much time as he mos needs. And he says he *will* contemplate the mos bottom of the bottle if *he sees* mos fit so to do. Because alcoholics are deeply *selfish*, Hester. And they know it. And they would much rather be kind. But all that alcohol does to them is mos *bring out* their selfishness. Which makes them drink even more. Because they hate their own selfishness. But *time*, Hester, *time* doesn't allow this. Time ticks by. He mos made his choice. And he allowed his now time to now tick by until he now *lost* our now dream. Now he has even lost his *time*. He's lost everything."

"But Jane!" Hester persisted, "it wasn't *his* choice. It was *circumstances*. The indifferent world has a callously short memory."

"It *was* his choice," Jane was beyond contradiction. "*Many* tried to help. But eventually, all of them, just stopped visiting. They stopped asking how things were. I think they couldn't bear to look. If they'd looked *properly*, then, mos they would've told themselves *they themselves* must stop drinking. But *they themselves* now did now not now *want* to now *stop drinking*. Like you and your children. You mos stopped coming to kuier. (visit.) Anyway, it wouldn't have made any difference." Firm lines entrenched themselves around the corners of her mouth "Nothing would've made any difference."

"Well, I cannot give up," Hester said, "Please Jane, if I'm able to keep him completely sober for one whole month, will you then give him another chance? For my sake, for your sake, for the children's sake?"

"No, sister-in-law!" Jane said. "I will not."

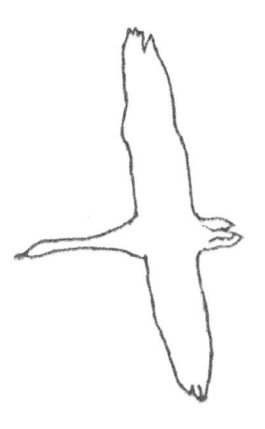

"So, Hester," Graph ceased staring out of the railway carriage window and looked at Hester, "we travel back across the mountains empty-handed. Do you not see that alcohol has the power to kill love? It killed Jane's love and destroyed her family. Now it threatens us."

"Arthur knows," Hester replied grimly, "that drink made him impotent and that he's a mere prisoner of his craving. He knows, drunk or sober, his world's ruined. Well. Jane may've given up. But I *have not*."

A few weeks after the visit to Jane, Graph once more took Hester to task.

"So, Hester," Graph spoke with grim concern, "we stopped visiting your brother and his family in Mossel Bay years ago because his drinking terrified our children. But *now,* that same terror has come over the mountains to Oudtshoorn to haunt us all, in our own house, every day. And every night. It's ever-present."

"I'm trying to persuade him to cut down," Hester said curtly.

"Hester. There's *no such thing*," Graph said firmly, "as *cutting down*. There's only *giving up*. And Hester. He shows no sign of improvement. He's unkempt and alone. And you continue," Graph complained, "to harbour him against my wish. Everybody's ill at ease, you, me the children, the servants. An unpredictable danger has settled over us like a black cloud. Our children used to live one long divine, light-hearted rough and tumble. *But now?* Their fun is a thing of the past. You're the only one who doesn't look on Arthur with unmitigated disgust. I'm sorry, Hester, but that's the only word for it. The children leave their beds at night and huddle together because they're woken by the sounds of porcelain being broken and dining room chairs being thrown at the wall. Pictures are knocked from the walls. You fell asleep last night because you were exhausted. And so I intervened. The children have *never* before heard the profanities he uses so loudly. Day and night. They're *young* children, Hester. And I heard him telling you my military service as a telegraph boy was nothing compared to his deeds in The Boer War and at Delville Wood. I'm sure he's correct. But, Hester, how did you respond? Hester! Look at me! I cannot believe it. Your response was to *offer* him another bottle of wine. What are you doing, Hester?"

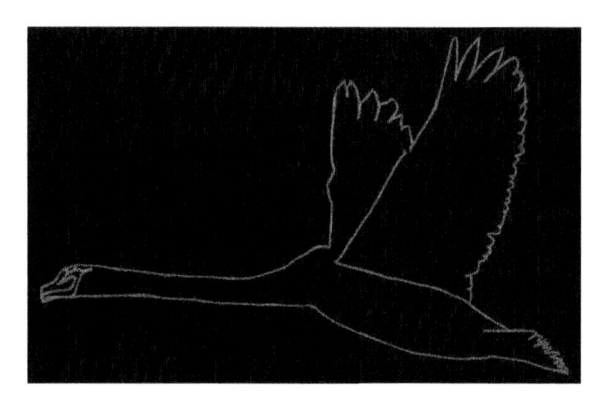

The eleven-year-old Natalie had spent the morning energetically helping her father clear the irrigation channel at the bottom of the orchard. They were alone and out of earshot of the rest of the family.

"I heard him again last night, Daddy," she said. "I often hear him yodelling at night when he's still far away, walking home from the bar. I know when to expect him. Most nights he gets here soon after the bar closes. The whole town sleeps but his voice can be heard over the rooftops, *singing* his head off. And then he sits on my beautiful bench that you put outside my window. And carries on drinking there. It's horrible. I hate it. And then ma (mummy) comes and sits with him. And they talk all night long. And he talks *such nonsense*. In a *loud* voice. But Ma always just sits and listens to him, hour after hour. Even when he's *very* cross. *No wonder* she's often so tired. She doesn't sleep at night. Well, not much."

Graph took the matter up with his wife. "Hester, you and Arthur are keeping Natalie awake at night when you sit with him on the bench outside her window. If you have to listen, night after night, to his poisonous ramblings, could you do it elsewhere? Anyway, I'm going to move the bench much further down the garden. But please! Be aware that all this obnoxious drunkenness is harming our children."

"Graph," Hester replied, an ugliness in her voice, "I have *only contempt* for the way you and the children and the world treat a man who's paying a high price for doing his duty on their behalf."

"Hester," Graph answered, a sadness in his voice, "One of a soldier's foremost duties is to stay alive. Even after the war he fought is won. Or lost. Arthur is drinking himself to death. He'll be no use to anyone dead. Including himself."

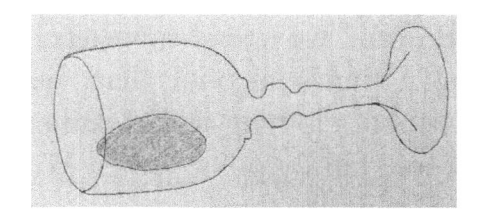

It was early evening. Arthur had taken himself to the 'kroeg.' (Bar.)

Graph raised his head from the ledger in which, in longhand, he kept the house-keeping records. "Hester!" his voice was filled with concern, "we *cannot* keep spending these large sums each week at the bottle store. They're ruinous, *literally ruinous*. Arthur should *not* be given the thing he most craves. In fact, if you hope to save his life and rehabilitate him, you should refuse his demands. But, instead, you *always* seem able *and willing* to find him another bottle. *No matter* the cost. Even when it's *obvious* he's had *far more* than he should. Even in the middle of the night. Actually, the doctor told me the proper amount for him now is nil. But you disregard all advice. So *now* we spend more each week on Arthur's alcohol than we spend on food, clothing and cleaning for the whole family put together. We *cannot* go on in like this."

"It's a stage," Hester said sullenly.

Natalie, who was present, looked from her father to her mother and back again.

"It's more," Graph said emphatically, "than a *stage*," The amount you spend on drink *increases* each week."

Hester rounded on her husband. "You took your wedding vows," she said intensely, "as did I." Do you *remember* your vows? You vowed, '*With thee my worldly goods I share.*' If you choose to break that vow now, at a time when my brother is in such need, I'll take him away and look after him elsewhere and then you'll have *not one*, but *two* households to pay for! Do you *hear* me?"

Graph knew Hester meant it. So fierce was she in her conviction that she made no attempt to conceal her wrath from Natalie.

Natalie shrank into her chair.

"I refuse to accept I'm doing any wrong," Hester continued. "In fact, the opposite's true. I'm looking after the person in the family who has the greatest need. As I always shall. I'd look after you or any of our children with exactly the same steadfastness if ever the need arose."

"In one part of my soul, Hester," Graph replied, "I cannot fault your compassion. You're right. Arthur *is* in *great* need. You believe Arthur has a *terrible* illness and you're *nursing* an ill person. You believe that like any ill person, Arthur deserves care and compassion. It'd be churlish of me to contest your stance."

"But, Hester," Graph continued, "in another part of my soul I focus on your neglect, your virtual abandonment, in fact, of your maternal and matrimonial roles. You sacrifice *everything else* so that you may give all your care to a hopeless case of alcoholism. I'm sad and frustrated by this, almost despairing."

"I'll do *whatever* it takes," Hester remained resolute.

"You demand, Hester," Graph acknowledged, "I be man enough to see it through, to care for you all, to look after everything and everyone, *no matter* the cost. Perhaps this is what being a husband and father means. Yet, the task seems endless, unreasonable, *beyond* my ability. But…….*Rejoice!*" he determined ironically, "at least I know this must be my work now even if it ends in complete failure and destitution."

"Yes," Hester answered. "That *is* what I expect and demand of you."

"Might it be too much to at least expect a 'Thank you'? For my labour?" Graph asked.

"*No more so*, Graph, than for me to expect a 'Thank you' from you for the labour of bearing you so many children," Hester said sarcastically, ironically and angrily.

"For that, Hester, I did at the time and have many times since, said a very clear 'Thank you.' In various ways."

Natalie leaned on the arm of her chair, the book she read forgotten. She looked long and hard at her mother.

Hester's dominee (priest) sat on his stoep (verandah) drawing deeply on his long pipe, exhaling slowly, concentrating on the matter before him.

"It goes on night after night, dominee, (reverend)" Graph complained. "When Arthur gets home he's always drunk. Teen daardie tyd het hy nog altyd diep in die bottel ingekyk. (By that time he's already looked deeply into the bottle.) And then Hester *always* brings him *even more* wine. And they sit on the garden bench and talk complete nonsense until dawn. He's always loud and aggressive and she's always soft and conciliatory. It goes on and on. After seven a.m. neither Hester nor Arthur are to be seen. He lies abed in the guestroom until mid-afternoon, sleeping off intoxication. And Hester mopes in our room to avoid the disapproval of her family. And to recover from the long hours of attendance. For my part, dominee, (reverend) I *deplore* the immense emotional damage to the family. But I do what I can. I work much longer hours than I did before Arthur arrived. Because I must pay the *grievous* liquor bills. Also I must fill in the *gap* Hester has left in the task of looking after the children. We're lucky to have Leonard and Naanie. They have deep understanding."

"Speaking of the children," the dominee said, "Rita tells me Natalie quite often comes to church in the afternoons. Not for the church. She comes to listen to Roger playing the church-organ. Rita says the girl seems very ….. *inside* herself. Troubled. Rita tries to engage her in conversation but she is polite and shy. Or scared perhaps? Apparently, though, she does speak to our neighbour, Susan Whelan, Roger's wife. In fact, those two speak a lot."

"Natalie's *scared*, dominee," Graph said sadly. "*All* the children are scared. Of course, I know the Whelans. If Natalie can speak to Susan about things, then that's a blessing. Because what my children are seeing …… it's *not* a good way for children to grow up. To see the things they see. Every day and every night. That's why I'm here again. Asking for your help. Asking for you to speak to Hester. Again."

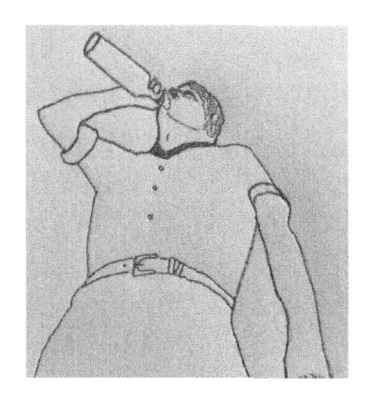

There came a night, months later, when, Hester absent for a few minutes, Arthur weaved his way indoors in search of more to drink, and, whether in possession of his faculties or not, found himself in Anastasia's bedroom. A scream from Anastasia brought not only Graph and Hester running, but also the terror-stricken faces of the other children peeping around doors.

"*Get out!*" Graph shouted and threw Arthur out of Anastasia's bedroom into the passageway. Being incapable,

Arthur fell to the floor with a thud and lay still. On his way down, the intruder's head hit the door handle causing a nasty gash and an instant and profuse flow of blood. Graph aged instantly. A pool of blood spread over the floorboards. Graph checked Arthur was still breathing before dragging the inebriate into the lounge and hauling him onto a chair.

"You administer the first aid, Hester," Graph said in absolute calm. "I'll go and be with the children."

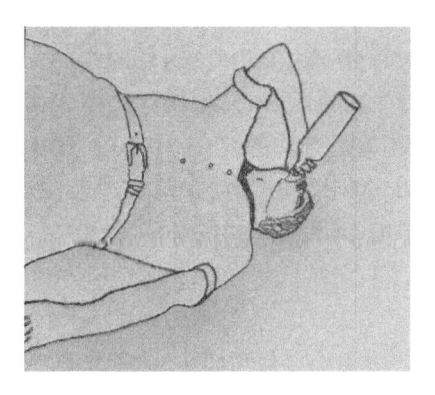

After this incident, Hester agreed to Graph's suggestion they go together to discuss their difficulties with the dominee. An appointment was made.

"Sit asseblief," ("Please take a seat,") the dominee said as he ushered them into his office. He took a long moment to pack the bowl of his pipe with tobacco and to light up.

"Begin jy, Graph" ("You begin, Graph") he said with his customary refusal to waste time on formalities and pleasantries.

"I'm tired, Hester," Graph said, looking at his wife. "Every family is struggling at present. People are calling it a 'depression' But, nowadays, as well as working harder than ever before, *and* for less money, it's necessary for me to sleep every night in an armchair outside the children's bedrooms. To protect them from your brother. We ought to be giving our children *much* more attention than we are. But the permanent presence of a drunkard in our midst prevents us from being the parents we should be. We're *exhausted.*"

Hester would hear no evil.

"Agh, what twak, Graph," ("Oh what piffle, Graph"), – ('twak' is pronounced 'twuck'), Hester was entirely dismissive. You're making a mountain out of a mos molehill to get your own way. Trying not to prove things are worse than they are."

The dominee swivelled around in his chair to look on Graph and to examine Graph's response.

"What could be worse," Graph asked, "than for a young girl to wake up in terror in the middle of the night with a drunkard in her room?"

"Gotts, man!" (pronounced ggggots with a guttural g). "Don't be mos bleddy *reedickuluss*, Graph!" Hester stormed. Her voice rose. "Arthur was heeltemal (completely) drunk. He didn't know *where* he was or *what* he was doing." Her voice rising to higher anger as she consolidated her view. "The next morning he couldn't remember *a single thing* about *any* of it."

"Hester," the dominee intervened. "You're now too heated."

Hester, ever respectful of any office-bearer of the church, silenced herself. But she sniffed a loud sniff. Which may only have been an inhalation of air. Or it may have been her refusal to back down. And then she sighed. Loudly.

"I've always assumed you know, Hester," the dominee pressed on, "that Susan Whelan, the organist's widow, has *long* conversations with Natalie? In fact I think we all know that Susan has played a big part in your girl's childhood. I *am* able to understand Graph's concern. Long ago when Natalie was still quite small, Susan noticed from her lounge window that the child came often to church to listen to Roger practising on the church organ. And one day Susan left her house and went into the church to speak with the child. And then, a day or two later, aware, because the child had told her so, there was a problem with strong drink, Susan asked me if I thought it acceptable for her to invite Natalie to their house sometimes. For tea. Knowing the circumstances, I said it seemed a *kind* thing to do. I mentioned this to Graph at the time. So you see, Hester, I too have long worried about your children's exposure to alcoholism. All your children. But especially I worry about a girl of Natalie's intelligence and character, a girl needing more parental input than you're able to give, being somewhat neglected. Because, Hester, your mind has long been on other things."

"Yes, well," Hester replied, "it was *high time* the community began to mos help us. Of course, I know Natalie often visits Susan. And I long since said thank-you to Susan. I could begin to think of this help as a small part of the recognition that Arthur *deserves* for the *sacrifices he* made."

"Hester," Graph sounded sad and over-burdened, "can you *not* see protecting children is *the primary duty* of a father? *That* is what this meeting's about. *We are here to talk about the importance of putting the needs of the children above the needs of a drunk.* And can you also *not* see how our marriage is compromised by this terrible drinking? *When* last did you sleep with me, Hester? Because, if you can remember that, well, all I can say is I cannot. We have lost intimacy."

Leonard and Naanie van Middel looked on with discomfort but made little comment as the family foundered. They went about their domestic duties and kept their servant's council. When the matter arose, as frequently it did because their duty was to keep the house clean, they would mention 'sulke dinge' (such things) amongst friends and family in the coloured 'lokasie'. (location or shanty town.) Their little acts of kindness, performed without thought of reward, went unremarked because they were unseen.

Just once, Len offered a suggestion. "Perhaps you must leave her, baas? And take the children with you?" It was an immensely selfless thought because dissolution of the Middler family could have disrupted, even destroyed the Van Middel's livelihood.

"There's *nothing*, Hester," Graph complained once more to his wife, "*nothing*, I can say or do to break the interminable pattern. Against my wishes, against my prayers, you *keep* bringing the *evil, evil, evil* green bottles home. There's a *huge* pyramid of green bottles next to the compost heap and *every day* an *astonishing* number of empties is added. Everyone, children and servants, keeps finding empty bottles hidden in the garden and turning up in the oddest places. Some aren't even empty, just abandoned."

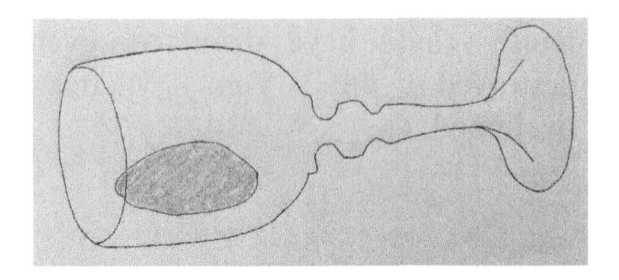

"As the months have passed, dominee," Graph again unburdened himself to the minister, "the family have learned not to comment. Instead, they've acquired the terrible art of saying nothing. *Nothing.* But, jointly and severally, they're assembling an *enormous* store of evidence against Hester. I don't know *where* it'll end."

"And, you know, dominee," Graph continued, "people are *very strange.* Our friends and neighbours *clearly* see what's happening, how strong drink *destroys* us. But *do* they change *their* ways? No! They just *keep* drinking *as if* the curse of alcoholism could *never* happen to *them*. They *still* even make *gifts* of *bottles of wine* to us, *to us of all people!* Even though I make it *quite* clear wine is the *last* thing we want. Which tells me just how dependent they are on the bottle. And how thoughtless. They have *not the first idea* of the degree to which the children and I *deplore* the presence of alcohol in our house. It seems *many* of our friends and acquaintances are alcoholics *without realising it*. They'd *never* consider giving up. *In fact* I think most w*ould be quite unable to* give up their evening brandewyn (brandy) on the stoep. (verandah.) Even if they *really wanted* to. Even if they *really* tried. Which they would not *think* of doing. It's as if their hands are *glued* to their wine-glasses. Watch them at a gathering! They're dismayed if they can't find their glass. They're deaf and blind. They *ignore misery*. Although it's there *right in front of them*. For all to see. They're *convinced* it's someone else's misery, *definitely* *not theirs*. They think it'll *never* be *their* problem. *Even though they see it. Every single time they visit us, they see it.* ….. They even think a drunkard's antics are funny!" Graph fell silent. And then he ended quietly, "They see it."

"Graph," the dominee sucked on his pipe, "it is not for us to see how this will end. Only The Almighty knows how it'll end. In the mean time you must keep being a good man. Keep looking after your children as you always have. *That* is your reward. For the time being. Your hard labour is both duty and reward. And always remember. Despite everything, there *are* good things in your life. Think of *them*. Study *them*."

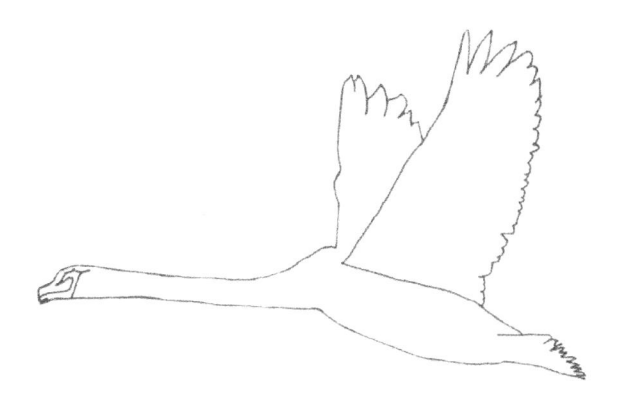

"Now. *Listen* to me," Graph said one day when Len, Naanie and all the children happened to be in the kitchen at the same time. "That pyramid of green bottles," he pointed at the huge pile of bottles in the garden, "must *never ever* be cleared away. Do you hear me? It must be *left to stand there* and to grow, day by day. It's already enormous. Surely the day will come when its sheer size pricks your mother's conscience? Or perhaps even Uncle Arthur's conscience? That mountain of bottles must be *our way* to register our plight and to contest this thing that's happening to us all. Perhaps even to stop it happening. At last. Although, I do understand it's a slender hope."

A few days later the thinker and poet of the family, Natalie, reverted to the matter of the pile of green bottles.

"Daddy," she said when she was alone with Graph, "our green pyramid is a very mos *morose* mos way to keep the score. We are mos building a *case*. But to *which* now *judge* will we present our case and *what mos good* will *come* of such a case? Are we not mos building a now glass-mountain of resentment and anger against the mos persons of my uncle and my mother? And do you think mos that will ever change ma's (mother's) determination to make her mos....*hobo*.... of a mos brother, the highest priority?"

Graph looked at his child and wondered, again, at her independence of thought.

Susan Whelan and Rita Van Der Westhuizen, long-standing neighbours and active members of the church, shared many secrets.

"Agh, Susan. This is mos *too terrible*, this alcohol business of the Middlers'," Rita said. "It makes me mos pieperig (sickly/weak) when I think of it all."

"At least," Susan agreed, "the music lessons we give Natalie take her, from time to time, out of her bad home life and put her into a world of harmony. Have you noticed her progress? She finds it a relief to leave the worry of alcoholism and to enter, instead, a world of music."

"Yes," Rita agreed. "It's mooi (pretty) to watch her play."

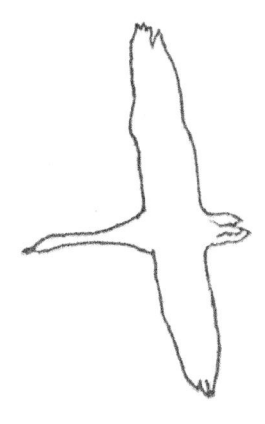

"Daddy!" Natalie asserted the morning after a raucous and destructive night, as she worked vigorously with Naanie to make the floor safe from broken glass, "I mos doesn't hate any actual persons. I believe I never shall hate *a person*. What I now hate is the now *substance* of alcohol itself."

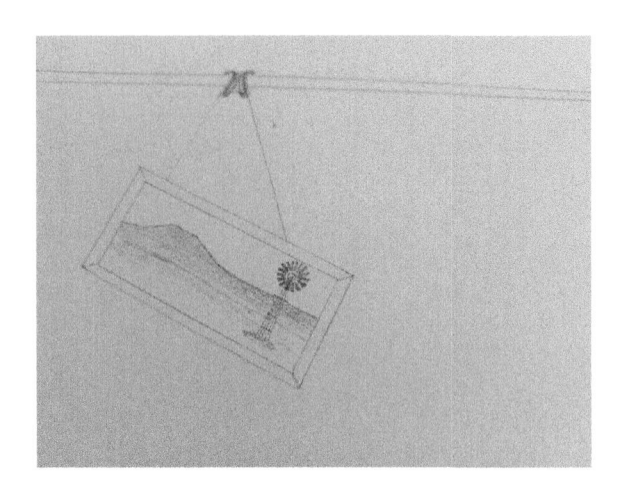

Graph looked at Natalie and then at Naanie.

"And what I wonder, Daddy, having mos looked *around* a bit…mos…" Natalie continued earnestly, "is whether alcoholism *runs in families* and whether any of your children, or my children, or our children's children, will have a …mos……tendency …to themselves become alcoholics.

"Funny you should ask that, Vygie," Graph looked again at Naanie and then at his daughter, "I've been wondering the same thing. Whether any of the offspring might one day be so blighted. And….how on earth to guard against such a thing……But…I wish my darling philosopher-daughter, *you* didn't have to think about these things."

"Well, Daddy, you and I are the only ones who mos *really* talk to each other about it. No-one else mos *says* much. Except when you and ma (mummy) sometimes shout at one another. Or if you aren't shouting at each other you mos go *for days* without saying *anything* to each other. Which, now in a way is now *worse* than shouting. You two seem to travel between being…mos…resigned…and mos …. acrimonious. With one another."

"I know, Vygie," Graph replied, "the family is besieged by this illness. And I cannot think it good that discussion is so *muted* and supressed. And sometimes entirely absent. But that's how it is. A growing silence has entered the soul of the family."

"Each one," Natalie responded reflectively, "knows and understands the worrying of the others, but because you mos look after us so carefully, Daddy, it seems mos … to all of us … mos … better to … harbour heavy thoughts than to talk about them. But do you know what, Daddy? Silence has become like one of those *electric dynamo engine things* that you mos always think are *so* clever. The silence is like a dynamo. It can give us the energy to … mos … *endure.* Each person finds … mos … *nobility* … in mos … noting details… but also in … mos … reserving comment. But, do you know what, Daddy? Each one of us is now encasing bad memories. Deep inside our now souls."

"Agh nee, baas!" ("Oh no, boss!") Naanie said. She looked

sympathetically from Graph to Natalie and back again. "Dit is *te* treurig." ("It is *too* sad.")

"Agh, don't worry, Naanie," Natalie went on remarkably lightly. "Nowadays we must mos work with what we've got. Just like every person in the world must. And do you know what? We have one another. And that's ... mos ... fair enough.... But," she reverted to her subject, "as time has gone on each one of us has found less and less wish to ...... *share* dismay. Although ... I think each one secretly .... relives .... the *ugly* things that happen. In their heads and hearts they relive it all. Every day. *Deep* inside. Over and over. But all that needs to be said these days can be ... mos ... conveyed ......by an understanding glance or by a mos nod or shake of the head. My sisters have found that a ...... supportive wink can deflect ...... a ...... *torrent* of argument and swearing ... make it all ... mos ... pass by harmlessly as the alcoholic nonsense that really it is.

What is now called … non-verbal … has become mos all that's necessary. This way we don't have to go through the …… tedium and self-analysis of … mos … frequent commiseration."

Graph communed with his daughter in that same silence of which she spoke. He knew she understood his silence to mean he accepted her words. "Let's go and see how the fruit in the orchard is doing," he suggested.

"Of course," Natalie continued as they walked, "their silence dissolves whenever Uncle Arthur's outrage takes him to new levels of fury and carryings-on. Because this … mos … brings out higher levels of anger in those who must watch and listen and … mos … *receive* it. So, new events make them break their silence and speak. But …"she ended slowly, "they mos soon retreat into silence again." They passed through the gate in the hedge that divided the orchard from the garden.

Natalie looked around the orchard to check no-one was near before continuing.

"Daddy," she whispered, "I must tell you a *terrible* secret. Sometimes when I've had no option but to listen to Uncle Arthur and when I've looked at how quickly his body is ageing from all the drinking and how he's often bruised and bandaged from falling and from … mos … other incidents, then, I must say, then I hope it's not going to be long before he dies."

"Naanie," Hester said looking in bemusement at the arrangement of bottles in the pantry and, unusually, doubting the methodical housekeeping of her close servant, "as I said the other day, we're to keep the full bottles on this side of the pantry and the empties, whether whisky or wine, must be put out with the rubbish."

"Yes, madam," Naanie replied steadily. "Boss Arthur takes the full bottle. And then he puts the empty bottle in its place. And sometimes he opens a few bottles and drinks a little from each one. And puts the corks back in again. He pushes the corks in *very* hard to try to make it look as though the bottles have never been opened."

"Hester," Graph stressed once more, "My patience is *gone* because I'm exhausted. Arthur has *again* been terrifying the children."

"Graph," Hester looked scornfully at her husband, "What *are* you talking about? You can see he's so bruised and battered that he couldn't hurt a fly, even if he wanted to. But you *know* Arthur's a *kind* man. He wouldn't deliberately hurt anyone."

"I know how you feel, Hester. And I understand," Graph summoned his mental reserves, "but you do understand, don't you, that a drunk man is capable of things he couldn't do when he's sober? And the *sad* thing is, Hester, people still *laugh* at Arthur's antics. *Even you*, Hester. You *laugh* at his dereliction. *Out loud.* When the whole situation should be *deplored. Consistently comprehensively deplored*. Even now, after *all* that's happened, you still laugh at your brother's drunken performances. Even though you can see your very own children are t*errified* by it all. And even though you know I find it …. *extremely* distasteful. Even though you know in your heart of hearts, it's all wrong. Everything that's going on is *wrong*."

"Yes, Graph!" Hester was vehement. "Because *I* see the *man*! All *you* see is the *illness*! I *allow* a man to be a man. Whatever that means. Being a man."

"That may be, Hester. But you need to know I've now told Arthur he's confined to the chair in the far corner of the lounge and if he strays from that chair into the passageway he'll be forcibly returned to the chair. By me!"

"You are offensive, Graph. Drunkenness is *not* a crime."

"No Hester," Graph said firmly, "it's not a crime. But it *is* offensive. Whether it's a disease.... Or not. *Whatever* it is. Stop being such a dummkopf."

It was past midnight. Arthur, in full voice, sang a distorted version of "Una Furtiva Lagrima" as he lurched around the lounge.

Natalie peeped out of her bedroom door in time to see her father overcome the drunkard's resistance and force him into the allotted chair. The resistance was stiffer than Natalie expected. A side table was overturned and a picture left hanging askew.

"Ma," Natalie pleaded the next morning, "I saw Uncle Arthur fighting with daddy last night. Uncle Arthur is quite strong. He frightens me. He might hurt daddy."

"Agh, Nattie," Hester looked askance at her daughter, "a drunk man is no match for a sober man. Your father is *quite safe*. An old English definition of a *coward* is a man who hits a drunk man. Because a drunk man cannot defend himself."

Natalie fixed her mother with an honest gaze. "Ma, is it not time to *admit the truth?*" she asked. "Aunty Jane loved Uncle Arthur. But she *couldn't* be with him, *not even for her children's sake*. So *you* cannot look after him. And you should look for some *other* way of ... mos ... *organising* things."

"*I myself* am the last place Uncle Arthur can call *home,* Nattie. *Do you not understand that?*" Hester stood firm.

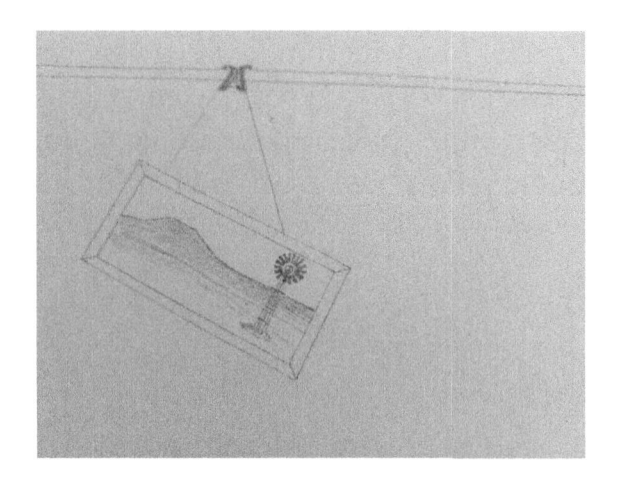

But Natalie remained unconvinced. Increasingly outspoken against her mother, the sixteen-year-old, fearing for her father's life, took to sleeping with a truncheon-like log under her bed and a kitchen knife under her pillow. Every morning she hid the knife in her bookshelf so that Naanie would not find it during the bed-making. With these weapons it was her intention to rush to her father's defence when next she heard a violent confrontation. One night, troubled by consuming nightmares which had disturbed the normal arrangement of pillows, sheets and blankets, Natalie turned rapidly in her sleep and the blade of the kitchen knife, no longer shielded by her pillow, pierced her cheek.

In an avalanche of shock she cried out involuntarily. Almost immediately her father was at her bedside. Graph stood aghast. A large circle of blood was spreading rapidly over his daughter's pillows and sheets.

Hester entered Natalie's room seconds later. She screamed at Graph, "What's going on? Graph! What have you done?" But Graph, frozen in disbelief at the knife in his daughter's face, did not immediately answer.

Anastasia appeared ahead of the other children and quickly shooed them away when she saw the blood and the knife. "Who stabbed you, Nattie?" she cried in profound dismay.

"No-one," came the gasped, sobbing answer.

Grimly, wordlessly, working as quickly as he could, Graph extracted the knife from Natalie's cheek. Natalie cried out in pain.

"Someone stabbed you," Hester screamed. "Who was it?"

"No-one stabbed me. It was an accident," Natalie wailed as the blood gushed.

"Anastasia, go and phone the doctor, tell him it's an emergency," there was more urgency in Graph's voice than any of his family had ever before heard.

For a moment Anastasia delayed. She was now crying profusely. "Who stabbed you Nattie?" she pleaded again through tears and huge heaving sobs.

"No-one stabbed me," Natalie wailed. "I keep a knife under my pillow in case I have to save Daddy's life when Uncle Arthur attacks him. I turned over in my sleep and the knife went into me."

"Anastasia! Go! Now!" Graph demanded.

Hester's appearance suddenly changed. She doubled over and then slowly subsided to the floor where she sat propped against the bedroom wall, staring at the wall opposite.

Arthur entered.

"Get out!" Graph said so savagely to Arthur, as he compressed Natalie's cheek to staunch the flow of blood, that even through his drunken haze Arthur understood the full weight of the threat. He turned and shuffled out.

Anastasia ran back in. "There's no reply from the doctor," she wept despairingly.

"Well then," Graph reacted instantly, now in icy calm, "go and wake up Len, and then *run* with him to the doctor's house." He pressed harder on the wad of sheeting he was holding against Natalie's wound in the attempt to reduce the flow of blood. His fear spiralled as Natalie spat out blood. "*Don't* get dressed. Just put on your raincoat over your pyjamas. *Run as fast as you can!*"

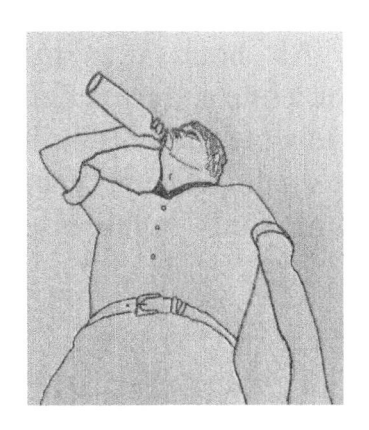

The doctor rushed in. Noting Hester's demeanour and inertia, he immediately turned his full attention to Natalie. While examining and dressing the wound, he spoke exclusively to Graph and Natalie. It was a small town. He understood. The Middler trauma and Hester's role in it were common knowledge. Being the family doctor, he had listened, over the years, to many accounts from the Middlers, children and adults of this pervasive case of alcoholism. When it came to *this* family, no matter what condition he was being asked to examine, the problem of Arthur seemed always to rise up and dominate the discussion. An hour after his arrival, the doctor wrote a prescription and departed in relative calm. "You'll always have a small scar on your cheek, Nattie," he said. "Otherwise you'll be fine."

Later, a while after the doctor left, Graph found his brother-in-law pouring himself a drink in the lounge. Without any further ceremony, without hesitation, without words, in the most controlled anger, Graph took Arthur by the scruff of the neck and marched him, still carrying the bottle, off the property. Arthur did not resist and, for once, did not even swear as Graph shoved him into the street, shut the wicker gate and told him in no uncertain terms that it would be a very big mistake for him ever to return.

Arthur shambled away into the first light clutching his 'friend', the still three-quarter filled bottle. "Oh, I've left your cork on the sideboard," he said to his friend. "But it doesn't matter. I'll look after you."

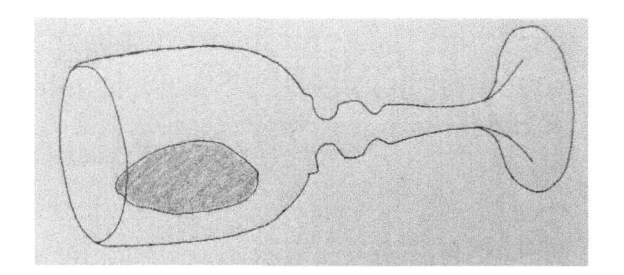

Hester sat a long while in the chair where Arthur would have sat had he ever finished pouring that drink, his last in the Middler home.

Natalie, while being tended by the doctor, asked her mother to leave her bedroom.

"Ma, please go away," she asked.

Hester stirred at this request. But did not move.

"Ma," Natalie repeated in a tremulous voice, her speech distorted by the wound on her cheek, "I want to talk with daddy in private."

Keenly feeling the justice of Natalie's rejection, Hester arose and went to the lounge. Which was two steps away along the passage.

The wine glass Arthur had been filling, when Graph collared him, lay on its side on top of the bookcase. Most of its contents had spilled and made their way over the rows of books until, reaching the lowest shelf, the red liquid fanned out and stopped. The wetness had not reached the floor.

"Just," Hester said to herself, "like the delta of a desert river. Too weak to complete its journey to the sea."

Aware her husband and children hesitated when they entered the lounge and saw her sitting in Arthur's chair, Hester began to acknowledge, with considerable contrition, her share of responsibility for the state of the family. Yet, still she mounted a moral defence.

"This isn't new," she began admitting to herself. "For a long time now they all seem to find reason to go elsewhere when Arthur is near or when anything concerning Arthur happens."

"It's entrenched," Hester told herself, "this habitual silence. My family. My servants. They've developed a technique. Over the years. When they encounter me, they study me. And say nothing. And go about their business. It's not disrespectful. It's a natural response. I refused to listen to things they *most* wanted to say. And it was reciprocated. Conversation became irrelevant when the *most* important subject was prohibited. I know now. *Just* how accustomed to crisis they've become. It's a cost of looking after my brother. I see it now as if one of those star shells Arthur often talked about, has exploded above me. It's lit up. And, in the floodlight, overwhelming isolation seizes my spirit. It's my lot. Even Graph doesn't approach. These days he makes less effort. Graph," she repeated. "My husband. Who always cares, *so*, for *all* of us. Leaves *no stone* unturned. Who *loathes* the thought of *any* harm befalling his family. Even *he* reels from events. And is close to speechless. But …… " she asked herself. "What could I do? What else *could* I have done?"

Graph however, still possessed the wisdom for which Hester had married him. He knew not to baulk at this hurdle. It might be a crossroads. Diplomacy must come urgently to the fore to hold the family together. Beginnings of recovery might be possible. "But, to tell the truth," he thought dejectedly, "I've little creativity left." At the moment of validation, he could not, however, allow himself to be beyond caring. Drawing on internal resources, fatalistic, stubborn, prudent, he rallied to make the exhaustive effort.

"En nou, Hester?" ("And now, Hester?) or ("What next, Hester?"), Graph asked.

A tear coursed down Hester's cheek. She leaned forward, sighed deeply, covered her eyes with her hands. She became aware, not for the first time, of wrinkles forming on her face.

Graph sat down next to her.

He tentatively touched her knee, expecting a rough brush-off.

Hester did not repel him.

She merely wept on.

Graph stayed beside her a long while, a silent presence, allowing her to grieve until, the moment feeling about right, he patted her knee, kissed her cheek, a long kiss, and left her.

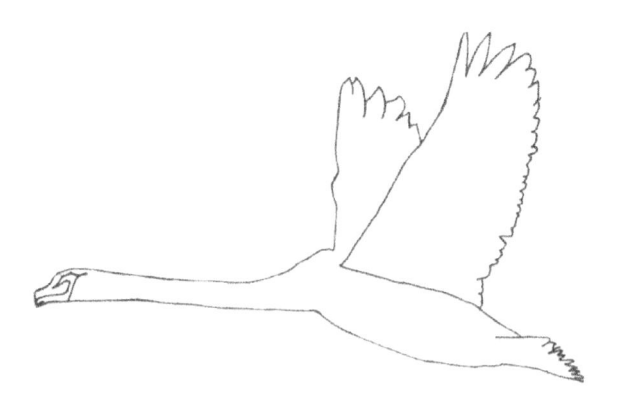

At church, Hester found help. Dominee Van Der Westhuizen, alert and conscientious, directed her. For months he had, often sub-consciously, enhanced plans for this moment.

The dominee arranged meeting after meeting. Hester went from office to office, considered various ideas. Eventually the best that could be done, was done.

Arthur went into an institution and then into another and then yet another. From time to time he absconded, always taking byways into the desert. He preferred freedom and the open road to official care.

One day, in the immense isolation of The Little Karroo, they found him dead, sunburnt and wrinkled. He lay a distance from a little-used track.

"Who could ever say," the dominee comforted the bereaved sister, "whether he went deliberately into The Karoo to die? He died where he wanted to die, Hester. In the desert. *Where he wanted* to die. Where he wanted to *live*. We know, you and I, how he loved The Karroo. It's enough. He has returned, now, to *his* place. The desert, Hester ….. it was your brother's *church*. God's will was done."

"Once again," Hester reflected, "the dominee has proved himself. So much knowledge. So much understanding. He sees *into* peoples' minds. Even Arthur's. Always a force for good. *Such* work and foresight. *So* quietly done. In the background. He listens to every point of view. Even to those who've 'had enough.' It's *not* for nothing the dominee is the dominee."

"Because," she reminisced, "for Arthur the desert was virginal. Clean. He loved that. But how did the dominee know? Arthur wasn't exactly religious. Perhaps the dominee learnt it when he visited Arthur in the homes? Perhaps Arthur thought himself lucky? Better to die in The Karoo than in France. In the trenches, he dreamed of two things. The English Girl. And The Karoo. Those thoughts kept him alive. Well. The English Girl was gone. Quite lost. Which left him the desert."

"I must think," Hester grieved, "at the moment he died, he was looking at the dry sparse veld. As he loved to do. He was watching *waar die pad* (where the road) passed on the other side of *die pan* (the dried lake) for *die slang* (the snake) and *die rolbal* (the tumbleweed). Certainly he was at one with the snippets of life, *die mier* (the ant,) *die akkedis* (the lizard) *en die aasvoel* (and the vulture,) which the cracked earth sent to entertain him. In his final moments. Perhaps there might even have been *'n* V*olstruis* (An ostrich) or two, *of 'n skilpad* (or a tortoise) or two. Or even a few."

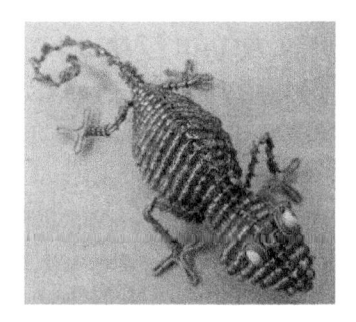

Die akkedis.
The lizard.

Graph, Hester, Len and Naanie were the only mourners at the funeral.

Dominee Van Der Westhuizen took the service.

Hester's reading was brief. It was all she could manage. Uncharacteristically, she chose an English reading. When the moment came she stood beside the coffin, touching the varnished wood, a tenderness in her touch. Sometimes she gasped for breath, but bravely she read, her voice a gruff monotone, her accent deep Cape Dutch.

Hester's reading,

"And some we knew, The loveliest and the best
That Time and Fate of all their Vintage prest,
Have drunk their Cup a Round or two before,
And one by one crept silently off to Rest."

"Indeed the Idols I have loved so long
Have done my Credit in Men's Eye much wrong:
Have drowned my Honour in a shallow Cup,
And sold my Reputation for a Song."

"And when Thyself with shining Foot shall pass
Among the Guests Star-scattered on the Grass,
And in thy joyous Errand reach the Spot
Where I made one – turn down an empty Glass!"

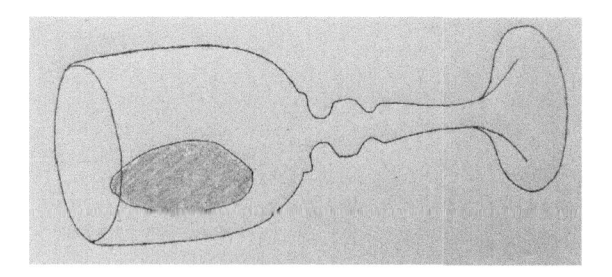

"But in my mind," Hester assured herself after the service, "the position I took remains, after all, defensible. For so long as God saw fit, I safeguarded my brother and ministered to his wounds. *He was a hero.*"

"Natalie's accident," she said to herself, "was *God's* way of telling me my nursing of Arthur must end."

"*But,*" she continued to herself, "I'll always believe Arthur's alcoholism originated in the trenches. Whatever others say. His suffering was as much a wound as would have been the personal ruin caused by an exploding shell. With all the ensuing gangrene and amputation. Worse. The wounded mind is more disabling than the wounded body, because the mind is hidden away somewhere in the skull. Unreachable. Invisible to many. Outsiders seldom see the full suffering. And because they cannot see the wound, they don't believe it real."

Her brother now dead, Hester consciously approached her own disablement. She did not expect easy reconciliation. The sword within her, still red hot, forged in anger and dismay at her family's disapproval, scorched and sizzled. But, mindful at last of responsibilities beyond the exclusive caring for just one victim, she worked conscientiously and steadily to cool her anger down. "I must try for a fresh perspective," she told herself as she struggled internally.

For at least one of her children however, the scorching left scars in the form of incontrovertible convictions.

"*Oh*," Natalie frowned at her mother, "so *now* you've changed. *Now* you want to be with *us* again. After you allowed our peace to be invaded by an aggressive *drunk*. After you nurtured a *monster*. For *years*. And all the while you thought it'd be okay to neglect your *children* while you looked after a *no-good, 'n rof.*' (A rough person.)

And you *used* Daddy. You used him *most single-mindedly.* He had to shoulder *all* the expense of your brother. You had no thought for how it affected *us.* How we had to do without. In fact you told Daddy you'd *leave* him if he wasn't prepared to pay. For all the drinking and the damage. You said he could 'gaan kuk en betaal' (an Afrikaans profanity meaning that Hester had said she did not care how Graph found the money but it was his job to find the money). I *heard* you say *it.* And you said it would be *his* fault if he found himself paying for two households instead of one. You *would* walk out on him! *How* can I forgive you this? It was *disloyal.* How can you *expect* forgiveness? It was *not* motherly, *not* wifely."

The censure of the other children was not so forthright as Natalie's. They were more accepting of explanations given them of shell-shock and trauma.

In the lounge one evening, Anastasia, the eldest, discussed alcoholism with the others. Hester was away over the mountains in Mossel Bay visiting Jane Calitz and Jane's children. But Graph and the other children were present.

"Yes, Nattie," Anastasia said mildly, "I agree with you. It *was* too much. When I remember it all, it was just *too* much. If I *think* of the now *intensity* of the mos ... alcoholic *onslaught* .... It's mos difficult to find *much* excuse. Or to think kindly about it. *We* had to *pay* with *our* childhood. And to watch Daddy's unhappiness. But at least we know *why*. We cannot mos blame Ma for The Great War."

"Nee, Anastasia!" ("No, Anastasia!") Natalie replied. "We mos know several families whose men were now wounded or now taken away from them by the war. Taken away for ever. And for *them* alcoholism was *not* a consequence. Daddy often told Ma that she ought now mos to have found *some other way* to mos look after Uncle Arthur. If she now wanted that badly to mos do it."

Graph intervened. "I see both points of view," he said. "But still. We must think kindly of your mother. *All* of us. She was loyal in her own way. She did her best. Her loyalty took her along another road. That's all. We're individuals. We react differently."

"Yes Natalie," Belinda remonstrated, "you *always* make *fuss!* All now *families* have problems. Children just have to mos accept parents for what they are."

"Ja, Natalie" Charlene looked Natalie full in the eye, "It *wasn't* Ma's fault. She was actually being kind, helping her brother."

Natalie glared at these incompatible sisters.

Graph, knowing the sibling rivalry of his children, looked for harmony. "Well. Uncle Arthur's dead. We're back to normal. At last."

"It didn't take us long to get back to normal. After Uncle Arthur left," Charlene observed.

"*Speak for yourself*," Natalie glared acidly at Charlene.

Other than a glance of contempt, Charlene ignored Natalie.

Graph nodded.

The five younger children, Delaine, Yvette, Frederic, Gavin and Garth, playing on the floor nearby, listened to the exchanges between their elder siblings with varying degrees of interest and comprehension.

"Where's Uncle Arthur?" Yvette asked. "We mos haven't seen him for ages."

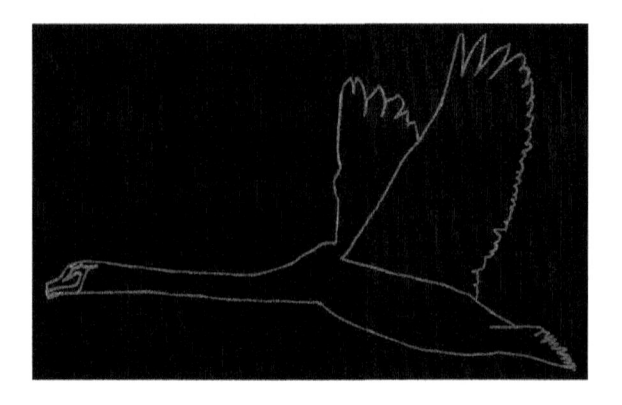

In Mossel Bay, Hester knocked at the door of her sister-in-law's house. She had written to Jane several times before, at, and after Arthur's death, and Jane had replied, but Hester was uncertain how, after the passing of several years, she would be received. She had journeyed over the mountains in some trepidation. She told herself it was imagination to think Jane saw her as a rival. She had not drawn Arthur away from Jane. Jane had expelled Arthur. And anyway. She was a sister. Not a lover.

Jane, drawn and grim, grey, prematurely aged, answered the door.

"Come-in," she said without formality.

"Thank you," Hester said with similar absence of formality. She entered the familiar, threadbare, sparse house. Although her visits had ceased, it was still family territory. But more destitute than she remembered.

Jane gestured at a chair. In silence. Hester took the seat. In silence.

Jane sat opposite her guest, waiting.

"You didn't come to the funeral," Hester said. Her voice was flat.

"Why would I?" Jane said. It wasn't a question.

"He was your husband," Hester said, also in monotone.

"Was," Jane stated.

"And the father of your children," Hester added.

"Was," Jane repeated.

They sat in dark silence for a full ten minutes. Not uncomfortable.

"Should'nt the children have attended their father's funeral?" Hester asked, still in monotone.

"I asked them," Jane said. "But they said he died long before he died. And they didn't want to go."

"And," she added, "they went out when they heard you were coming."

Hester looked around. The house was not only empty of furniture. It was empty of Life. Hardship resounded from every bare corner. But it was thoroughly clean. Proudly, rigorously clean.

"And he'd long been dead to you, as well?" It was not a question.

"Yes," was the simple, impecunious answer.

It seemed profane to say more.

The two women sat on in silence for another half hour.

Then Hester arose. Opening her handbag, she looked for her purse. Self-consciously she extracted a folded five pound note. She unfolded the note. It was a large and ornate piece of paper, full of its own importance. Jane watched. She knew what the paper was but had seldom seen so large a denomination of money. Pensively, Hester placed the five pound note on the dented table-top. She used a fisherman's lead sinker lying near at hand to weigh it down.

"This is for you," Hester said.

"Thank you," Jane said. But she did not move and her lined face remained, like her voice, expressionless.

Hester leaned against the table. She looked out of the window at the sea.

Jane looked at nothing in particular.

Just as there had been no formality in arrival, there was none at departure. No word at all.

Hester walked to the front door. She let herself out. Respectfully and quietly she closed the door after her.

And then she walked back to the railway station.

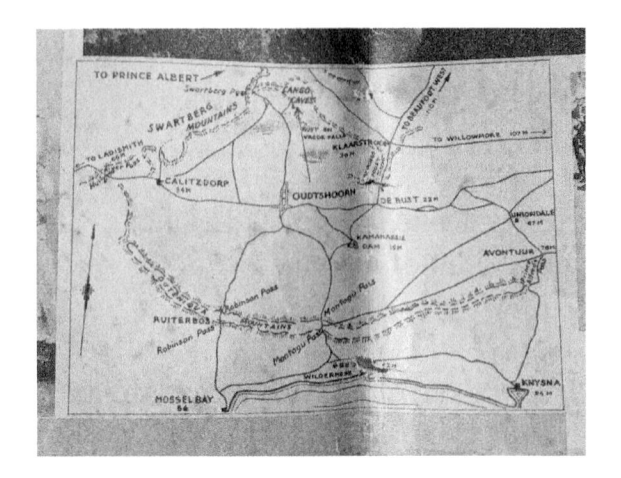

Dominee Van Der Westhuizen concentrated hard. Hester and Natalie Van Middel were in his office and at loggerheads. Again.

"Agh" Natalie said forthrightly, "whether it's Charlene's nature or some self-defence mechanism strengthened by the now alcoholic turmoil, only God knows. She sees differently. We've never been close."

"Look at your mother, Natalie," the dominee directed. "Can you not see she's exhausted and sad?"

"Of course she's sad," Natalie's voice rose in rebellion. "My *mother* looks through a now bewildered haze on the outcome of her own now voluntary *neglect*. We're *all.....exhausted*, dominee. Can *you* not see? It's *obvious*. The outcome of her now *obsession* is the children grew up *too fast*. Whatever Charlene and Belinda say. Or think."

Hearing raised voices, Mevrou Van Der Westhuizen came in. She knew, too well, the differences of opinion. There was no split-second pause in the argument for the suggestion she held in reserve. She knew to bide her time, waited her chance.

"Natalie," the dominee unaccustomed to any challenge from someone so young, especially a girl, spoke sternly "*forgiveness* and understanding would befit you. Your mother always does her best."

Vividly, Natalie increased her offensive. "I'll *forgive*," she said, "when my mother admits she caused the now *extremities* of emotion which my father's ... mos ... *active* tolerance engendered. Have you *not* seen, dominee, the now *pyramid* of green bottles that sits in our orchard? Do you not see what it cost in now money and in mos *love*? And in mos family *life*? Dominee?"

"There are many things you don't know, young lady," Hester said.

"And there are many things you take for granted, Ma," Natalie instantly replied.

"You're a headstrong girl," the dominee said. "You need disciplining.

If you were my daughter, I'd give you *a good hiding*."

"No, dominee," Natalie replied undaunted and icy, "I do *not* need disciplining. In fact, *perhaps* you should *note* that I *shall* go to the law if anyone touches me. In *thought* I am, unfortunately, already old and strong. I can tell right from wrong. *My childhood* made me old. Which is why you should *expect* me to resist. Circumstances have made me what I am. *Circumstances* which it seems *your theology* has never now *understood*. And now I begin to *scorn* your theology. *And* your authority. The *lack of discipline* lies with *other* parties. *Definitely*. With other parties."

Dominee Van Der Westhuizen glared at Natalie.

Hester, horrified at confrontation between her daughter and a man of the church, *her* church, covered her mouth with her hands.

"What I *need*, dominee," Natalie stated forcefully, "is to *leave* home."

"No," the dominee repeated, "what you *need* is to learn how you yourself would gain from forgiving your mother. Not that I'm convinced she's done anything which requires forgiving."

"Why," Natalie asked no-one in particular, "do intelligent people so often make *such* wrong decisions?"

"Forgiveness is a double-edged sword," Mevrou Rita Van Der Westhuizen interjected, thinking it a good moment to bring out her plan, "*but* ….. *instead* of repeating discussion of these *sad* things, Nattie, we *could* talk instead about you becoming our reserve organist. It's sometimes mos *so* difficult to find people to play on Sundays and also for weddings and christenings. Especially when I have to be away. And it would be something creative for you to work at, a way to take your mind off all *the hard things* and to think about *nice things*. We're *so* impressed, Susan and I, at the progress you've made with your music."

It took Natalie a moment to adjust to Rita's change of subject.

"Thank you, Mevrou," (Ma'am) Natalie said appreciatively. "I'd *like* to play more. And it's mos *very* kind of you to offer. So, *yes* please. I'll be happy to play at weddings. And funerals. But count me out for church services and christenings. And, while I love your kindness, I have to say, in any case, the reasons for leaving home, will *not* change."

"And as for my *mother*," Natalie added, "she shall wait a *very* long time before I forgive her."

The younger children gawped at the fearful jarring clashes between Natalie and Hester. To them Natalie's insubordination seemed inexplicable and foreign. Distasteful.

"Belinda," Delaine asked, in dismayed innocence, "why are Ma and Nattie always *so* cross with each other?"

Graph was present. Telling himself he had much to learn from keeping silent, he looked from child to child with curiosity and concern, wondering what explanation Belinda would give.

"Agh, Natalie thinks she's *big* stuff," Charlene broke in before Belinda could answer. "She tells Ma our life's *not good enough.* It's good enough for *us* but not good enough for *her.* She says sport isn't *intellectual.* And she thinks our friends are dull because all they do is 'waste time on tennis and swimming.' She says fitness matters but sport doesn't. She *keeps saying* she's going to leave home. *Well, let her*! If she thinks she'll do better without us, *well then, good riddance!* Let's *see* if she finds *real* friends wherever she's going. *Let's see!* Anyway, what's *wrong* with swimming and tennis?"

Graph stirred, but kept silent.

"Agh nee, Charlene, that's a bit harsh," Anastasia said.

Anastasia had grown into a graceful young woman. The Arthur years had pressed her into care-filled maturity.

"Well," Charlene insisted before Anastasia could continue, "Natalie says the Cape platteland (countryside) suits girls like us. She says no proper demands are made on us because servants do our chores. And all we have to do every day is while away the hours with bosom friends. And do sport. She says our lives revolve around looking pretty, not eating too much and attracting a rich husband. Because we need someone who will let our now lazy lives continue forever. She says we're massively simple and we don't read. And there isn't even compulsion for us to play the piano. We only have to practise if we feel like it. According to her we're mos boring and will turn into mos '*dumb clucks*'."

"Natalie's *kop toe* (arrogant) and obstinate," Belinda agreed.

Anastasia compared these descriptions with her own feelings. She vividly remembered her drunken uncle affecting everything. "You're forgetting Char," she moderated, "how *terrified* Nattie was of Uncle Arthur."

Graph tried for a positive turn in the conversation. "That's the theme! That is *the* theme! Even though Uncle Arthur's dead, Natalie's memories are *bad* enough to make her long to leave home. As soon as she can. Justifiably. And on *that* score, Anastasia, I *cannot* tell you *how* proud I am of you. When drunken mayhem blighted us day and night, you spun a cocoon for your younger siblings. You gave kindness and protection under which they laughed and played. *Unbidden.* I didn't ask. Without prompting, as *young* as you were, you assumed parental responsibilities! I hope you'll *always* remember how the younger children came to you. Your mother and I are glad you *accept* us for what we are. You aren't cynical. You didn't have to *learn* forgiveness. It came naturally. You never resented the huge task of standing in as mother."

"Thank you, daddy," Anastasia blushed. "But Char, Nattie hasn't been happy for a *long* time. Even before she stabbed herself, she wasn't *happy. Especially* she was of course unhappy about Ma and Uncle Arthur. But *I* think she would have now seen things *differently* even if Uncle Arthur hadn't made life difficult. Because of *other* things. Things that happened when she was little. She was *always* going to be different. That's just *people*. People are mos individuals."

"What are individuals?" Delaine asked.

"Yes … well … why can't she be like us?" Belinda insisted. "The dominee tells us to 'honour our father *and* mother.' Natalie doesn't have friends. The only person she honours is *herself*."

"*Because*, Bee," Anastasia said in a soft voice, "she is *just not* like us. And Bee … look closely and you'll see she *has* friends, loyal friends."

"Agh," Charlene said in active contempt, "she's just '*anders*.' ('*otherwise*'.)

"What're individuals?" Delaine repeated.

Hester, too proud to admit being weakened and diminished, looked sadly on the outcome of her work. "Graph," she said mournfully, "Natalie actively increases her now unforgiving stance. She loses no now opportunity of flinging reminders in my face. Yesterday she told me *again* it was *not* really lucky for *any of those concerned* that I've a tolerant husband. It's *not* right for a now daughter to say such things."

"Vygie," Graph took up Hester's concern, "Uncle Arthur's *gone*. He's *dead*. He'll *never* return. We're *out* of it. Circumstances have changed. Your brothers and sisters have recovered their sense of humour. They bicker normally. Isn't it time you, too, forgave your mother? To be more at ease?"

"I know how you feel, Daddy," Natalie replied. "I feel a little of it too. And I *have* been thinking. But different thoughts. One of several things I've been thinking is there was a silver lining to the alcoholic strife. And do you know what mos that silver lining was?"

"What was it, Vygie?"

"It was the closeness between you and me in the now *midst* of chaos. We were mos allies when the family finances were being depleted, when the green pyramid was built, when the now furniture and crockery was thrown about and broken. We consoled each other. Just mos by being together. And this happened because mommy was as she was. To you and to me. Mommy never afforded me a high priority. I was not her fifth, not even her now tenth priority behind the needs of her drunkard. Well. Uncle Arthur's gone and I'm back to being fourth daughter. A parent must give time fairly to mos each child. *You* are fair. Which means since Uncle Arthur died we don't work and talk together as much as we did when he was alive. As we did," she became reflective, "*because* he was always drunk. Which is good. Parents shouldn't mos have favourites. But I *miss* our talks. I really *miss* them. And," Natalie hesitated, "I still remember how I once told you I wished he would die."

Graph stroked his chin. "For you especially, Vygie," he said, "it's obvious settling back into normality is proving difficult. Perhaps you should mix more? Spend more time gossiping? Like your sisters? *They* spend *enormous* amounts of time *gossiping*," he looked good-humouredly at Natalie. "Like most men I often wonder *what* they find to talk about. Hour after hour. But *then*. I tell myself the gossiping of womenfolk holds communities together. It spreads news so we all know what's what. Which must mean gossiping is actually very *good*, even though it often seems a pointless waste of time to most men. *Men* extract the gist of *hours* of wives gossip in a matter of seconds. But women *initiate* it. That's the important bit. Women *create* the good atmosphere in life. Gossip is a blessing."

"I'm glad you see into things, Daddy," Natalie laughed. She gave him a hug, "And glad you've persuaded yourself about gossip. It's good you forgive mommy. But I can't. And. By the way …… Some gossip is mere scandal. And idleness."

"But ….. for me, *gossip* is mos *not* the answer. *My* answer is different. I see how times are *hard*, how there's never enough *money*, how we're in a depression. For me the answer is to leave home and go out to work. Which'll take some pressure, at least, off you. You've enough to look after. I must be self-reliant and free. My *'Eroica'* must mos become a *Polonaise!*"

"Oh *no*, Vygie! I still don't like that idea," Graph twitched involuntarily at the thought of his daughter fending for herself. "You're too young."

"Daddy," Natalie replied, "There's no alternative. Actually it'll make me happy. I'm tired of being with lesser beings. I'm of an age and we can't ignore the *big* question of money."

She paused for a moment. "You know, Daddy," she went on purposefully, "the more I think of it, the more I think our family should *not* have had to pay all the doctor's bills for Uncle Arthur's illness and injuries. Or even for me when I stabbed myself. Those should've been paid by the state. Like they do in Russia nowadays. What else is the mos state *for? Our* doctors charge *as much* as now they like. Which is a *very* poor state of affairs when people are mos sick. To make mos *profit* out of *sick* people."

"Gosh, Vygie," Graph answered, "that's advanced thinking."

"Agh, not really, daddy," Natalie said, "It's just that most people are devoid of imagination. *And* don't read the news."

"Graph!" Hester's voice filled with disbelief. "You *cannot seriously* be thinking of letting her go out into the world *by herself!* She's too *young!* And, though I say it myself, too good-looking. It'll be *inviting* trouble. Not only is she attractive, she's also *headstrong*. But *not* so forceful as to be able to take care of herself."

"I keep telling her we don't want her to go, Hester," Graph replied. "None of us want her to go. Not you, not me, not the other children. But she says the thought entered her head as a breeze, grew into a wind and is now a hurricane. She says nobody can hold back a hurricane. She doesn't like the way young women, including her sisters, are cosseted and says she's legally old enough to leave home."

"And what age *is* the legal age?" Hester asked.

"I'm not exactly sure," Graph answered, "but she may be right. It can't be far off. We do know other girls about her age who work in offices. And shops."

"She knows nothing," Hester fretted. "*Nothing!*"

"Not quite nothing. Did you know Mevrou Van Der Westhuizen and Mrs Whelan have taught her shorthand and bookkeeping?"

"Oh!" Hester was surprised. "No, I didn't know."

"She says young girls have been going out to work since The War. And now it's her turn. It'll change her troublesome 'Eroica' into a polonaise, she says."

"Hmmph!" Hester scorned the metaphor. "What would *she* know about the polonaise at her age?"

Graph smiled.

"Graph, for *goodness sake!*" Hester suffered bemusement. "What're you *smiling* about? This is *serious*."

"I'm thinking, Hester, about *you* and the polonaise when you were her age," he answered.

Natalie's aspirations were not the only sign of children growing up. On top of Natalie's decision to leave home, the family's attention now also focussed on another matter. Anastasia was showing interest in a young man.

"Graph!" the outraged Hester protested one Sunday in her stentorian tones, "I spied Anastasia today, sitting on a bench in the churchyard after church, *holding hands* with a *man*! *Gotts, Graph*! (Good God, Graph!)"

"Who was the man?" Graph asked.

"I don't know," Hester replied, "their backs were to me."

"Well, didn't you go and speak to them?"

"I was thanking the dominee for the service. And I *certainly* didn't want to draw attention to them."

Graph went straight to Anastasia. Then he returned to Hester.

"I've told Anastasia in no uncertain terms not to make a fool of herself," he said to his wife. "I think she *does* understand, Hester. Because she's contrite. She's no fool, our Anastasia.

Just a bit *too kind* for her own good, that's all."

"*That's all*, Graph!" Hester protested. "I *hope* you told her *never* to do it again."

"I didn't have to tell her. She knew immediately. But also, Hester. Do you want to know who the young man is?"

"We'll have to *watch* her," Hester seemed unconvinced.

"I know who the young man is." Graph repeated.

"Who is it?" she asked.

"It's Walter Whelan, Roger and Susan's son."

"Oh," Hester said, as if contemplating something foreign.

"Yes. How much do you know about Walter Whelan?" Graph asked.

"Not much," Hester replied.

"*Walter Whelan*," Graph sounded impressed, "is the man who's just inherited the Whelan's shop."

"Oh?" Hester questioned, "I thought the business was being taken over by Roger Whelan's brother."

"So did the whole town. But apparently not. People say Walter plans to expand from the family-run haberdashery shop into a much bigger concern. He's moving to bigger premises which'll be a department store. There'll be departments for tailoring and outfitting, kitchen and household goods, furniture, toys, and goodness knows what else."

"Oh!" Hester said.

"So, a budding romance mightn't be a bad thing, you see, Hester?"

"Oh yes, I *do* see," Hester agreed. She suddenly wasn't distraught.

Arthur Calitz was dead. The ever-present disturbance of a drunk had ended.

In the relief of quietude, Graph reinstated the Middler routine of Sunday lunch.

Leaving time for church attendance, Sunday lunch began at 3pm. Typically, English roast beef and Yorkshire pudding or roast lamb and mint sauce were served with home-grown vegetables. Always roast potatoes, carrots, green beans and rich gravy. This would be followed by fruit salad. The fruit, freshly picked, came from the Middler orchard. And then ice-cream, cakes, cream and coffee. And koeksusters. Since Arthur's demise, no alcohol ever appeared. Naanie excelled. Judging by her culinary skills, she might have learnt her art anywhere between Stirling and Truro. Although, of course, she had never left the Cape of Good Hope.

Invariably two or three guests were invited.

"Sunday lunch," Graph would say, "is *the* high point of the week. It's a time when *all* the family *actually assemble*. I love the opportunity for everyone to stop doing things and actually sit down to *talk* to one another. Of matters small and large. A moment for finding out inner things, little and big things that matter."

Natalie however, was not sure. To her father she commented, "I don't know daddy. It's not like when I'm with my friends. I find Sunday lunches to mos be a time when I must polish up my *diplomacy*. I don't so much find out what others are thinking as spend time defending myself."

"Everyone, Vygie, has to make an effort," Graph responded. "Some days it's more difficult than others."

"But daddy," Natalie replied, "when I'm with *real* friends, like Mrs Whelan, it doesn't take *any* effort. Conversation's easy and endless."

One Sunday, lunch lasted longer than usual. Guests that day included Walter Whelan, Aunty Kitty and Uncle Pieter.

Things got off to a less than promising start. Shortly before everyone arrived, Hester took Natalie to task for being absent from church.

"But Ma," Natalie argued, "I learn *more* from my books, sitting on my lovely bench in the orchard, than perched on a pew listening to *the dominee*. In fact I'm *closer* to God on the bench daddy gave me, under the trees, than on any church pew. In the open I'm better able to wonder "where the wind comes from."

"Ummm……., guests are arriving," Graph intervened.

Hester, not relishing discord in the presence of guests, let the matter pass.

As ever Hester sat to the right of Graph, and Anastasia to the left. Natalie next Anastasia. Walter had been placed at the far end of the table with the youngest daughters Delaine and Yvette on either side of him and the two boys, Gavin and Garth, opposite. Although Anastasia and Walter were seated a distance from one another, their palpable attraction to one another brought new excitement. All felt it. Belinda and Charlene nudged one another. Aunty Kitty munching foodlessly, looked over her spectacles. Pieter disguised his keen interest. Naanie lingered over serving, observing tiny details, exchanging pleasantries as she came and went about her work. She pointedly included Walter in her mothering.

Walter was a big presence, burly with a moon face and receding hairline. His conversation and impeccable manners, while genteel were marvellously worldly. The eight year age gap between himself and Anastasia presented no obstacle. As for Anastasia, years of standing in for her mother had given her circumspect maturity and an aura of authority. All could see she was bursting with happiness. Conversation ran along smoothly.

The Middler children responded to Walter with shyness at first, and then with delight. Walter, quite at ease, knew how to amuse them. South African born but exceedingly British, he bantered in perfect English, effortlessly adjusting exchanges to the age of each child.

After a while, Graph, held up his hand. "Anastasia, will you say Grace please," he asked.

"All hold hands," Delaine spoke up quickly. Rather loudly.

"Agh, *nee wat,(No!) not again*," Charlene glowered at her younger sister.

"*Yes. All* hold hands," Delaine insisted.

Graph humoured the young request.

"*All* hold hands," he repeated firmly, winking at Charlene.

"*And* close eyes," Delaine demanded of everyone, especially Charlene.

"Agh *sies!* daddy," (difficult to translate – a dismissive protest) Charlene rolled her eyes.

"*And* close eyes," Graph repeated.

"*And! close! your! eyes!, Charlene!,*" Delaine venomously echoed her father while looking daggers at her older sister.

Charlene smirked.

"*No! peeping! Charlene!*" Delaine insisted fiercely.

"Charlene!" Graph insisted mildly.

Belinda found herself invaded by an army of giggles. Which, with all her might, she struggled to repel.

Charlene, infected by Belinda, also began giggling. Small suppressed giggles at first, but then bubbling. She shut her eyes tightly, attempting to be at least superficially respectful, but lost her battle.

Anastasia amused, waited patiently, looking from one to another.

At last everyone held hands with eyes closed, ready for the important religious proceeding. Belinda was last to comply. Especially with closing eyes. At last, Anastasia too closed her eyes and said grace.

"For what we are about to receive, may the Lord make us truly grateful."

"Amen," everyone said.

Charlene and Belinda welcomed the end of the religious moment with an explosion of suppressed laughter.

Walter turned to Delaine. "I can say that in Latin," he said.

Belinda and Charlene, in hysterical mirth, rocked forwards and sideways on their chairs.

Naanie brought in more serving spoons, clucked with religious outrage at Belinda and Charlene and went out again.

"In what?" Delaine asked.

"In Latin."

"What's Latin?" Gavin asked.

"It's an ancient language. The Romans used to speak it," Walter replied.

Belinda and Charlene making strenuous efforts, reduced hysteria to mere giggling. But it still came in enormous waves. Self-consciously.

"Well why didn't they call it Roman then?" Delaine asked, clearly bored, but making allowance for the importance of the big, clever new guest.

"I don't know. Would you like me to say it in Latin?"

"All right then," Delaine said grudgingly.

"Benedictus, Benedicat, per Jesum Christum Dominum Nostrum Amen," Walter said.

"*What?*" she asked, but she sounded bored. She obviously thought the subject a nonsensical waste of time. "What does *that* mean?"

"It's the Latin grace," Walter answered. "Would you like to learn it?"

"No," Delaine said.

"Oh all right then," Walter responded unruffled. "What shall we talk about now?"

"Let's not talk rubbish," Delaine said.

"Ek se maar niks," ("I am not saying anything,") Hester said, her Calvinist disapproval in play.

Kitty looked at Hester and also said 'niks.'

Anastasia's eyes danced merriment at Walter. Just for once, she noted, his verbal supremacy had met an obstacle.

Walter noted her amusement. And was glad.

Natalie inspected, digested and absorbed the nuances. She shared the amusement. But remembering this kind of talk did not always end merrily, she withdrew imperceptibly and said nothing. The family, accustomed to her silences and entertained by the current conversation, left her to her hinterland.

Graph held up his hand again, requiring attention.

"I have news," he said.

Had Anastasia been anything less than the de facto mother of the family she might, at this moment, have revealed a touch of shyness. She knew what was coming.

Natalie, also in the know, stole a glance at Anastasia and marvelled to herself. "She doesn't seem nervous. A little tense, perhaps. But, instead of reticence there's an aura of confidence about her. And happiness. Especially happiness."

Graph looked around the table. "Anastasia and Walter," he said formally, "are engaged to be married."

For an extended moment the family sat stunned. But then there were shrieks, much tumult, and a waiving of the rule children must remain seated until excused. Excited sisters hugged and kissed Anastasia and one another. Belinda and Charlene caught up Yvette and Delaine, linked arms at the elbow and began a circular dance.

Gavin and Garth, wondering what it meant, joined in.

Aunty Kitty remained seated. Her jaw worked but her mouth remained closed. This was too much news. Belinda approached and gave her a small hug. "Is this the *haberdasher*, the *man of the churchyard bench?*" Kitty asked her niece in an audible whisper.

Len and Naanie came in from the kitchen to see what all the excitement was about. Once they understood, they performed a dance of their own. To one side.

Uncle Pieter pushed back his chair, folded his arms and sat legs outstretched, beaming at the carry-on.

Dinuzulu and Cetshwayo, the watchdogs, and Lady, the lapdog, stood up from where they had been lying on one another and began their loudest barking trio. Dinu and Cetsh wagged their tails fast which made their bodies zig-zag.

Hester smiled. Which made a change.

After a while, to restore calm, Graph held up his hand. The laughing girls returned to their seats. Even Dinu and Cetsh, coaxed to a calm by Natalie, followed the human lead and lay down. Although they kept licking Natalie and whined when she returned to her chair. Hoping for more uproar, the dogs looked up at the humans. Their tongues lolled, they smiled and their tails thumped the dog basket.

Graph spoke. "Welcome to the family, Walter," he said. "Just one thought," he added to the company at large, "for us all. In marriage, we should do our best to make our spouses laugh. Every day." He arose and went to shake hands with Walter.

"Hmmrph," Kitty said. But when Pieter also shook hands with Walter, she followed her husband's lead. Walter received a damp, elderly kiss on the cheek.

After lunch Graph, Pieter, Walter, Anastasia and Natalie wandered off to the orchard to 'see how the clingstone peaches are coming along.'

"There's much to discuss," Graph said. "But let's leave that for another time. For now," he added with a wrinkle of amusement, "I've a small piece of wisdom for you, Walter. You need to understand that marriage, these days, is a democracy. And this democracy contains one commanding-officer and one soldier. The art is working out which is which. *But*," he paused, "for today, let's simply celebrate."

Walter, much impressed by Naanie, turned to Graph when they were out of earshot of the kitchen. He nodded towards the coloured matron who could be seen working away, "What a wonderful servant you have! She's a diamond! Did she really produce that lunch all by herself?"

"I know," Graph replied in low tones. "She's very capable."

"Daddy's set up a pension for her and her husband," Natalie volunteered youthfully, pleased at Walter's observation.

"Yes. But," Graph declared, "they hardly gave me thanks for it! They say they want to live with us and work with us until they're completely physically incapable. Only then will they stop work. And even then they don't want to leave our household."

"So," Natalie enthused, "Daddy's also made legal provision for them to keep their accommodation rent-free until they die, even if he and ma die before them."

As Walter was leaving, Garth came up to him.

"Walter," he asked, "What does 'engaged' mean?"

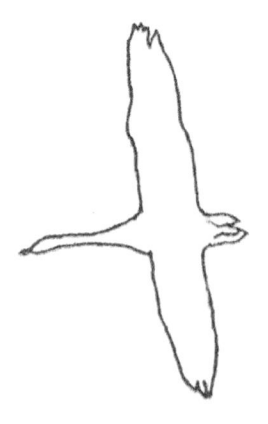

"I've made another appointment," Hester said to Graph, "for us *both* to meet the dominee in his office. At least we both accept him as counsellor and adjudicator."

"It'd be counter-productive for me to disagree with *that*," Graph replied. He frowned.

"I think it better to ignore such remarks," Hester said testily. "You're frequently less than reverend about my church. But if we're to find agreement with one another about Natalie, we need all the diplomacy we can find. And the diplomacy must begin within ourselves. The dominee suggested Susan Whelan and Rita Van Der Westhuizen also come to the meeting."

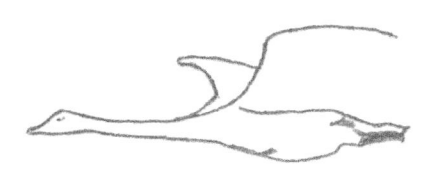

"I'm glad, Graph and Hester," the dominee said as the meeting settled down, "you agreed to Rita and Susan joining us. Susan's the right person to have with us today. Her long friendship with young Natalie gives her *insight*. Sometimes a child tells a friend things she won't tell parents. And, now that Walter's engaged to Anastasia, Susan is, after all, part of your family."

"Yes," Graph nodded. "Thank you, Susan. I often thought it a great blessing Natalie confided in you during those long years when Hester and I were preoccupied with Arthur Calitz."

Hester shifted uncomfortably on her seat.

Susan felt at ease. "Actually, I always wanted a daughter," she said. "The age difference between myself and Natalie wasn't an obstacle."

"Susan has," Rita said, "a wide acquaintance. Not only in Oudtshoorn, but beyond. Which will help us find the right accommodation and opportunities for Natalie."

"Of course," Graph began, "we all know too well how we reached this point. So, I'll go straight to the matter at hand. Natalie recently received a written offer of employment from Donald Barker. This brings within reach her long-standing dream of fending for herself. To me it seems prudent we agree how to *help* her. Rather than *contesting* the whole idea."

"It *is* a big step," Susan affirmed. "However, between us we know *most* of *our* people in Oudtshoorn. By working together we *will* find something suitable. And I mean not only a safe place for her to live, but a way of giving her the independence she so desires…… without losing her … to…….. ugliness."

Earnest discussion ensued about Natalie's determination to leave home, about her ambitious nature and whether it was legitimate for a girl to have such ideas.

Hester's beliefs were bluntly asserted. "*Natalie* must live *at home* until she marries. I know people think I've done wrong. You all think Natalie's problems were caused by my *excessive* care for my brother. But I say my caring for my brother was *right*. Unfortunately it resulted in my daughter feeling as she does. Makes no difference. It's *wrong* for a young girl to go out on her own to work. A girl's place, and a woman's place, is *in the home*. Wherever possible." Hester, glaring at the assembly, folded her arms and sat back. "This is *my daughter* you're talking about. *En* dit is ons se volk. (*And* it is our people/culture.) Ons is *nie Engels nie*. (We're *not English*.")

The dominee understood. Turning in his chair, he looked steadily at Hester. For the moment, as was his nature, he kept silent.

But Graph, who also turned to face Hester, knew his own mind. "Agh, nee wat, Hester," ("No, Hester,") he insisted, "we've *discussed* this a thousand times. Natalie will soon be *legally* entitled to leave home. We can't stop her. If we oppose her, she'll go away thinking us the people who stood in her way rather than the family and friends who helped her."

"Hmrph," Hester said. "I don't know the law. But I *do* know there's the law of the land, dis 'n Engelse wet, (it's an English law), *and then,* there's *our family* law. But perhaps you forget? There is also *morality!* There is also *decency!*"

"Hester," the dominee said, "you and I've spoken many times on this matter.

I'd like to give you my full support. I agree with your views. But Graph's right. Natalie will soon reach the age at which she's legally permitted to leave home."

"What we *have* to do, Hester" Graph stood his ground, "is find some way of making Natalie's departure *harmonious*, so she thinks we have *her* interests at heart. We *don't* want acrimony at her departure. She must feel comfortable about coming home from time to time."

"Hmrph," Hester said, more to her husband than to the dominee. "I don't know what Natalie says to you. But to me she says she wants to escape what she calls 'our world of music-less triviality' where, she says, 'trinkets prevail above thought.' But she's wrong. Our world is *not* trivial. Our world is *not* music-less. Our world is *not* thoughtless. Our world is thought*ful*. Our world is good. *In the eyes of God*, it is *good*. The code by which we live is *not* a trinket. All the modern thoughts about women, *those* are trinkets. One day Natalie will learn just how *thoughtful* our world *is*. *Our* world. The world she thinks she knows enough about to *dismiss!* At *her* age. I ask you! She's still wet behind the ears! If she's not *very* careful this *ugly* world will turn *her* into a trinket!"

"The tumult of our lives," Graph spoke to all the company, "didn't allow Hester and I to bring Natalie's talents to the surface as, in more favourable circumstances, we could have. She's intelligent, our Natalie. And her intelligence has been stifled. Or rather, neglected. By her parents. She knows it. That's why she respects you, Susan. You gave her the intellectual sustenance she always needed. She needed, and still needs, intellectual sustenance," he ended wistfully, "every single day."

"*Sophistication!*" Hester dissented. Currents of controlled anger coursed through her veins.

The dominee observed everyone closely. "Hester," he sympathised, "*many* things in this world do *not* go as we wish. But don't you worry. As always, you and I'll work together. For now we must give Natalie freedom to go. That's how we shall keep her!"

"The time has come," Graph said, "to pay the price of our dereliction. Because, after *Arthur*, Natalie believes she *doesn't* owe us obedience. None whatsoever. She thinks her parents were wrong to put caring for a drunk above caring for children. She's careful not to say as much to *me* but she's outspoken to others."

"Arthur was a *hero!*" Hester said forcefully with palpable anger.

"Natalie will thumb her nose at *any* form of coercion," Graph continued as if there had been no interruption. "So we must be careful. I'm certain she would *not* obey an instruction to live at home. And I'm not going to insist. Not with *this* girl, anyway. She's *different*."

"Hrmph," Hester said again. "Girls are girls."

"*Because*, Hester," Graph turned to his wife, "the reality is, no matter what you or I or the dominee or Susan think, Natalie's alive to, and will remain convinced by, the new thinking of the twentieth century, that women should make their own way in the world…… her childhood did nothing but reinforce that view." His voice tailed off.

"Twak," Hester said. ("Twaddle.") "It's all complete *twak!*"

"I'm sorry, Hester," Susan spoke up, "but I *fully* agree with Graph. Natalie and I've been *good* friends for years now, ever since I met her when she was little …. when she used to walk to church by herself to listen to Roger playing the organ. We have *long* conversations. Our talk isn't just about music and recipes and book-keeping and marketing and administration and all that. We talk about *Life!* And not just about running a home and a business. But about *all sorts of things!* She *often* admires the freedom women gained during The Great War. Her general knowledge is *way* beyond what's normal for someone her age. She *envies* the status of women in the new Russia. Actually, *in a nice way*, she *can't wait* to leave home so she can become *involved* in it all."

"So," Graph said heedfully, "you equipped her with an *independence* she wouldn't have learned at school, taught her how to run a business. But also … broader things. How to be happy. How to look after herself. It's a very *big* blessing."

"Hrmph," Hester said.

"I did the teaching," Susan agreed, looking with concern at Hester, "but *Natalie herself* went out to find work. She has *energy!* She'll go far because she *initiates* things. Donald Barker said it took only two probationary Saturday mornings to see Natalie was not merely an ornament."

"Donald Barker," the dominee said reassuringly, "is a good man, Hester."

"I *believe* a woman's place is in the home," Hester repeated soberly. "Ek twyfel nie daaraan nie." (I do not doubt it.") "But *my own daughter* tells me," she continued critically, "the world of the Middler family is tiny. She says the world beyond our garden gate is scarcely vista enough to contain her. To embrace her. Her and her *big ideas*. …….. So ……. 'Hoogste saal, ergste val' ('the highest saddle will result in the hardest fall')". She folded her arms firmly.

"Yes, well, Hester," Graph observed gently, "there's *tradition* and then there's *progress*. What do you suppose Vygie *actually means* when she tells me it's time to clear the green pyre? She says she often asks people what it is they need to make them think of their homes as *home*. It takes many things to make a home. She says the first requirement is security, and the less safe a person feels the harder it is to call a place home. She felt threatened for years. The legacy of the threat is she'll make a home somewhere else, in her own way. She'll build a way of life in which she feels safe and happy. Especially she's tired of criticism. She'll leave bad memories behind. She *long since* gave up any thought of *being* with us."

"I've said what I've said," Hester's downcast voice reluctantly recognised defeat.

"Well," Rita looked around, "the time Susan spent teaching a *special* child has made many things possible. And Hester, I *do* understand your concerns. But please don't worry *too* much. It occurs to me I should start by asking Mrs Van Niekerk if *she* can offer Natalie a room. Her house is respectable. Both Mrs Van Niekerk and Mr Barker are respectable. Natalie will be safe. We're all nearby if ever she needs us. So …. if we're all agreed, I'll approach Mrs Van Niekerk. I'm sure she'll agree. She has vacancies at present. Mrs Van Niekerk's place will be only a short walk each day to Mr Barker's motor works. Do you agree, Jacobus?" she asked her husband.

I *do* agree," the dominee said weightily. "It seems best."

A few days later, Graph took Natalie aside. "I've had a conversation, Vygie, with your mother and with Susan. To discuss your plans. We met at the dominee's, so, of course………" Graph watched for the change in Natalie's expression he knew would come, "……… the dominee and his wife were also there."

Natalie grimaced and rolled her eyes. Graph knew the rebellion was not directed at him. "Yes, I know," he smiled wryly. He glanced upwards at white-ribbed high altitude clouds in the blue Karoo sky.

"I know you appreciate it's my duty to hold the family together. Your mother is pretty kwaad (cross) about you setting yourself free. And kwaad with me for allowing it. So it was best to agree to discuss it with the dominee. You know how she respects the church. I was looking for a neutral place to repeat to her that the law is on your side. Or soon will be. Luckily, Rita heard of my request and proposed Susan attend. Rita knows how well you and Susan get along."

Natalie looked enquiringly at her father. "Neutral?" she asked.

"Well," Graph laughed, "as close to neutral as I could find…….. *If* you're *really* determined Vygie, to go, to leave home, then we've a plan. Are you really, *really* determined? It's a *big* world you know. You're young. It would be okay to change your mind. You could still, if you wished, as a temporary alternative, live at home and work at Mr Barker's."

Natalie's reply held the certainty of intelligent emergence from long constraint. "Daddy, I'm *determined*. I've *thought* about it *such* a lot. I *will* earn enough to support myself. I've checked. So I don't *have* to stay at home *any* longer. And I'm *not* going to wait for the clock to tick all the way to the legal age. My waiting days are *over*. Mr Barker says the sooner I start the better. Having worked at his office several times, I see the mos *terrible* state it's in. It'll take time to put things in order. But Daddy. Because you *are* who you are, you *already* know *all* about it. You and I *know* things without much speaking. *You're* the exception, Daddy. I'll *miss* you. But, for the rest, I'll be less lonely on my own than in this music-less house. Even though there'll be fewer people around. At least I'll be able to choose not to live with people like Charlene. Wherever I go."

"Vygie," Graph latched onto the opportunity, *"Where exactly* you might live was discussed. I recoil from the suggestion of you going. But I understand. So I agreed to the meeting to discuss where you might live. *Especially* that. Rita's now *found* a room for you at Mrs Van Niekerk's place. Your mother finds the arrangement easier to accept because it was made by the dominee's wife."

"Oh," Natalie glimmered amusement. "That explains something. Yesterday I went myself to ask Mrs Van Niekerk if I could have one of her rooms from the beginning of next month. She said I could. I was surprised that she didn't seem surprised. It was as if she expected it. As if young people leave now home and move into her house often. Now I see why. She already *knew*. Although she didn't let on she knew!"

Graph nodded slowly, registering the logical progression.

"Agh Daddy," Natalie continued, "I'm like you. I see a lot. Especially I see you've *much* too much to mos *look after*. You've mos *lots* of children, a wife who's done the *exact opposite* of helping you, and now *enormous* money worries. I *wish* I could help more. I'll be mos better able to help you from afar."

"And, Daddy," she romanticised, "you know……. *our* people, everyone from our own Louis Tregard of Oudtshoorn, to the mos Thirstland Trekkers and Retief and Potgieter and Maritz, so many of them, they suffered from *trekgees*. (trek fever, a need to keep moving on.) I think *I'm* like them. I want to *see* and *be* in *many* places. I would mos *love* to be a wanderer. But *not* a wastrel. I want to be mos *constructive*."

"Oh well, Vygie, my Thirstland Trekker," Graph spoke slowly, coming sadly to terms with the immediacy of the change, "we'll always be soulmates, you and I, wherever we are. Distance won't change that. But I hope you'll stay at your first outspan *a long time*. I like to think you'll be only ten minutes' walk from me."

Natalie left home.

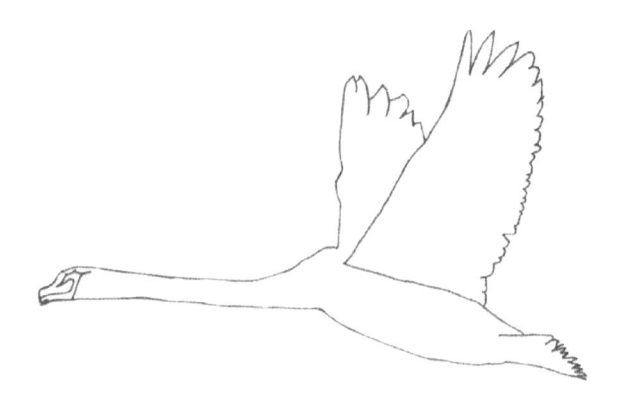

Natalie thought it about right to visit the family home on Tuesday and Friday evenings. A fortnight after leaving, she paid an evening visit to Graph. They sat on her bench in the orchard.

"Mr Barker is very good at fixing cars," she said. "That's obvious. *But.* He mos doesn't know *the first mos thing* about mos accounts. About how *important* book-keeping is. Just by writing to a few customers and sending out statements I've mos, in *two weeks* mos, got in enough money for him to pay my salary a mos *hundred times over*. And if I *hadn't* sent reminders those people might *never* have paid. Because if people think they can get away with not paying, they'll now *just not pay!* So you see, he urgently needed me to work full time. And it's not only getting money in! *Everything's* in a now muddle. Suppliers haven't been paid. Huge numbers of letters are sitting in boxes, waiting to be answered. The bank account has *never* been reconciled. Tax is overdue. *All* the ledgers are behind. Especially the nominal ….. So….. further education can *wait*. Given our mos circumstances and the opportunity now mos presenting itself, I *must* continue with *this* now work! I'm going with him next week to visit his bank   manager!"

Walter Whelan drove his car to the small motor works owned by his friend, Donald Barker. Several squeaks and rattles in 'my old jalopy' needed attention. More worryingly, a new expensive grinding sound had begun somewhere below the driver's seat. Walter found Donald's workmanship reliable and reasonably priced.

He parked in the yard amongst a collection of vehicles. Some rotted in the sun, derelict. Others more or less viable, awaited attention. One or two glittered ostentatiously.

Hoping to speak to Donald, Walter entered the office. He saw his future sister-in-law, entirely alone, surrounded by ledgers, filing cabinets, tables, paper trays, two typewriters and a telephone. Seated at a desk, engrossed, she wrote at high speed in a ledger. Piles of envelopes and newly sorted documents lay neatly around her. The boxes of motor spares which, on Walter's previous visits, had occupied every desk and table, were stacked in a corner of the room, out of the way.

"Hallo, Natalie," Walter said, "Heavens! This place is much less chaotic than usual. You've been *busy*. Mother mentioned you'd started. How're things?"

"Oh! Hallo Walter," Natalie looked up. "Yes. I've been here several weeks."

"And? Do you like it?" he asked.

"I *love* it," she replied. "There's *so* much to do. Mr Barker says he's happy for me to run the office alone if I can cope. I'm pretty sure I can."

"Gosh!" Walter noted the place had been cleaned as well as tidied.

"Life is suddenly enjoyable," Natalie enthused. "It's *interesting* …. all this," she gestured around the office. "Although ….. I'm only at the beginning of getting organised."

"New brooms sweep clean!" Walter remarked.

"It's coming on," Natalie nodded. "Are you looking for Mr Barker?"

"I was hoping to speak to him about my old Model T," Walter said.

"That's alright, Natalie said. "I'll write a note and give it to him when he returns. He drove to a farm this morning to help someone with a tractor."

"Graph," Hester asked irritably, "why do you sigh like that?"

Seated at his desk, Graph pored over the family finances.

"I've no idea how we are going to pay for Anastasia's wedding," Graph's forehead wrinkled.

Hester tilted her head back and regarded her husband through narrowed eyes. "Graph!" she scolded, "You worry too much. Remember, we don't have to support *Natalie* any more. And even if that's *not* a saving

I'm *keen* to make, is it not now nevertheless a saving? And soon *Anastasia* will be gone. So that'll be *two* less mouths to feed."

"Yes," Graph agreed, "but The Great Depression is damaging *everything*. I'm not sure I'll bring in enough money for the next year or two. Have you *read* the newspapers? Have you *looked* around town? There are destitute *white* families everywhere. Men without work. But what do *we* do? We push out the boat! Hester! You really *must* learn to be realistic about money."

"Hallo Walter," Natalie said when Walter returned for his car. "I'm just going to the bank. Mr Barker's in the workshop if you'd like to talk to him. Your car's ready."

"Thanks, Nattie," Walter said cheerfully. He found his friend in the workshop streaked in oil and working stretched out under a Model T similar to his own.

Donald, hearing footsteps, emerged from the confined space under the car, put the spanner he had been using on the running board, stood up and began wiping oil from his hands. "Too much oil to shake hands," he gestured at the blackness.

"Business picking up?" Walter looked about at the array of vehicles waiting for attention. "There're more cars here than I've ever seen at your place."

"Yes," Donald said slowly. "I know we're supposed to be in a depression but I can't complain. According to my bank manager, I'm doing better than ever."

"You even have an assistant, these days," Walter grinned.

"*Invaluable*," Donald said. He clearly meant it. "My paperwork's *never* been this good."

"Not just an ornament, then?" Walter chuckled.

"God, no!" Donald agreed, "*definitely* more than an ornament. Never stops. Even asked if she can work on Sundays until she has everything up to her standard!"

"And. She *looks* pretty good too. Quite an assistant you've found yourself," Walter chuckled again, a little louder.

"*God*, yes!" Donald nodded. "But honestly, I don't look. Well. I should say I *try* not to look. But you know, *she* found *me,* I wasn't looking for anyone! She just showed up one day and asked if she could work in my office on Saturday mornings. I said I'd let her try every Saturday for a month. See how it went. Offered her a pittance. After two Saturday mornings I told her she'd a Saturday job for life if she wanted it and gave her a big increase. Next thing she's saying she wants to leave school to work for me *full time*. Said she had her father's agreement to do just that. Naturally I said 'Yes.' Next thing Dominee Van Der Westhuizen and his wife turn up enquiring about the arrangements. Because Natalie's still young. I explained what she would do and how much I'd pay. They seemed satisfied and went to talk to her mother. So now it's settled. And," he added with some disbelief, "we're *both* getting rich. She's always here. It's never been so good. Everything's running like clockwork."

"Good!" Walter said. "Excellent! Did you know I'm engaged to marry her oldest sister? So Natalie'll be my sister-in-law."

One Sunday the lunch guests were several of Graph's business associates. The conversation about flour milling and crop prices was of no interest to the young who made an early escape to the orchard. The older girls lay on the grass looking up at the fruit trees while the younger children argued over rules for a game they were inventing. The 'irrigation' could be heard bubbling tunefully at the far end of the orchard.

"It's Sunday," said Anastasia. "I wonder if we'll see Nattie today?"

"Agh, Natalie only comes *late* on Sunday afternoons," Charlene commented scornfully. "And only to give Naanie her laundry. Lazy cow."

"She doesn't come to visit *us*! That's for sure," Belinda agreed. "Aunty Kitty was talking about her yesterday. She said Natalie's paying Naanie *much* more than should be paid for laundry and ironing. She thinks Natalie's *throwing* money around like the new-rich and her misplaced generosity will upset the wages structure. Because other employers will have to pay more if wages go up. People will be cross with Natalie."

"Agh, Natalie's gone completely *'koptoe.'*" (A misplaced sense of importance has gone to her head,) Charlene grumbled. "Just because she works in a now *office*. Have you seen her *rokke* (dresses) these days? I think she only lives the way she lives as a way of scorning us and our ways."

"I'm not sure, Bee," Anastasia gently disagreed, "I think it's nice of Nattie to help Naanie at a time when daddy's struggling to pay for everything."

Sounds from the kitchen interrupted their conversation. Naanie could be heard clapping her hands and ululating in wonder. Dinu, Cetsh and Lady barked and squealed continuously.

"Agh, God," Belinda said, "it sounds as if Natalie *has* honoured us with her company. That's why Naanie is carrying on. Again."

"Speak of the devil," Charlene said.

The three older sisters stirred. Leaving the comfortable warm grass, they walked to the kitchen.

They found not only Natalie and Naanie, but also, to Anastasia's delight, Walter, who, by chance, arrived at the same moment as Natalie. Anastasia embraced her fiancé.

"Naanie, do you *have* to make that noise?" Charlene demanded. "You sound more like a *black* than a coloured. What are you? A Fingo?" Taking a step back she made a scene of scrutinising Natalie's outfit, "Te pronkerig," she said. (Too gaudy.)

Walter's face showed shock and involuntary disapproval, not only at such sisterly discord, but at the very idea anyone should speak so rudely to a servant.

This was exactly what Charlene intended. The corners of her mouth turned upwards.

"Is that so?" Natalie grimaced at Charlene. "I see you're *still* drawing attention to yourself by being unpleasant. I don't expect *you'll* ever change. I suggest you go out to *work. Perhaps, if* you actually spent time doing something *useful*, then, *if* you're any good at what you do, *which* you probably *won't* be, you might actually *earn* some money. *Then,* instead of envying my success, you, too, might be able to afford decent clothes. Rather than your present now *hand-me-downs.*"

"Is nie hand-me-downs nie," ("They're not hand-me-downs,") Charlene was unprepared for so vigorous a defence.

"If you're *so* jealous," Natalie's flare-up heightened, "just understand this. I'm *not* scared of you *any* more. Not like I was when I was a child and you bullied me. Probably *you'll never* understand what sheer *character* can achieve. Because it takes force of personality to overturn conventions."

Charlene held up a middle finger to Natalie.

"I think you've never even *thought* of the self-sufficiency for women. You'll always be sommer (just) a *wall-flower*. You'll *never* see how, *just by visiting this house* I introduce, for a few minutes, *active* life into your *endless* routine. But. No use falling out of the tree! Let's just accept we'll never have time for one another."

"Agh, your *adventure* of going off by yourself won't last, Natalie," Belinda said. "You'll soon get tired of living in a poky pondokkie. (cottage.) And then you'll come home with your tail between your legs."

"On the contrary," Natalie's expression changed to jubilant defiance, "my boss says because I do the work of two people, and because I prefer working alone, he's decided against employing an assistant to help me. And as a reward he's increasing my salary by the amount he would've paid such a person."

Naanie, having listened involuntarily to this exchange, turned away to continue her work. She made a fatalistic Nguni click of disgust.

Natalie brushed past Charlene and Belinda to the corner of the kitchen where the small children had entered and stood watching. "Here you are! *Sweeties* for the sweet!" she said handing them each a paper bag. And, here's a little present for each of you which you must only open tomorrow."

"Nattie," Anastasia said demurely, "We *do* miss you *really* you know I hope one day you *will* come back home. To *us*."

"No, we really *don't* wish that," Charlene countered.

Walter looked bemused.

Natalie turned to stare at Charlene.

"Gavin and Garth," Anastasia intervened, "Yvette and Delaine, say 'Thank you' to Nattie for your presents."

"Thank you, Natalie," the children, obedient to their de facto mother, responded in simultaneous monotone.

"Well, Stazie, it's kind of you to say you miss me," Natalie softened, "I'll remember that. But. Too much happened in this house." She gestured at Charlene and Belinda. And at the chair to which Graph had confined Arthur. "In Life it's better to go forward. Coming back here would mos …. be … *dismal*. Really." She glanced at Walter and then at Belinda and Charlene. "*Definitely*," she said darkly, "there's *only* going forward.

I'll *never* again wear Charlene and Belinda's hand-me-downs. *Never!*"

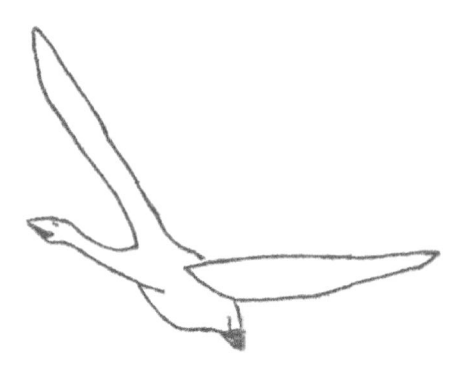

"She's *leaving!?*" The friends met by chance in the street. Walter could not believe it. "Only a fortnight ago, when I saw her at The Middler's, she sounded so *happy* in her work."

"Yes," Donald Barker answered delicately. "It's a *great* disappointment. Things were going so well. But she's *determined* to leave."

"*Why?*" Walter asked.

"Well…… It's a sore point. To say the least. A top dog from Port Elizabeth visited last week," Donald explained. "I'm an agent for some of his products. So he visits from time to time. Likes to keep an eye on his outlets. He was impressed by the transformation Natalie's brought about at my place, admired her energy and efficiency. Said it rare to find anyone, let alone 'a mere girl', who could read and interpret Profit and Loss Accounts and Balance Sheets. More than that, could actually start from scratch to create them herself. And…... he admired *her*. So…… he didn't waste time. Offered her a job then and there. Five times the pay. And *much* more besides. Perks. She's to have a swanky office of her own in central Port Elizabeth and will be required to travel. She'll be given a whopping great travel allowance. It's the bit about travel which *really* appealed to Natalie. Posh hotels and restaurants and all that. She has itchy feet, that one. I wish I could keep her. But Oudtshoorn's too much of a dorp (village) for her. Her talents seem *endless*. She's able to give *much* more than *Oudtshoorn* demands. She *needs* the *city*. I can't compete with his offer. And I can't afford to fall out with *him*, either. I'm going to miss her."

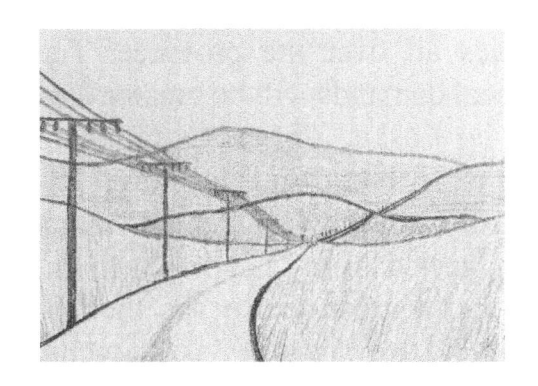

South African Road

"What work will she do for him?" Walter asked.

"Actually, she told me quite a lot about that," Donald answered. "She's always open and honest with me. Perhaps she told me more than necessary because she felt bad about leaving. We've worked closely during the time she's been with me. Neither of us wanted to damage our …. respect ….. for one another. So ….. some of the work, if I understand correctly, will be the same as she does for me. Secretarial and financial. But there'll also be sales work *and* monitoring agencies all over the province. The technical demands will be greater than anything I asked of her. Or anything she's experienced up to now. His organisation is *much* bigger than mine. He suggested in my hearing it might profit her a great deal if she thought *'definitely'* of herself as 'a chic addition to a smart operation.' Didn't seem to care I was listening. One of her tasks will be to 'vet and control incoming communications so he doesn't have to waste time deflecting the wrong people'. He told her he'll require her to use her intelligence because she'll have to learn a lot about his product range. He even said there was no doubt glamour and direct smiles make for profitable first impressions on customers. And 'mysteries of dancing eyes' may be 'irrelevant forces' but they are the path to 'big deals'. I think he *really* noticed she, like himself, doesn't want to be restricted to office hours. She prefers to work seven days a week and eighteen hours a day, thinks sleeping a waste of time. Sets little store by holidays. Likes staying on after others have gone home. And arrives before them. She's going to be *busy*. She'll travel all over The Cape. There'll be weeks in Cape Town and visits to East London, Kimberley, De Aar, Clanwilliam, Colesberg. And everywhere in between. All sorts of Twee Buffels and Putsonders."

x   x

[[Twee Buffels Met Een Koeel Doodgeskietfontein (The spring where two buffalo were killed with one bullet)

and

Putsonderwater (Hole without water)]]

x   x

"They'll be away a lot. Stay in the best hotels wherever they go. So we may actually see her from time to time when work brings her to my place. It's not difficult to imagine how he'll use her to make *a lot* of money. Mind you. He already has a lot of money."

"They?" Walter asked.

It was fairly late. The evening meal at the Middler's was all but over. The family lingered around the table. Naanie, carrying plates and bowls to the kitchen, joined in the conversation as she came and went.

There came a "hulloooo" and Natalie walked in.

"I've just come to collect a few books," she said. She stopped and glanced around. "But also," she added nervously, "as everyone's here, it seems a good moment to say goodbye."

Conversation stopped.

"Daddy knows about it. I'm leaving town. Going to take up a better opportunity. I haven't told many people."

Naanie stopped in the kitchen doorway. She turned to look at Natalie.

"I've been offered exactly what I've been looking for. It's a position in a big motor company in Port Elizabeth. It'll entail travelling. Which I've *always* wanted. And so ….. I'm going away, to live in Port Elizabeth."

"Graph!" Hester exclaimed in shock and disbelief. She looked to her husband seeking assurance that Natalie's outrageous plan would not be countenanced.

But Graph was nodding.

A gleam of understanding crossed Hester's face. "You already *knew!?*" she upbraided Graph, her voice rising. "And you said nothing."

Graph's forehead wrinkled involuntarily. He leaned back in his chair and scratched his pate while

Naanie, the childless servant and midwife, wounded by the thought of her favourite being so far away, ululated dismay in a shrill key. Anastasia, Belinda and Charlene were scandalised. "It would be *immoral*," Belinda said, "for such a thing to happen in *our* family."

"Well now, Belinda," Natalie responded. "I seem to remember it was *you* who said I'd soon tire of living in a poky pondokkie. So. Maybe I *would* have tired of it eventually, and maybe I wouldn't. But now we'll never know. Because, with my new position in my new company, I'll be able to afford to live in a posh hotel in Port Elizabeth. I'll never be like you, a puddle-duck looking for a puddle. Call me immoral if you like but I'll never accept a life in which the single objective is comfort and in which ambition is relegated to some underclass."

"Agh!" Belinda replied, "you think you're a *situation*."

The younger children, gathered around Natalie, waited impatiently for the conversation of elders to cease so they could ask their own questions.

"Did you bring us presents, Nattie?" Yvette seized a split second in which no-one was speaking. She looked hopefully at Natalie's handbag.

"Are you sleeping here tonight?" Gavin asked. "You always go away so quickly!"

"Why *don't* you sleep here any more?" Delaine protested. "It's *misgusting* that you don't you sleep here any more?"

"*Dis*gusting," Natalie corrected her.

"No, Gavin, I won't be sleeping here tonight," she answered. "But……" she searched in her deep handbag, "somewhere in here, I *do* have something for each of you." Extracting small bars of chocolate she handed them out like a mother bird to open-mouthed nestlings, smiling down on them from some height of compassion while they clustered around her as if she were an angel or goddess.

"Isn't Nattie sleeping here tonight?" Garth asked Gavin in his small voice.

"No!" Gavin answered, "pay *attention*, Garth!"

"Oh, *dit!*" Garth said.

Natalie started at Garth's innocent profanity. But concealed her amusement. "Garth," she said seriously, kneeling down to focus on him and to look him in the face, "you really *mustn't* use that word. It's *not* a nice word. Where on earth did you learn such a word?" She looked to Anastasia for support.

But Anastasia stood arms folded, a picture of serenity, smiling a wide smile. She surveyed the family, her bickering parents, the censorious Naanie, her de facto children, the rival siblings, the rebellious Nattie. "Worse things have happened," she said.

"Kinders grootmaak is nie perdekoop nie," Hester sighed and grumbled. ("Raising children is not like buying and selling horses.") Perturbed, she turned to her husband, "Graph," she said, "I really *cannot* accept this."

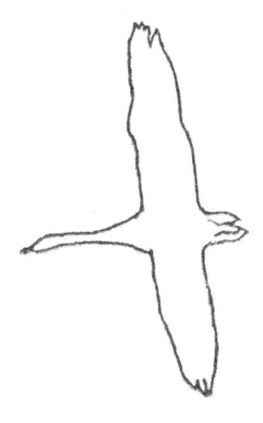

In the house neighbouring the church, Susan and Walter Whelan discussed the family to whom they would be tied by marriage.

"*Nothing*" Susan said, "is going to stop Natalie. Or even impede her. She's a perfectionist. She's only at the beginning. Her ascent will be fascinating. Nail-biting. I *pray* for her. I wonder *how* high she'll go, how she'll handle success. If she succeeds."

"I see now ….. how you love Natalie," Walter said. "And ….. thinking back, I realise how much a part of our lives she's been. Until recently I took little notice. I simply thought her to be part of your endless church work. You were looking after a child with the misfortune of having an alcoholic uncle. But. It was more than that."

"Yes." Susan agreed. "Natalie's the daughter I never had. An intelligent angry child. Struggling amidst the troubles of her large family. My work with her was rewarding …… her gain was my gain. She's a *keen* learner. With a *huge* imagination. *Long* ago I realised she's able to *think* her way out of difficulties. Of course no human is omnipotent. But … we hit upon the idea of *using* trouble as an energy source. We would focus on problems. Focussing brought ideas. Some ideas became solutions."

"She has a *brain!*" Walter said. "Donald thought her a gem. Most people never fathom the logic of double entry accounting, or fully grasp its usefulness for business and trade. Oh well. At least the worst of the Middler difficulties are over now. Because …… dare I say it? .... Arthur Calitz is dead."

"The *acute* troubles are over," Susan agreed sagaciously, "but the aftermath will endure. For decades. It's engrained."

"Will you miss her?" Walter asked.

"Oh, heaps and *heaps*," came the wan reply. "But we'll be in one another's thoughts. Mere geography cannot separate us."

"Do you approve of her going to Port Elizabeth?" Walter asked.

"Why? Do you think I should *disapprove*?" Susan asked.

"It's just that …. well ……. her decision has ignited a conflagration amongst the Middlers. Because …….. and I don't know how much the family knows, but….." Walter chose his words carefully, "Donald implied the new employer intends to use the feminine form to increase his sales. Apparently 'the mysteries of dancing eyes' will be useful in clinching deals. And … the business trips will be a duo, they'll journey together ….. in his car."

"*Really*, Walter!" Susan looked at her son, "do you *have* to be so specific? … But of course," she relented. "I understand. These things are real. All I can say is Natalie *will* manage. She knows where to draw the line. She's young but she knows what's what. We often discussed expectations of the life and work of women. And whether women might do better without men.

Our most interesting talk concerned what on *earth* women *actually are*! And how grass can be surprisingly greener. And how we might protect ourselves. And what it is women would actually prefer to take from existence. We decided," Susan remembered with amusement, "women often simply prefer feminine company ….. the moments when they make a pot of tea and natter over buttered scones …… those can be peaceful moments."

Walter stared at his mother.

"Oh, don't be alarmed, dear!" she soothed. "We never advocated the convent. We decided men are probably essential. Not expendable."

"Well," he said, "I'm glad my Anastasia is as she is. Dependable and home-loving. Unflamboyant."

"Nee wat!" (Oh, no!") the dominee sighed. Another meeting had been called. This time to discuss Natalie's departure for Port Elizabeth. "It *is* a *terrible* mistake the way the English let women into universities. All these notions of the equality of women! It's a liberal *quagmire*. The world will pay a high price for such an immense liberty, for disturbing the natural order of The Almighty."

Rita Van Der Westhuizen looked glum and said nothing.

Susan Whelan glanced around, weighing up, once more, the personalities and the issues. She decided there really was no point in debating liberalism with the present company.

"Nothing good," Hester said grimly, "will come of it."

"We might at least applaud Natalie's remarkable success?" Susan suggested.

"But skoonsister (sister-in-law)," Hester replied, "*surely* it's *our failure* rather than *her success*?

"We've been over this ground so *many* times, Hester," Graph suppressed impatience as he tried to close with the immediate issue. "Natalie's of an age at which *the law* permits her to make this decision."

"*The law is stupid*," Hester said. "*Very, very stupid*!"

"Hester," Susan intervened, "I agree with Graph. The law is clear. The best hope is to give Natalie freedom to go. *That's* the way to *keep* her. *That's* how *we* shall remain in *her heart*. Even when she is not in our *houses*."

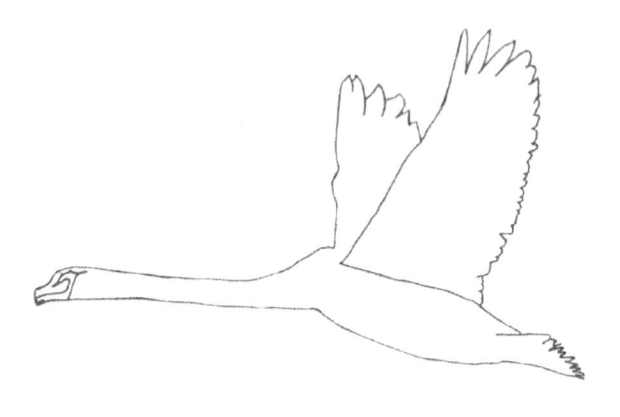

Graph called on his daughter at Mrs Van Niekerk's boarding house.

"I have the reservations for our fortnight at The Grand Hotel," he said. "The letter came this morning. Also, yesterday, I collected our train tickets and coupe reservations from the SAR travel office."

"Oh, I'm *glad* you're coming, Daddy," Natalie read the letter. "I'd have struggled to pay for it myself. Although, I could have. Just about."

"I couldn't think of doing less," Graph replied. "Wish I could do more."

Natalie hugged him.

"Have you started packing?" he asked.

"I'll pack the night before we leave. Just two small suitcases for clothes and a few books. Easy for one person to carry."

"Oh!" Graph scratched his pate. "I'm used to the ways of your mother and

Aunty Kitty. They require one porter each. Just for the hat boxes."

"Yes, daddy," Natalie accepted the family joke. "But I'll be living in hotels. And spending my time working. So I'll need only work outfits."

"I looked it up," Graph said as they boarded the overnight train. It's two hundred and seventy-nine miles by train from Oudtshoorn to Port Elizabeth."

Their train crossed an immense semi-desert. From a plush carriage they rejoiced in a realm they called home, ostriches, giant tortoises, cacti, the empty expanses, lonely farm houses, antelope.

"The scene reminds me of Perceval Gibbon's 'GREAT KAROO'", Natalie said. She quoted,

"Years and years I've trekked it,
Ridden back and fore,
Till the silence and the glamour
Ruled me to the core;
No man knew it better,
None could love it more."

By late afternoon, having gazed on splendour for more than an hour, it was time for a tete-a-tete.

"In this place," Graph gestured placidly at the passing scene, "God's Hand is visible."

Natalie admired the myriad flat-topped koppies. "Our homeland," she agreed. "Just to look at it is a tonic." She settled back in her chair, crossed her arms. "Merely looking at it," she repeated quietly.

"Did you notice," Graph also leaned back on his seat, "those chaps in the SAR ticket office gave me exactly what I asked for?"

"What did you ask for?" she asked. "Oh! You mean the coupé?"

"Not just any old coupé," he said. "I asked for the coupe′ which I knew would be the last compartment in the last carriage of the train, followed only by the guard's van."

"Daddy!" curiosity and delight belied protest, "being in the last carriage meant we had to carry our suitcases further along the platform than anyone else. Why did you ask for *this* one?"

"It's a remnant of a childhood obsession," Graph explained. From this trailing vantage point, in this last carriage, there's a quietude. Almost …. a detachment. …… Here, we're *last* to arrive at any landmark, *last* to clatter onto a viaduct. By the time we arrive the engine's already gone on. We're *last* to enter a tunnel from which the locomotive might already have emerged! And …. from time to time, when it thunders around a curve, we have silver-blue views of our indefatigable 'iron horse.' Then, as the rails straighten out, so does the string of brown coaches. We no longer see the engine. The bluster of soot and steam melts away. A distant pattern of cylinders resumes. Haste and energy are muted, become merely a pulsing of carriage wheels, a melody and rhythm. All we do is watch. And listen. And ….. this far back, if we put our heads out the window we're less likely to get smuts in the eye. It was *big* stuff to me when I was a child. Still is."

"I love you, Daddy!" she nestled up.

"And I love our country. The farmers' homesteads are *specks*," she looked out at the landscape, "so *remote*. And the desert's so *big*. So *yellow* …… and *brown*. It's even *blue*. And the purple mountains are so *distant* …. jagged horizons ….. etching the sky. The only green places with a *few* trees are the farmsteads. I *wish we* lived on a farm. Like some of our relatives."

"Yes," Graph's brow crinkled. "The farms……" For a moment he was not with his daughter. Transported involuntarily back to crises of youth, violent flashbacks and horrifying images invaded his brain. "Beautiful, *poetic* farms," he mused. "*What need* have *South Africans* of *poets* …?" he made a partial return to the present, "or poetry …..? when their farms ….."

he sighed, "when the *farms* are the poetry? …. Ah! …. the veld …… but ….. alas ….. in war the farms are …. *impossible* to defend …... A *nightmare!* Too *vulnerable!* Too distant! The farms are *too* remote! Too *isolated*…… A strategic liability ……. I have misgivings about the future."

Natalie stared at him. But said nothing. She had long known much of what he was thinking. And imagined a terrible deal more. The passing scenery and the conversation were bringing to the surface of Graph's mind, memories of The Boer War.

Graph thought of 1901 and of lines written at the time.

NOORDKAAP

Flying in the wind
we leave our dying bleeding
on stones.
Also in the grass they lie,
stretched out.
Or doubled up.
No time.
Rifles recovered. Death imminent.
Must pass.
Move out.
Now what use friends?
Uniforms?
Badges of rank?
Kameraderie?
The end will be soft.
Leave them to it.
No choice.

But he did not mention the poem. He
must put it out of his mind. Silence it.
This was his daughter's moment. Not
his.

But the thoughts would not be driven away.

"There are many, many, such farms," Graph said, suppressing wistfulness. "Invaluable, unique. *Spread* over *vast* areas. Those ver verlate vlakte! (remote deserted plains). Sanctuaries of the veld! The *distances* you understand, the *distances* are both the glory and the downfall. Because, in time of war the defenders are often too late. When the farms are under attack. *Vulnerable*, you see. *Very* vulnerable. The defenders are few and the attackers many. The bravery of farmer and wife is seldom enough. Brave though they are! Often, the outcome is the worst. Especially was it so in the Kafir Wars. When the farms themselves were the border. Murder, pillage, burning. Savagery. The English administration's refusal to defend their own colonial frontier caused The Great Trek. And. Sixty years later, in another war, history more or less repeated itself. The English burnt the Boer farms and put the boers (farmers) in camps. Where many died."

"And *I*?"

"I *fought for* the English."

He was silent for a moment.

"Accident of birth."

He was silent for another moment.

"Don't think about it, Daddy," Natalie said.

But Graph could not help thinking about it. "Each farm is a poem," he said. "And poetry is a force. But poetry succumbs to savagery. Poetry," Graph repeated, "is weaker than savagery. Savagery overwhelms goodness……. 'Bulalani abatagati' ('Kill the wizards') and 'Rule Britannia' Somehow we *cannot* progress beyond Dingaan and Arne. Many believe Ndlela was a cannibal. Being of high rank he *must* have owned *many* cattle. And would not have been driven by *need*. To eat human meat."

"Unless he was campaigning somewhere, I suppose," Natalie shuddered.

"It's no thanks to *anyone* but ourselves that *we're* still here. Unfortunately," Graph continued, "the circumstances in which people find themselves drive them to take fixed intellectual positions. It seems to be human nature. Sometimes, people even sacrifice friendship to these attitudes. Some sacrifice their *lives* for mere beliefs. It's like going swimming in a heavy suit of armour. A burden and…… a loneliness. And *beliefs change!* But," Graph continued, "we survived. We did our best. And our best was just about enough. Somehow we squeezed through between all the mishaps. And yet. ……. those who lose a country live always in a crisis world. Even if fortunate enough to be granted another country. Because the loss of a country is the pain of its dead soldiers and the mourning of their families and the depression of the displaced all put together. Those who've not lost a country have no way of comprehending this. Least of all the British. They haven't lost their country since 1066."

"We've done better than squeeze through," Natalie said. "Our history has proved it *impossible* to live peacefully together. *So we must find a way to live apart!* In peace. The English, the Dutch, and the tribes."

Graph did not respond. But his bleak thoughts were dispelled by the balm of his daughter's company. And by the gentle rocking of the coupé. However fragile or temporary civilisation, life itself, might seem to Graph, the train was a brief haven. It afforded momentary shelter from the chaotic rush of history. And from the demands of the world. Even as it took them to the next endeavour.

"Apparently," Graph voiced his response, long-since calculated, to the emergencies of life, "creation requires us to be positively cheerful as we confront the insufferable! So. Hard-work and determination shall be our physic. And …… in the face of the insurmountable ……. detachment."

"Actually," he continued a few moments later, "the art of continually making the wife laugh might be, under heaven, the ultimate civilisation, the policy to trump all policy."

Natalie laughed.

The train meandered on through pure semi-desert.

"We benefit from the toil of those who went before," Graph indicated the swaying carriage, the passing cacti, the land, the sky. " …… Those whom Sir Percy Fitzpatrick called 'the nameless pioneers', *they* were the ones with so great a longing for freedom that they packed up and trekked, left the rule of The Dutch East India Company far behind."

Logo of Dutch East India Company

"And in turn, when the time came, another generation of pioneers moved far away and left the British to their British colony."

Flag of The Cape Of Good Hope Colony

"Even though Sir Percy eulogised over his days of transport riding, all the wagons, the oxen and the hunting, I'm not sure he grasped the full drama of trekkers trekking a thousand miles into completely unknown territory. Oftentimes disagreement amongst themselves caused them to trek away from each other. And although the administration they detested eventually caught up with them …… more or less ….. they *did* succeed in laying the foundations of several very big wonderlands. But Sir Percy wasn't interested in all that. He was interested in the money to be made from supplying gold mines."

Flag of The Orange Free State

"The lands those pioneers came to call their own were several times the size of the European countries from which they came. Transport riding was different from trekking. Transport riding was for profit. Trekking was for the soul. Sir Percy was a youthful transport rider for a brief period. Trekking was forever."

Father and daughter marvelling at the landscape, listened to the rhythms of the train.

"Our times, it must be said," Graph continued, "are safe compared with the days of the pioneers."

Flag of The Republic Of Natalia

"We no longer fear poisoned arrow and assegai. And attack by Zulu and Matabele hordes. But the peace of our wide, wide empire was not easily built. We're fortunate. Our magnificent desert is orderly. But. *Never* can we relax our guard. *Never!*"

Natalie had heard this before. She didn't mind. She liked to hear it. She nodded and thought about the origins of things.

"And, thank God," Graph said fervently, "the iron horse has replaced the ox-wagon. I know the ox-wagon is a fond memory. But, when I think about the era of the trek-boer and of two hundred years of trekking and transport-riding … and of The Great Trek … I marvel at the speed things happen these days. Now, it takes less than twenty-four hours to travel a distance that took a week or more in your grand-parents time. In those days one might have waited two or three days for a flooding river to subside. Before it was safe for a wagon to ford or a horse to swim. Now we build a bridge. That's the difference between 1860 and 1930. Civilisation, after all, owes *much* to the *inventiveness* of the empire. It brought us steam-power, electricity, the postage stamp, the internal combustion engine …….. the end of the slave trade. *That* most of all. It adds up to freedom. Yet, even with so much progress, human beings are seldom free. Humanity hasn't learnt 'to live and let live.'"

Graph studied a page of his pocket notebook.

"What're you looking at?" Natalie asked.

"When I bought our tickets I jotted down all the station names along our route and the times we're supposed to depart those places," he said. "I used to do this as a kid, to check whether the train was keeping time."

Natalie reached out for the notebook and ran her eye over her father's copious notes.

TIMES

NOTE : "S" means train will stop only when required to set down or pick up passengers.

Oudtshoorn	4|0
Stolsvlakte	S
Vanwykskraal	4|37
Hazenjacht	4|48
Le Roux	5| 5
Delport	S
Middelplaas	5|18
Marevlakte	5|22
Stompdrift	S
Vlakteplaas	5|46
Rooiloop	6| 2
Scholtz	S
Snyberg	6|25
Barandas	7| 3
Toorwater	7|26
Vondeling	7|43
Antonie	8|29
Willowmore	8|59
Skerpkop	S
Oven	9|35
Solitree	S
Knoetze	9|55
Fullarton	10| 4

Draaiberg	S
Eensaam	S
Miller	10|35
Fern	11| 0
Humefield	11|12
Klipplaat	12|50
Hardwood	S
Mount Stewart	1 17
Baroe	1 43
Haasfontein	2 2
Wolwefontein	2 22
Kleinpoort	2 46
Cockscomb	3 1
Sapkamma	3 13
Glenconnor	3 32
Kartega	4 2
Steenbokvlakte	S
Bluecliff	4 35
Centlivres	5 6
Fitzpatrick's Valley	5 36
Uitenhage	6 11
Despatch	S
Perseverance	6 24
Redhouse	6 35
Swartkops	D
New Brighton	D
Sydenham	D
North End	D
Port Elizabeth	7 0

"Very neat," she said handing back the notebook. "'Oven' is the right name."

Dusk fell. Secure in the rocking coupé they wondered what scenes were passing in the darkness outside. Their conversation was interrupted by a waiter walking the length of the train striking a dinner gong. At his entry to each carriage he called out, "Second sitting!"

Graph slid open the varnished coupé door. Balancing against the train's momentum, they launched themselves along the swaying corridors of several 'long-distance' carriages until they reached an ageing dining car.

Built before 1900 for The Cape Government Railways, the dining car with its galley, still proclaimed an old logos. Etched on the windows and carved in the wood were the letters 'CGR'.

"Gosh!" Natalie said. "How beautiful! And how *hushed!* Is it the red carpet that muffles sound? This is lovely, daddy!"

Graph squinted at the detail of a carved crest and then stood back to admire the wider impression. "My! It's a work of art, this dining car. I wonder whether those etchings and carvings were deliberately preserved. Or whether their survival was just a dictate of economics."

Wide windows along the varnished mahogany walls were set in gold frames. Cut-glass lampshades cast variegated light over everything. Pure white ceilings, mahogany beamed, brought into relief the darkening night outside.

"It's a mobile museum-piece," Graph enthused but before he could finish examining it all, they were shown to one of the tables for two that ran the length of one side of the dining car. The table top, covered in a cloth of brightest white, was secured to legs of decorative wrought iron which in turn were bolted to the floor. Mahogany swivel chairs with burnished red leather backs and padded seats were also bolted to the floor. The chair padding was outlined in gold filigree. Tables for four lined the other side of the dining car. The white staff wore black uniforms with navy lapels. White shirts. Somewhere beneath the floor, steel wheels kept time.

"Everything in this dining car was designed to *last*," Graph said appreciatively. "All the furniture is fixed to the floor and walls."

"*Naanie* would be impressed by the whiteness of *this* tablecloth," Natalie said, running her finger over the fabric. And she'd *love* the conically folded serviettes. *And* the silver place settings."

"I'm just going to take a look at that thing," Graph said rising from his chair almost as soon as he had taken his seat, and immediately standing aside for a waiter. He made his way towards an ornate wall-mounted clock at the far end of the carriage.

"I couldn't see who the maker was or where it was made," he said when he returned a minute or two later, "but in the world of clocks that one's pretty grand. Surprising that it keeps time, considering the motion of the train."

For the young Natalie, travel was a novelty. Her imagination responded to the novelty of the continuously changing scene. They studied the menu.

"Would you care for a glass of wine, Vygie?" Graph asked.

Natalie stared at her father aghast. "But, *daddy*, you *know* I'll *never ever* touch alcohol," she said, amazed at his offer.

"Yes. I *do* know that," he said. "But I was interested to see how you'd react. You'll soon be on your own in the world. Such offers will be frequent. It's simply hospitality. So, be prepared. Think of, and keep ready, an inconspicuous way to decline."

"Oh, certainty makes the response easy," she said dismissively.

They tried to give attention to the menu.

But the dramatic setting through which they passed was more compelling than the menu. "Look daddy," Natalie gazed excitedly through the window, "the moon has just risen behind those clouds. It's *huge*."

Silent moonlit veld, a blue-silver majesty, whispered past the dining car window. Smoke from the engine cast moonlit shadows which flitted alongside, dancing on the scrub. Away on the veld, in the darkness, horned heads lifted to scent the approaching intruder, started at the sudden piercing headlamp, cringed as the thunderous, clanking, smoke-pouring locomotive burst upon the peace.

"It's lighting up that wind-pump. And the whole farmstead. Do you see?"

"Oh, yes I *do* see," he said. "A golden wind-pump!"

"I wonder how many generations have lived there?" she mused. "It's *the essence* of home."

"At *least* ten, on average, I should think," Graph replied. "Once people settle in these parts they tend to really *settle*. And. Permanent settlers they may be, as are we. Individuals. *But* like us, they're expendable. It'd be folly to lose sight of that greater cultural truth. Terrible as it may seem, we're all merely ants whose primary duty is to offer up what's asked of us. As do ants. Priv*ants*. Serge*ants*. Serge*ant*-majors, Lieuten*ants*. Capt*ants*. Command*ants*. Within that outrageous limit, we're free to find what happiness we can. Duty bound, in fact, to find it.

Natalie knew of old her father's ant metaphor and its wartime origin. "Each soul," she said, "is sometimes a Lilliputian and sometimes a Brobdingnagian. That's how human beings are." She looked at her father expecting a response. But his mind was, once again, elsewhere.

After a while he did respond. "Because," he mused, "there's really no such thing as A Promised Land. On the very day the Boers scored their spectacular triumph over the Zulus at Blood River, thinking they had thereby, that day, secured Natal as a Boer republic, *on that very same day*, which I think of as the birth of the Natalian Republic, unbeknown to the Boers, British redcoats landed at Port Natal and hoisted the Union Jack. So much for a promised land."

Natalie left her father to his thoughts. She understood silent communion and knew the calming effect of sitting quietly beside him.

"Daddy," she said after a while, "we must be sure to find ways to bridge our separation. I don't want long periods when we don't see each other."

"Oh, I *wouldn't* worry about *that*," he replied. "Our bond is immutable."

"Yes. But time and distance will be enemies now," she said, showing the first sign of real apprehension since taking it on herself to leave home.

"Don't worry," Graph said reassuringly, "we won't allow them to be insurmountable enemies. There's every chance we'll spend week-ends together once in a while. Sometimes in Oudtshoorn, sometimes in Port Elizabeth, sometimes perhaps, temptingly, at halfway houses."

"Money'll be a problem," she fretted.

"We both have livings to earn," he agreed, "free time is scarce. But the reason I earn money is to look after my family. Keeping in touch will be a way to look after the family."

"Yes, better to spend money on togetherness than on alcohol for Uncle Arthur," she observed. "And, I can hardly believe it. But if things turn out as I'm told they will, *I'll* be able to treat *you* to halfway-house weekends. That'd be a welcome change. Instead of depending on you to pay for every last thing. But, of course, the money isn't mine until it's been in the bank four days."

"Oh!" Graph looked surprised. "Do you have a bank account now?"
"I do," she said, determination tinging her answer.

"Goodness! You're grown up! I wonder," Graph continued, "whether Hester would join us for halfway-house weekends? And whether she'd accept the expense of the other children coming along."

"Probably not," Natalie's mind was clear. "She *doesn't* approve of what I'm doing and she'd begrudge money spent visiting me. She neglects responsibilities, especially the mundane, and puts time into things which suit her. And, to be fair, it *would* cost a lot. Especially if the whole family came."

"Let's be optimistic," Graph said. "Both you and I are industrious. You might prove you're doing the right thing. Financially. Your mother's sometimes persuaded by financial success. Also. Fate could be on our side. The South African economy is not without promise. Engineering, industry, endeavour of every kind may boom. It might be possible to do well. Think how Port Elizabeth has gone ahead recently. Completing the mile long breakwater five years ago made a huge difference.

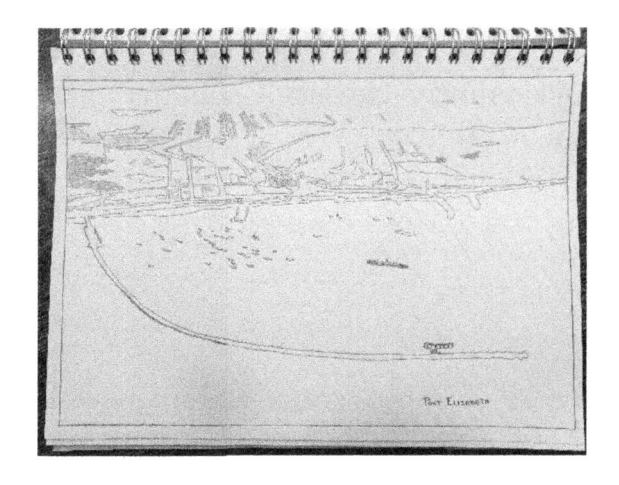

Shipping is now easier, quicker and cheaper. And these days refrigeration makes it possible for people in Europe to eat fruit grown here. That's astonishing. We might, ourselves, benefit from the increase in trade. Of course the European news is bad. But there's everything to play for."

"Agh," Natalie agreed, "European news is invariably bad. The Saar plebiscite and German rearmament and all that. It's front page every day. But Europe is six thousand miles away. Two weeks by the fastest steamers. The Great Depression will be beaten. By us. Look at us. Look at our railway carriages and our giant locomotive. We still move. Everything functions."

The coupé with its mirror and steel basin and heavily varnished fold-away table gave them all they needed.

"I feel excited and tranquil at the same time," Natalie said, snuggling up again to her father.

The train wound on through serene darkness. Despite pro-Boer sentiment, father and daughter believed their trouble-free journeying to be a tiny part of immense imperial progress. They believed this security to be world-wide, repeated throughout the European empires and made possible by them. Frequent stops at ghostly, brightly-lit, deserted stations seemed more for the sake of good order than for any purpose apparent in the utter stillness of the night. No passengers alighted or boarded. Nothing was loaded or unloaded. "No wonder they call this train a 'skilpad' (tortoise)," Graph grinned. "Oh yes," Natalie agreed, "the children at school used to call this route the 'Toet, hier gaan ek, toet, hier staan ek' train." (Whistle, here I go, whistle, here I stop.)

Their bedding, sets of unyielding white linen and heavy blue blankets, standard issue of The South African Railways, was spotlessly clean. It was carried in, unpacked and unfurled from canvas bags by a burly coloured attendant. He made up two of the three bunks in the coupé.

Under the cold firmament they rocked and swayed through semi-desert until, the night advancing, profound sleep enfolded them.

Into this deep slumber came, much too soon, a metallic wake-up call. A customary brisk rattling of keys on compartment doors and loud official announcements in the corridor outside about arrival times and breakfast times rose above the clicking of carriage wheels. The rousing, an infringement of soft morning, was eased when the waiters of the night before unceremoniously entered each compartment wielding heavy pots engraved 'SAR' and announcing, *"Koffie, coffee!"* Steadying themselves against the swaying carriage, they dribbled and splashed coffee into small cups. "Milk, madam? Milk, sir?" "Sugar, madam? Sugar, sir?" And were gone.

Natalie, wrapped in heavy SAR bedding, jarred to wakefulness, looked down at Graph from the top bunk, "Somehow," she said sleepily, "I wasn't so pleased to see them this morning as I was last night."

She descended from the top bunk, raised the blind and looked out. The landscape had changed during the night. They had descended into unfamiliar coastal scrub and grassland.

There came another announcement.

"Arriving at P.E. in one hour and thirty minutes."

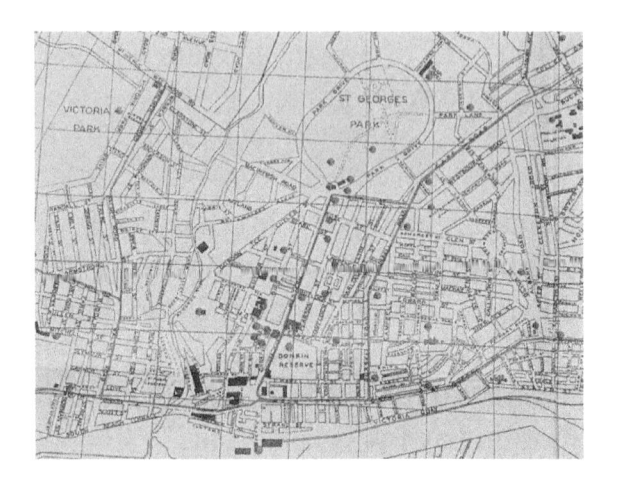

The sounds changed. Instead of sweet rhythms offered to the open veld, the bogeys began irregular clatter against suburban and then city walls. The pace slowed. They saw the sea. Flanges wailed against curved rails, signals fell back to 'halt' even as they passed. Points interrupted the rhythm of the track. At last, their carriage haven, clicked a final few meticulous clicks and came to a halt. They stood motionless at a long platform. The stillness seemed odd, too quiet after long journeying. But their beautiful brown train with its yellow lettering seemed to want to expel passengers and baggage, to be left alone. Walking away they looked back. The giant engine, near the buffer, panting still, was already uncoupled. Several yards now separated it from the first carriage. Reversing heavily over a set of points onto the adjacent track, it began making its way rapidly to the engine shed. The long carriages settled into loneliness.

Graph and Natalie carried their suitcases the short distance up Jetty Street, across Market Square and up Whites Road until they reached The Grand Hotel. Their arrival was expected. Within minutes the formalities were complete. Graph had been painstaking in the arrangements.

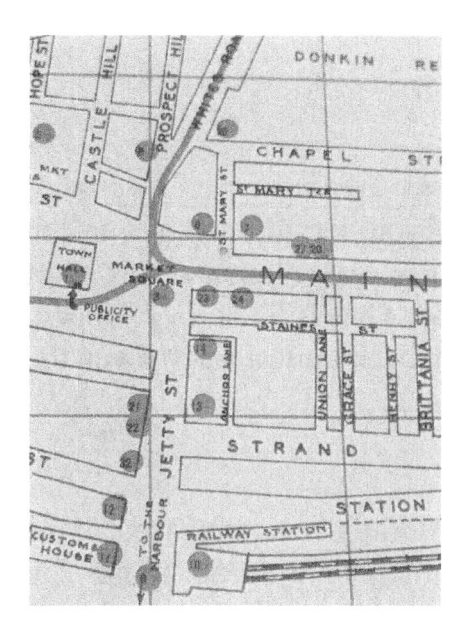

"What a beautiful *place!*" Natalie exclaimed as she came into her father's room after unpacking. "Such lovely rooms! So modern and clean! Every detail neatly designed!"

"Yes, well," Graph responded, "it seemed important to make your first impressions of P.E. as pleasant as possible. So I asked for rooms with

427

balconies, French windows and sea views."

"The views are *immense*," she said. "And did you see the pictures in the foyer? There was a lunch at this hotel in 1887 for Queen Victoria's jubilee. Must have been quite a party. Even the mayor came."

"Really!" Graph was impressed. "I've often heard people speak about The Grand but I've never been here."

"Not only that," Natalie continued, "past guests include Mark Twain, Sir Alfred Milner, Cecil Rhodes and Field Marshall Lord Roberts."

"All the big wigs, hey?" Graph commented. "Well. Where else would they stay? Now .... What shall we do today?"

"Time is precious," Natalie was positive. "Let's have tea and then begin looking at hotels. I want to compare *all* the options. Going to my office had best wait for tomorrow after a night's sleep. And. Daddy. I *do* want you to come with me to look at *all* the hotels. But when it comes to my work ……. *that* I'll do by myself."

By the third day, things at work were falling into place. Elated, Natalie returning to The Grand Hotel, found her father in the lounge, darkly engrossed in a newspaper. He presented his cheek for the usual kiss and went straight back to reading.

"What is it?" she asked.

"Oh, just the news....... the world's gone mad," he replied.

"Yes, but you're *unusually* preoccupied," she reacted to his mood.

"Well…….. Hitler is claiming more land. According to this article, he's saying *all* German populations should be brought under central German rule. If the land they live on is part of another state, then that land should be occupied by the German army and become part of Germany. Berlin must be in control."

"Oh?" she asked. "Is he making a *new* claim?"

"I'm not sure there's really anything *new*," Graph said, "but it's not exactly peaceable is it? He grows ever fiercer."

"Actually, combining all German speakers in one state makes sense to *me*," Natalie said. "Just as we have Basutoland for the Basutos, Bechuanaland for the Bechuanas and Swaziland for the Swazis. I think Zululand should follow that pattern and revert to a separate colony for the

Zulus. *That's* how to keep the peace. To my mind it's a pity the Matabele and Shona have to share Rhodesia with each other and with the white settlers. The path to peace is to give each tribe its own land where it can have its own government, language and culture. What could be more natural?"

"In Europe people have generations of cultural and family ties to lands in which they're a minority, so it's not straight forward," replied the gently unconvinced Graph"

"I don't know Europe," Natalie said brightly, "but in Southern Africa it's straight forward. All the white South Africans need do is make sure the tribes live peacefully in their own lands. And protect their title to those lands. Replace the tribal 'virtue' of war with settled civilisation."

"Oh ….. war, disease, flood, famine," Graph looked out the window, "that's Africa. It's nature's way of keeping numbers down."

"But daddy, this is the twentieth century. *We* have to ask ourselves where nature ends and civilisation begins."

"The divide is wide," Graph's brow furrowed. "It's a shifting frontier."

"The *answer*," Natalie asserted "is there *is* no answer. Culture is common decency more than money or power. But in Africa where differences in civilisation are *so* big, it's now werklik (really) easy to see what to do."

"Only by truly understanding," Graph thought out loud, "……. the past ….. will we *begin* to comprehend the present. Find a good way forward."

"Well, daddy, Europe is Europe and Africa is Africa. And in Africa, *Dingaan* (King of the Zulus) made the issue *quite* clear. Dingaan's words were, 'I see that every white man is an enemy of the black man and every black man an enemy of the white, they do not love each other and never will.' And he said those things even before he murdered Retief. The Zulus are *warlike*. They attack other tribes. And they respect only the *power* of the white man, not the whites themselves. *That's* why I think the Zulus should have a state of their own …. to make it easier for the whites to stop them attacking others. The Xhosa's need the same treatment. To this day black children are taught to believe that preparation for endless 'faction fighting' is crucial. No! The whites must keep the peace by keeping the tribes apart."

"Maybe," Graph said. "But Dingaan *was* only one man. After all."

Natalie frowned. "He controlled the Zulu nation. To our detriment. And how many Ndlelas were there? And how many are there still? *And ......*" she went on "then there is Rehobothia. The English and their missionaries will not rest until they have built Rehoboth 'in *England's* green and pleasant land.'"

Graph laughed.

"The English have *never* understood our predicament," Natalie said intensely. "They only came to The Cape Of Good Hope because they didn't want the place to fall into Napoleon's hands. It was a reluctant investment. The Dutch were here a hundred and fifty years before the English."

"And since *the day* the English arrived we've lived without proper protection from the state. English laws work against us. The English just *don't see* the things we see. Because they're not forced to put up with them. *Every single day*. The English don't live *with* Africa. We *do*. They're nice and safe in their *faraway* island."

Graph's brow moved upwards and wrinkled even more. "History is memory of intense perceptions ……… we're in a different era now. Europe's still licking the wounds of The Great War. We've a need for something greater than 'civilisation' and 'culture' put together. I don't think there's a word for it. Maybe I'll call it Natalianism. Or, better still, Vygieism."

Natalie laughed.

"But," Graph frowned, "'Lady Chatterly's Lover' is symbolic of what's happening to our empire."

"Have you *read* it?" Natalie asked surprised.

"Yes," Graph answered.

"How did you get a copy?" she asked.

"From a friend of a friend who went to Italy last year," he said.

"Was it good?"

"Yes. To me it was less about morality and more to do with Europe's perpetual class struggles. It made me, as an aside, think the class-wars of Europe as bad or worse than the race struggles of Africa."

"Books!" Natalie commented, "they look forwards, and backwards. They keep alive, sometimes for centuries, thoughts that otherwise would die. Worlds within worlds. Nothing human lasts forever. I wonder how many people, in a hundred years' time, will remember things like The Battle of Blood River and the Republic of Natalia? Let alone a person called Ndlela."

"Or Smellekamp," Graph chuckled.

"Or Smellekamp," Natalie echoed. "Even at this distance in time, it irks me that true to form, the British with their incomprehension of racial matters, threatened to assist Dingaan against us if we went into his territory. Even after the murder of Piet Retief. Even after Weenen. Even as Dingaan continued murdering our emissaries."

"I forget some of the detail," Graph wondered once more at the extent of detailed knowledge in one so young. "But we mustn't forget one thing. In war both sides commit atrocities. Anyone who believes otherwise has fallen for the propaganda of the victor….. Anyway ….. for better or worse, we're in The Pax Britannica now. Perhaps we're lucky?"

"To me," Natalie insisted with the calm of one accustomed to a certain thought, "the fall of the Natalian Republic was just another instance of Dutch-Germanic civilisation being thwarted."

At any rate," Graph winked at her, "reading this newspaper makes me think you should find yourself a nice German South Wester. Go live on a farm in South West Africa. Out of the way. South West might be a German colony again, one of these days. Quite soon if things keep going as they're going. Better still, marry a nice Portuguese merchant from Luanda. Or Beira. Move into neutral territory."

"I'm not ready for any John Donne yet," she protested.

"Only joking," he said. "But……. changing the subject, shall we walk into town to see if there's anything worth seeing at the theatres and bioscopes? By the way. Who's John Donne?"

"This fortnight" Graph said on the last night at The Grand, "passed quickly."

"Best times always go quickly," she agreed. "I loved the tram rides. And the motor buses. I'm *glad* you were here."

"Not that I did much," he said.

"Yes, you did. You told me I couldn't afford any of the places I liked."

"A *fat* lot of good *that* did," he said.

"Daddy, I *appreciate* all you said and did," Natalie said seriously. "As always, I appreciate it. But Daddy. The point is from now onwards *I* set the standards and make the decisions. It's a new life. I already see I'll have to be strong. It's a *man's* world. As if I didn't know. Men *don't* take kindly to women giving instructions. Or to women having the final say. *Fortunately*, the people in my immediate office are all women. But … beyond that …… I'll have to *confront* some headstrong, self-centred, dismissive heads of other departments. I'll *do* it. I'm used to being in the minority. They'll find out I give better than I get. Like the silly old dominee found out."

"Yes. The 'silly old dominee' as you put it, *did* find out," Graph agreed. "Not that he's inclined to accept your views. But I worry in case all this becomes too much for you. I think I should return in a month, make sure you're not cracking up!"

"I won't be cracking up," she stuck her chin out.

"Oh well, at least I persuaded you to opt for The Palm Grove Hotel instead of this place. Or The Park! Or The King Edward!! Although I'm *dumbfounded* at the amount you'll be spending on accommodation."

"In a way, daddy, it won't *'cost'* me anything. Because I *love* the whole idea." She reached out to touch his face. "After all, what's money for? I *think* I've now persuaded you I'm *no longer* a boarding house person. It's *not* my *style*."

CHAPTER FOUR

NOCTURNE FOR THOSE NEVER BORN

by

James Horner

For

Molly

DRAMATIS PERSONAE

BELL MISS MONIKA
Wimbledon friend of Rosemary, Eric and John Carpenter in the 1920s. Godmother to John Carpenter.

CARPENTER MRS EILEEN, FORMERLY GREEN, NEE MANDELSONN
Neighbour to Eric and Rosemary Carpenter. Married Eric in later life.

CARPENTER ERIC 1879 TO 1952
Father of John Carpenter and Neil Carpenter. First wife Rosemary. Widower. Second wife Eileen.

CARPENTER JOHN 1910 TO 2002
Father of Colin Carpenter. Colonist. Elder son of Eric and Rosemary Carpenter. Attended Exeter College 1929 to 1932. Emigrated to South Africa 1937.

CARPENTER NEIL 1912 TO 2001
Younger son of Eric and Rosemary Carpenter.

CARPENTER MRS ROSEMARY 1880 TO 1926
Mother of John and Neil Carpenter. Wife of Eric Carpenter.

GREEN NEILL
Son of Eileen Green.

KALM GLEN
Fellow student 1929 - 1932 of John Carpenter at Exeter University College.

LUNDY PAUL
A friend and fellow student of John Carpenter from Exeter University Days. Cousin to Katherine Ilchester who first appears in a later chapter.

MANDELSONN HEINZ
Father of Eileen Green. Prussian Jewish by birth.

SNOW ANDREW
Wendy's baby.

SNOW SONIA, MRS
John Carpenter's landlady in Exeter.

SNOW WENDY
Sonia's daughter.

1928 TO 1931

WIMBLEDON AND EXETER

Monika stopped what she was doing. From her kneeling position she looked steadily at her young friend. "How did it go?" she asked. "Did you like the room?"

"It's a quiet house," John replied.

"Well," Monika persevered, "I hope you liked it. You'll be away for three years, so it's *important* you feel comfortable. What did your father say?"

John's voice was flat. "The room is large and the landlady seems ……………nice. I know I *must* go," he continued, "It's the fate of youth. To be ordered away. Called away.

Sent away ….." He gestured deprecatingly. "I'm not sure I'd have *made* the decision if you hadn't been so sure. *Three whole years!* Away from you and 'Clear Sky.' From our garden. I can't think it. *Why am I leaving my best friend?"*

"What did your father think?" Monika repeated, rising to embrace him.

"I don't care what he thinks. I'll do better away from him. And from Eileen. *Especially* from Eileen…….." He frowned. "At least in Exeter I won't witness, every day, the deeds of the step-family."

How long will it take to walk to the university?" she asked.

"Twenty minutes, more or less," he stared through Monika. "If I have to go ……… I'll simply retreat into solitude."

"It *is* a big change," Monika agreed, an icy hand enclosing her heart, "but your decision was good. You had the forethought to imagine your *whole* future ….. work, play, money….. everything…. The world will always need engineers. You'll make a good living."

A similar conversation took place at the Carpenter house on Wimbledon Common.

"It'll be a step in the right direction. And serve a number of ends," Eric affirmed. "Exeter's a long way from Wimbledon."

Eileen nodded.

"He'll graduate in engineering from Exeter College. That'll be an external degree from The University of London. He'll be able to choose a position anywhere in the world. Far from us."

"I've thought more about going to Exeter. Being away from home may help my father and I avoid complete estrangement. It's not perfect. But things might improve. Sometimes I even feel sorry for the old man. When I was young he seemed so ….."

powerful. Now he seems ... lost ....
confounded ...... although of course
he'll never admit it. To me, nowadays,
he appears consigned to the mere
nothingness of the idle rich."

Monika nodded slowly. "Knowing
you all as I do, it makes me sad. So
much has been lost. And .... yet
more could be lost if we're not careful.
Sometimes it seems inevitable. Still,"
she brightened, "at least we have today
...... Surprise!!......... I have tickets for
'Pygmalion.'"

"Are we going to the theatre?"

"Yes."

"In London?"

"Yes."

"Oh grand! A comedy!" he hugged her. "The best comedy is about serious things, isn't it?"

"I've always been struck," Monika agreed, "by the timelessness of Pygmalion. When he found he couldn't live in harmony with any of the women he knew, he carved himself a statue of the most beautiful woman you ever saw and fell in love with that instead. It's amusing to think the ancients found it amusing!"

"Hmmmm," John thought about it. "An ancient solution to a *universal* problem …. and yet ….. I feel sorry for him……. poor chap, it must be awful to be unable to find *any* woman with whom to make a go of it …….. at least a statue would be cheap to keep. ……. No need to buy food …….. *and* ……. " he pointedly admired Monika, "no need to spend vast sums on *her* clothes. *And* ……… no less unyielding than a *real* woman."

Monika blushed and ignored him. "Are you ready?" she asked. "We've plenty of time. Let's catch an early train and spend time in London. I fancy another ride on an open-topped omnibus."

"I read somewhere," John reacted slowly to the urge to hasten, "some think Shaw's 'Pygmalion' a kind of class propaganda, they think his idea of class hierarchy based on dialect and accent a false premise. It made me wonder about propaganda and comedy." He combed his hair. "Perhaps, it's not too cynical to think propaganda is unwittingly often comedy and comedy is often propaganda? .... But.........." he knelt to tie a shoelace, "one thing's certain. There's *no* propaganda about us, my Monika. We follow the pattern. I'm your Pygmalion and you're my most *beautiful* statue. 'Ich dien.' ……..Although ………I have to note *again*…….. you're *always* fully clothed…………..well……*almost* always ….and…….*almost* fully.

Unlike the ancients. Who *obviously* knew *far* more about such things than *you*... *Un*fortunately for me."

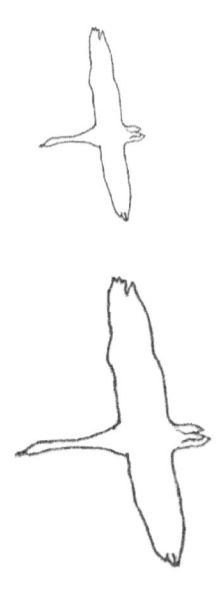

"You want to buy him," Eileen's voice was querulous, "*a motor-cycle*?!"

"He's long dreamed of this Triumph Ricardo machine," Eric explained. "It'll be a going-away present. And as his departure is likely to herald long periods of separation of father from son, I think it should be a substantial present. I need to do *something*. I feel superfluous to the lives of my children. It's *uncomfortable*. Somehow I never managed to draw them into things that interest me. We've lost touch. They've their own thoughts."

"Hmmmph," Eileen said. "You never ask for anything and so *of course* I agree the expenditure. Also, give him your grandfather's stamp collection. You've better things to do than play with stamps."

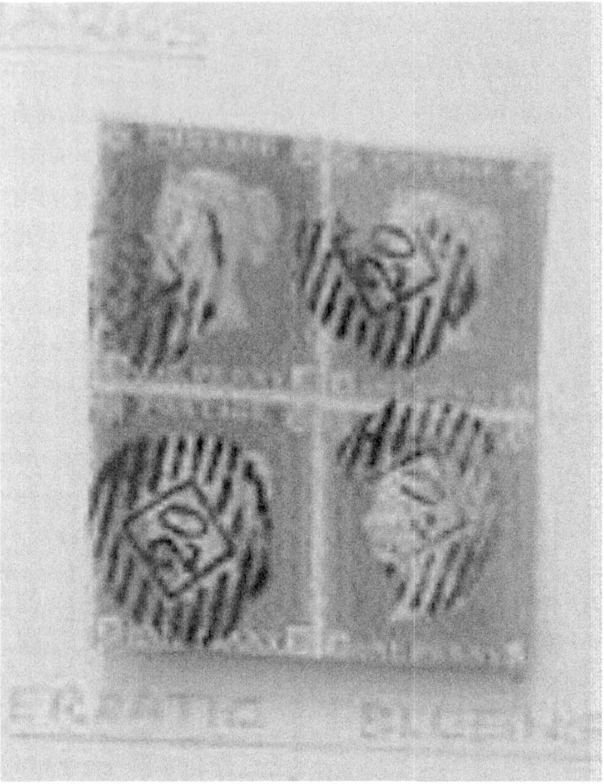

459

"May I?"

Monika nodded.

They embraced. A long embrace. Intensity at parting signified belonging. "I love you, boy," Monika acknowledged the crisis. "Maturity," she thought, "does *not* lessen *this* predicament."

She suffered another twinge. Her role as John's godmother had not been mentioned for years. "Perhaps he's forgotten? Did it never register during childhood?"

"I can hardly cope," John did not relax the embrace.

Monika wiped away tears. "We must do our best. *Always*."

John touched a tear on her cheek. He mounted the motor-cycle, the gift from Eric. "I'd never-*ever* wish, Monika," he strapped on a pair of goggles, "to make you, *you* of *all* people ….. *cry* …… All I want is to be here with you. But ….. since I *must* go ……as *you* urged and I agreed …… I now think of this fair machine as my lifeline to you. It provides independence and mobility. Its *real* significance is …… that ….. at *any* time ….. I could start it up and ride to you, *wherever* you are. It's an embodiment of Dialectical Materialism. In a world where little inspires, it's an inspiration." He touched the throttle. "It can both roar and purr …………….. However," he returned to the moment……., "the *truth* is…… all I have, Monika ….. is *you* and 'Clear Sky and our garden ……. the rich earth we dug. It *flowered*. Under *our* hands. I know every inch of this ground, every stone and shard, where the fertile bits are, where it's a waste of effort to plant and where it's often too wet, where it's iciest in winter and where hottest in summer, where to scrape out the moss, where to look for the first signs of spring, where the ants nest, the places snails hide. And …………. in the orchard………. where best to put our chairs when we read to one another, where the softest grass for our blanket grows…"

"For the time being, however…… I have to go. In leaving I suppose I should, *attempt,* to cast away the bad things since mother's died. But the fact is, my home is *not* my home. *You're* my home. Wher*ever* you are."

"Thank you," he leaned over to touch her arm "for keeping me sane. And don't you worry. The key to your door shall be *always* in my pocket. *Even* when we are both *very* old. Just as it is now."

From his pocket he withdrew the iron key, held it up to show her, kissed it, and returned it to his pocket. He tapped the pocket reassuringly.

The Triumph Ricardo responded with a roar to another touch on the throttle. "You see, it roars and purrs."

Still Monika wept.

"I'll make sure we're often together," he consoled her. "You'll see. We'll go to theatres and picture-houses again. And to restaurants. Just as before. When the holidays come and the flowers grow we'll work in the garden, just as before. Send those silly snails packing. You'll see. We'll have multitudes of *moments*. Because we'll *create* them. It *will* be as it was. This machine," he tapped the fuel tank, "makes it possible. *All* of it."

"Your mother," Monika spluttered above the thudding of the Triumph, "would have been *so* proud! Going to *university!*"

"Yes," John agreed. He turned off the engine. "Mother would've guided my progress ……. with maternal clarity. But ………. in her place…… I have you …… My father hardly features. And yet, curiously, for different reasons, neither my father nor I, as it turns out, are overjoyed at passing this milestone. Yet it must be."

"Work hard, boy," Monika reached the moment of parting. "I know you will. But also. Keep in mind. At the end of it all, at the *very* end, once the exams have proved you know a great deal, the best thing you'll know is how little you know."

John restarted the Triumph. He touched Monika one last time and rode away.

In Exeter, Mrs Sonia Snow sank into her armchair. She looked through the French windows at The Haldon Hills. From time to time she glanced down the road. Her new lodger, another student, would arrive shortly.

"Judging by his father, they're a nice family," she said to Wendy, her daughter. "They're well-to-do. So the rent should be paid. On time."

Wendy, not yet twenty, a study in lithesome youth, petite with falling coils of bright auburn hair, easily balanced her thirteen-month-old son on her hip. Supporting the child with one hand, weight on one leg, eyelashes coated in black mascara, she looked at her mother out of sparkling blue eyes.

Andrew, secure on his perch, a cherubic representation of his mother, his face fresh-soft, chubby pink-white legs, a shock of auburn-red curls, stared unblinking at the world.

"But I'm not sure about the motor-cycle," Sonia added.

"What's wrong with having a motor-bike?" Wendy, a tearaway, challenged her mother freely.

"It's the thought of noisy comings and goings at night. If he goes out much. Young men with motor-cycles can be cocky."

"Cocky! Mother! You don't know that!" Wendy protested, a twinkle in her eye. "You've only met him *once*. You liked him. Give the boy a chance. Be nice to him and he'll be nice to you."

Sonia leaned forward. "This must be him now."

Both women looked intently. "He's stopped," Wendy said.

"Must be him," Sonia agreed. "Seems to be looking for a place to leave the motor-cycle."

"Let's go and meet him." Mother and daughter walked down the path.

"Hallo Mr Carpenter," Sonia said hospitably. "Is this all you brought?" She looked at the bag slung across John's back and held out a hand for him to shake. "This is my daughter, Wendy," she continued, "and her son, Andrew."

"Pleased to meet you," John said still astride the motor-cycle. "Especially you, Andrew," he extended a finger to Andrew. The baby showed no sign of shyness. Instead, taking John's finger in his tiny saliva-coated hand, he smiled and gurgled. To Sonia, John's deference confirmed the decision to accept this student in preference to other applicants for her room.

"Yes," John answered, "I couldn't carry much on a motor-cycle. Two suitcases arrive by train tomorrow. But that's it."

"That's okay," Sonia said. "Wendy'll show you where to keep your bike while I make tea and flapjacks."

"We've never had a motor-cycle before," Wendy, still carrying Andrew, led John around the side of the house.

"I'm sure," Sonia asked as they came in, "you'd like a flapjack before I show you around. I'm a widow and Andrew's father is away at sea. Put your bag down there, love, next to the dresser. So, it's just we two women and Andrew. But we're used to company. Over the last nine years I've have had three other lodgers, all nice quiet students. I hope you'll be the same."

"Yes, of course," John said immediately. "I'll do my best." Sonia looked on him approvingly.

"I do believe you will," she said. "So we'll get along well. I don't tolerate unruly behaviour and told your mother and father as much in my letter. But I see you're no ruffian."

Wendy rolled her eyes. "Andrew needs changing," she said, obviously contented with motherhood. "It's nice to meet you. See you later."

Taking no notice of Wendy's eye-rolling, Sonia gleefully kissed the baby. "See you soon my gorgeous baby boy." Andrew dimpled. Mother and daughter were close.

"She gets lonely," Sonia confided, "with her husband away so much. But the baby keeps us busy."

"They both have the reddest hair I've ever seen," John observed.

"Yes, I know dear, shining red," Sonia's adoration showed. "They're in the next room to you. But Andrew's a good sleeper so you won't be disturbed. Now, tell me about yourself."

"My mother died two years ago," John began.

"Clean towels every third day," Sonia said as they entered John's room with its view over The Haldon Hills. "The laundry basket's there, in the corner. Mrs Edwards collects laundry on Mondays and returns it on Thursdays.

Clean linen every Tuesday. You can use the lounge and kitchen any time. Here's the front door key. Toilet's downstairs," she indicated an annexe visible through the window, "bathroom's at the end of the passage. Supper's at six. So. I'll leave you to unpack. Let me know if you need anything."

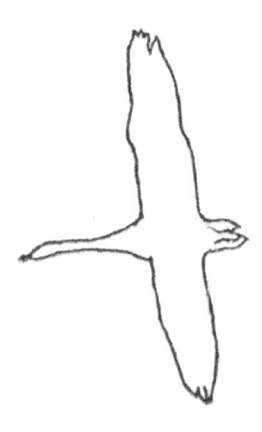

Exeter
25th October 1928 Almost midnight.

"Beloved Monika,

Arrived mid-afternoon. Fascinating journey. <u>Long</u> road! Kept stopping to consult map and signposts. All well. Lovely landlady. Mrs Sonia Snow. Good sort. Her daughter is lovely too. Wendy. They made me welcome. I am the only lodger. There have been other lodgers before me. Wendy has a tiny son. Andrew. No human being ever had hair so red!

Missing you.

John

Wimbledon
27 October 1928.
A reasonable hour.

My darling boy,

Received your letter. Glad you arrived safely. I worried about you on that infernal machine over all those miles. Cannot believe your father bought it for you. Your digs sound nice. University is a place to make friends. But I know you will put studies before sport and entertainment. It is important you succeed. For your mother's sake and your own. And for my sake.

I look forward to seeing you whenever you return to Wimbledon. 'Clear Sky' is your home. In fact it is our home. Always I love you dearly.

Monika.

Exeter
Friday
2nd November 1928

Dearest Monika,

I am forlorn and desolate.

Homesick.

I see it now. University was a stupid idea. The people are nice. But they are strangers. Everything is unfamiliar. You are my family. I long for your bustle and wisdom and neatness and all the small things. The way you breathe, your genteel coughs and sneezes. The way you endure. In life small things are big things, don't you agree?

Why on earth am I doing this? How will it make things better? Am I not, like a conscripted soldier in the trenches, being forced by a demanding society to squander precious days of life? This education ambition is a mere survival technique. Things could not have been better than we made them last year. At 'Clear Sky' we had everything. We had one another. Leaving Wimbledon was a mistake.

Should I not stop this and live with you? I could do clerical work in London. We could do what we do. Go to places we love. Be gardeners in a paradise called 'Clear Sky.' Most especially, share thoughts. Sharing our thoughts is what I miss most. And reading to one another! That is special. Not many people read to one another. We created our own university, a university of beatitudes. The institution I now attend pales by comparison. It is a kindergarten to our university.

Why is everything so wrong?

John.

Wimbledon
Sunday 4th November 1928.

My darling John,

I wonder whether you know how hard it is to say no to your request. What we share was and shall remain, a beatitude.

But the answer, John, is No!

And …………….. regarding your comparison with soldiers …… 'squandering life'….. I know………… too well …………. the dread and the agony, the obliteration of the trenches. The loss of my man was unforgiveable, cruel, unjustifiable, obscene. It made no sense at the time and it makes no sense now.

However, attending university is not squandering life. It is nurturing. Your life shall not be wasted. Not if I have any say in the matter. Your education shall serve you all your life. You must stick at it. I have taught you a few things. Use them! When I am in my seventies (!) and you are in your fifties, (!), then you may live with me if it is still your wish. But until you have your qualification your visits must be confined to holidays.

And…….. over holidays, 'Clear Sky' shall be your home. Even as it is now while you are away. There is no doubt in my mind. You must stay at university, be studious, take every last drop of knowledge your lecturers give you, become an engineer.

I love you my boy
Monika

Exeter
Wednesday 7th November 1928

But Monika,

Visiting only in the holidays is too limiting.

I want to ride the Triumph to you each Saturday. And return each Sunday.

Love
John

Wimbledon
Friday 9th November 1928
Sunlight.

Well My Boy,

I yield. You may visit. But not every weekend. That would restrict development of university friendships. I think every second or third weekend would be fair.

And. We need to be careful. People might talk.

Love
Monika

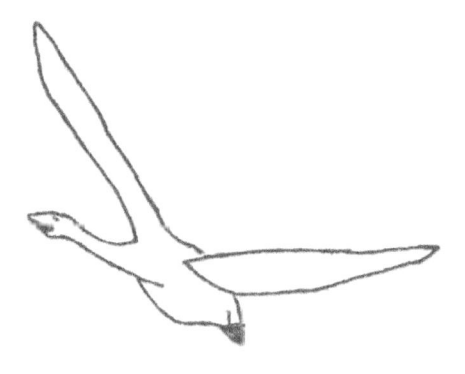

Exeter
Saturday.

What Happiness!

Your letter was waiting when I returned from a walk along the river to Topsham.

I shall ride my life-giving Triumph to you next Saturday. Please be home. If I leave 'Clear Sky' early Sunday morning before anyone is about, my visit shall be completely secret. Please write to say this will be okay.

Love
John

Wimbledon
Tuesday 13th November 1928

My Boy

I am glad.

This Saturday it shall be.

I need to tell you several things.

Not now.

One day.

In words.

Not in writing.

See you Saturday.

Love
Monika

Exeter
11pm
Sunday 18th November 1928

I am back at the house of Mrs Sonia Snow. Physically. But my soul is far away at 'Clear Sky' with Monika.

Please may I visit again next weekend?

All my love,
John

Wimbledon
Saturday 24th November 1928

Well Youth,

It troubles me greatly to think your visits will mean long journeys on icy roads.

There is a better way.

I shall visit Exeter now and again, perhaps once a month.

Stay at a different place each time.

And you shall come to Wimbledon but rarely.

Please keep this secret. You do understand how very difficult our lives would become if people jump to the wrong conclusion?

Next Saturday I shall travel to Exeter by train and return on Monday.

I have booked two rooms at The Imperial Hotel, New North Road. It is five minutes' walk from Exeter St David's railway station. Just around the corner and up the hill. Meet me in the foyer at 6pm on Saturday. We shall have dinner together. And make plans for Sunday. We must be discreet. To anyone who asks you are my nephew, I am your aunt.

Perhaps we shall take the train to Exmouth or Dartmouth on Sunday? A day out elsewhere for the sake of privacy?

Write to me.

With love,
Monika

Exeter
Tuesday 27th November 1928

Dear Aunt,

What a lovely idea! Eureka! Thank you! Life returns!

Saturday at 6pm!

Your loving nephew,
John.

Exeter 6pm
Thursday 29th November 1928

Beloved Aunt

Only 48 hours to wait.

You are my next of kin. All my life I shall look after you as you have looked after me. Of course I will be discreet. Everything, sweet 'aunt', shall be as you ask. I need you to be confident I shall never do anything which leaves you feeling insecure. But, somehow, concerning your anxieties, I feel certain all will be well. Because we shall make it that way.

Until 6pm on Saturday,
John

"This is so *beautiful*," Monika enthused as John handed her down from the train that Sunday morning at Dawlish. "A railway station *next to a beach*. Powderham Castle ….. the railway beside the river ……….. those forests and fields … the *reedbeds* ... and then the beaches, the waves breaking next to the line ….. And *so* many birds! …. Shall we walk along this promenade?"

"Yes," John agreed, "this side of the river with its castle is grand. Unlike the Topsham side which is industrial and smells fishy."

"And," he continued, "the line we've just travelled was where they experimented with the atmospheric railway. More than eighty years ago!"

"The what?"

"The atmospheric railway."

"Never heard of it."

"They built trains drawn along by a suction in a pipe that ran between the rails," he explained.

"John," she said, the beginnings of a smile around her mouth, "I may be a mere woman but I can tell pumpernickel from bread."

"Don't you believe me?"

"Not actually."

"Truly," he insisted, "they actually *ran* those trains for a couple of years. But in the end the leather they used, to maintain the vacuum at the joins in the pipes, wasn't strong enough. It kept failing. So they gave up. But it was a great idea because instead of having many steam locomotives pulling trains along, you had a few stationery steam engines at intervals along the route. The problem with the idea was ……. that it didn't work."

"Pull the other one," her smile widened.

"I can prove it to you," he said, "but I must say, I marvel at the way history fades from memory. Or is unknown. No wonder people hold erroneous views."

"Yes, well youth," she said, "you'll have to prove it. But I can't imagine you will."

"Prove it I shall," he insisted.

"And………. it seemed to me," John changed the subject as they set off along the promenade, "nobody took any notice of us last night at the hotel. In the dining room. Do you agree? Are you comfortable about how it went? You've been *so* worried about discretion. *Unfortunately*, of course, the truth is there's *still* nothing to feel uncomfortable about."

"Yes," Monika replied, "it went smoothly, didn't it? We actually *look* the aunt and nephew we hold ourselves out to be. Which is important because things are different now. Until recently, in Wimbledon, you were simply making daily visits to the home of a close family friend. Everyone knew and accepted that. They weren't wrong. But now, my boy, I'm visiting you instead of you visiting me!"
"And you're happy about it? You do want to visit me, don't you?" John

fired questions. "Is the hotel expensive? It does seem extravagant. I want you to be happy and ……… " his voice fell in uncertainty.

"Oh! *Truly!*" Monika patiently dispelled doubt, "I am *happy*! But it's just ….. I'm *old* enough …. to understand ….. everything…. *Happiness* attracts attention ….. people form wrong impressions ….. and …… rest assured," she smiled wanly, "when it comes to paying, money is *not* a worry. I have," she hesitated, "an *embarrassingly* large amount of money……*embarrassingly* large. I'd be happy to neglect money altogether were it not I feel profound responsibility to all the generations whose cumulative effort I've inherited. It would be a breach of their trust, dishonourable, if I didn't do my best to handle my fortune wisely. My *very* best. I have advisors………it takes effort………..much effort," she tailed off.

"Gosh," John replied. "I've never given it much thought. I mean I always knew you came from a well-to-do family…… I just didn't know *how* well-to-do. But when it comes to wealth, what I *have* thought about, *a lot*," John continued seamlessly, "is how *rich* we are in *non-monetary* ways. We now have *our own* form of Dialectical Materialism. It's *priceless*. From the wreckage of the trenches, where you lost your first love…… and from the….."

"My first and only lover," she interjected flatly …. "at the time ….. and since ….."

"And from the wreckage of my family, where I lost my mother ….. and more ….. we have *rebuilt*. Fate dealt us violent hands but we've forged peace. Against the odds we've created a haven. We *are* the haven. Vile doings of the iron world can't touch us. Isn't it *wondrous?* Isn't it what everyone wishes for themselves?"

"We have, my boy," Monika agreed introspectively, "reversed ill fortune." She paused. "But our safety is internal, not external. It will endure *only* if we remain platonic. Our safety is our trust in each other. The world *isn't* like us. The world is nasty."

"I understand," John response was uncharacteristically curt. At Monika's uneasy expression he quickly added, "I'm angry at the world, sweet, judicious aunt, *never* at you. We have your reputation to consider. I care a *great deal* about *that*. Living, these days, amongst lecherous students, I understand your concern even more. As if I didn't already understand." He grinned. "I've been reading about modern Russia, where, for a while, the slogan was, 'Family life is dead.' If we lived in Russia you wouldn't have to worry about your reputation. Women are free there."

"*John*," Monika protested, "Family life will *never* die. Women are never *completely* free. Perhaps men aren't either. Even if Bolsheviks believe differently. It's the nature of things. Think of the harmony your mother created. Such *priceless* harmony is guarded by all who benefit from it. Women need the family. Especially when children are born. But usually all their lives. The family is the safe structure in which they guard those they love."

"Mmm…..children……" John mused.

"Yes, John, *children*," Monika confirmed with quiet certainty.

"I've been thinking about you and children," John turned to her. "I worry about you not having children."

"You're kind," she replied shyly, "and young …"

"So, let's have children."

"*What!?*"

"You were deprived of the chance by The Great War. Now there's a second chance," he opened his palm in reasoned offer.

Monika blushed. "No! Oh no! No, no, no! *Too* fast, my boy. Too fast! That wouldn't work! Many things stand in the way."

"What *things?*" John asked. "What could be more important? One legacy of The Great War was millions of unborn children. War stole conception from you. It's a militarist crime although militarists hardly give it a thought. I'm offering restoration. We'd have beautiful children. Neither of us is *that* bad looking. Especially *you* aren't!"

"Don't joke," Monika said. "It's no joke."

"I *promise*, I'm *not* joking."

"John, John, *John*," Monika drew him to a sheltered bench where weak wintry sunshine gave some warmth. "I can give you *only* the status quo. There are *big* reasons for not doing what you propose."

"*What reasons*? Isn't procreation part of existence? We have the equipment."

"Big reasons."

"Such as?"

Monika looked at him intently. "Must I spell it out?"

"Yes. You must."

"There's the age difference between us."

"I don't care about that."

"And I'm too old for childbirth."

"Not if we don't waste time."

"Youth is a time to be young …. You're too young to be a father. We'd have to marry."

"Many a man in the trenches would've thought our love the ultimate blessing! I *want* children! And I want them *with you*!"

"No, John," Monika insisted gently, "it would wreck our haven. ……

And," she surveyed him apprehensively, "there's another reason….."

"Which is?"

"I cannot surrender my financial independence."

"What!"

"Money."

John stared at her. "Are *you* telling me you think money more important than the chance of *your own children? You* of *all* people!? I thought we were *romantics!"*

Monika drew a deep breath. "I am a romantic. Even though I prefer spinsterhood."

John laughed a hard laugh.

"I'm not a *loud* suffragette, John. But I *am* a suffragette. I've watched marriages. Soon after marrying, women find themselves unfree. Money, you see, is *not just money.* It's independence. I'm one of the lucky few. I have money *and* independence. I *cannot* give them up. *Ever.* I don't *want* to give them up. I enjoy them too much ….. you see." There've been precious few women in history who've had independence. The *trick* ……. is *not* to marry. No matter *how* tempting. Because ….. marriage becomes a prison in which spouses hear but don't listen. Or listen but don't hear." She dimpled. "After a while they cease acknowledging one another's credentials. They hold one another back. But, I can still *love,* you see. I don't have to *marry* in order to *love.* I have no wish to rely on an antenuptial contract."

John regarded her in silence. "Well ……… I hope," he finally said, "you don't think of me as dominating. I would like us to discover for ourselves how something so fair as the human female squeezes out something so abominable as the human male and goes on to love him for ever."

"I know what you're thinking," Monika spoke carefully, "but if you think me hard-hearted, and if you think not wanting children is rejection, let me prove otherwise. From deliberate spinsterhood I tender you *enduring* friendship.

John looked at her.

"*Accept* it my boy. Unconditional, friendship is what you shall have from me. Is it not *enough*? You may, being young, find it insufficient. But if you think intelligently, you'll see it amounts to *more* than most men have. Because platonic friendship neither

lapses nor loses its mystery………..
and …… I wasn't going to mention it
…… but as things turn out ….. this is
the moment to tell you …….
something else."

"Something else?"

"So………," she touched his arm to
bring him back from disinclination to
hear more, "So ……… listen
carefully."

"You have my attention," he said
sardonically.

"I visited my lawyer again. A copy of
my will is in the bottom drawer of my
bureau. Signed and sealed. The lawyer
has the original. You know the bureau.
Where you keep old parts of 'My
Tables.'…… I've left everything to
you."

John looked into the distance. I hope and trust you understand," he said, "my wish to inherit my father's money is *territoriality*. You don't have to compensate me for monetary loss. I don't covet money for its own sake. The *quantity* of money isn't the issue. What I want is recognition. Eileen's invasion and occupation of *my territory* sticks in my throat."

"I understand," Monika responded. "Completely."

"*You*, however, never fail to fascinate me. You draw me in. You preoccupy my preoccupations. I adore you. *You.* Not your *money!* Your money never came into it."

"I know," she knew this ground, "which is why you're my heir. ….. In time you'll discover a pitfall. Being an heir doesn't itself make a person great. Rather the reverse. Sadly. Anyway …… one day …. you'll have a few drops of my amber tears …. spilt from the chalice of our very own sun …... But your precious love must remain unrequited. Platonic."

John sat in silence.

"It's an act of trust," Monika affirmed. "One day it'll be yours. All of it."

"I love home," John said, "and you *are* home. Monika! ………… can't you see? ….. The gift of children is greater than the gift of inheritance?"

"They are different things, my love. The one I give you. The other I cannot."

"Well," John said, "Now I know what Orsino felt when Cesario insisted, 'You tell her so. Must she not then be answered?'"

Although it was Saturday night, the well-to-do part of Wimbledon was silent. Hoping not to draw attention to his arrival, John turned off the engine at the top of the hill and allowed the Triumph to free-wheel swiftly in the darkness down past the last ten or more houses. Without the engine's roar, the wind rushed in his ears. He came noiselessly to Clear Sky, dismounted and pushed the machine over the grass past the wintry flower beds to conceal it behind the shed.

Monika was waiting. She hurried out to enfold him. "I've been *worrying* about you on those icy roads," she fretted. "Come into the warmth."

"I enjoyed the ride," he ignored her concern, slumped contentedly on the sofa and welcomed the fire in the ornate hearth. "Very cold and a little tiring. When I stopped the bike to go behind a hedge, I watched hailstones compete with my pee. Which was a novelty. But the engine ran well. Not sure what I'd have done if there'd been a breakdown. But ……… here I am. Exactly where, in *all* the world, I *most* want to be."

The long cold road had drained more of his energy than John admitted. In a matter of minutes he fell asleep, leaning against Monika on the sofa, leaving untouched the food she had prepared. The fire burned low. Careful not to disturb him she remained motionless for a long time. Her arm, caught in an awkward position, ached with the effort of keeping still.

"*Three hours* you've been asleep!" her eyes shone as he awoke. "I *cannot* put you through this *winter journeying*. On *icy* roads. It's silly. From now onwards our term-time meetings shall be in Exeter. *I'll* do the travelling. By train. I should've thought of it sooner."

"Oh?" John accepted. "*That'd* be *perfect.*" Tranquil after sleep, he watched the fire.

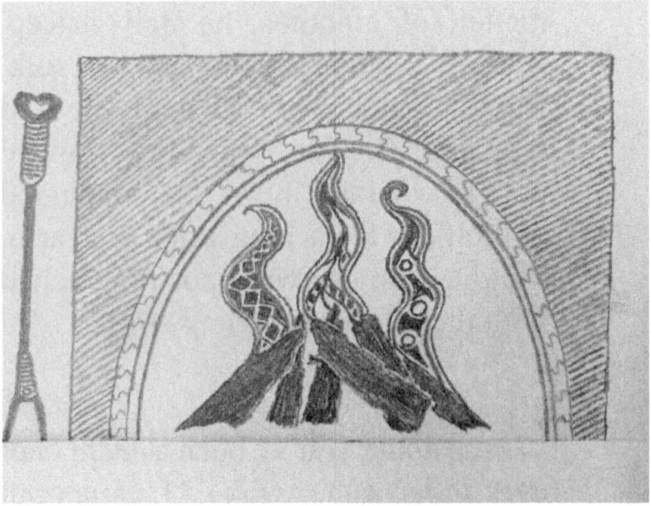

May Glen join us for breakfast tomorrow?" John asked Sonia Snow one Friday evening.

"Oh, I do *like* that young man. Yes, of course. He's welcome. I'm glad when he visits. Did you know him before university? At first I thought him too small and too young to be a student. But I was wrong."

"Thank you, Mrs Snow. I'll let him know he's invited. And that you think him too young and small," John teased, "to be a student."

"Oh …….. I didn't mean …………"

"And tell him you like him for being well balanced and normal. And for his bright smile of reason."

"You're blushing, Mum," Wendy sparkled.

"Oh *go on* with you both. I only meant he seemed very young."

"Did you now?"

Andrew cooed and gurgled.

"He's clever, our John, isn't he darling?" Sonia bent over the child. But Andrew ignored her and held out his arms to John.

John picked him up, hugged Sonia and winked at Wendy. So fully had he been included in the lives of the two women.

"I'll go to Glen's, then. To invite him. See you soon. Toodleoo," he returned the baby to Wendy. Andrew protested loudly, squirmed in Wendy's arms and reached again for John.

"Oooh, you really like them, mum, don't you?" Wendy continued when John was out of earshot.

"I do," Sonia admitted, "Good boys. And, by the way, I saw you look at Glen."

A shadow flitted over Wendy's face.

Sonia sighed. "I love you, my Wendy, and I love *you*, my baby," she cooed at Andrew, "but you are *the* most *worrisome* girl and *this*," she said, "is the most *worrisome* predicament I've *ever* known!" She hurried off to the pantry.

"Andrew can't be *unborn,* you know," Wendy called after her.

"Do you sometimes let your room to women students, Mrs Snow," Glen asked, "or is it always men?" It had gone eleven but Glen Kalm and John were still breakfasting. The French-windows alternately rattled to the spatter of raindrops or let in rays of February sunlight. Sonia and Wendy divided time between tending Andrew and preparing food. In the distance The Haldon Hills were partly cloaked in cloud. A treble rainbow arched above the woods.

"Oh, call me Sonia, my dears. When it comes to lodgers, I'm fussy about behaviour, not gender."

"That's nice," Glen approved, "At first I thought Wendy must be a lodger. But then I thought she might be a niece or younger sister."

"Really?" Wendy fluttered her eyelashes audaciously. "So do you think I'm young then?"

At that moment, for no apparent reason, Andrew, in Wendy's arms, leaned back and roared with laughter.

"Glen's a funny boy, isn't he Andrew?" Wendy asked.

Andrew, reached out to John who took the child and raised him high before pretending to let him fall. Andrew squealed. "*You* know what you like, don't you mate?" "More!" Andrew said. John obliged. Andrew kept repeating, "More!" They were entertained for a while.

"I've noticed your landlady's taken a shine to you, my friend," Glen remarked several similar breakfasts later. They waited outside an ivy-clad lecture hall for their lecture to begin. He looked on John with his usual aura of reason.

John nodded. "She's an angel. But. Age difference. And. Anyway. I'm spoken for."

"Oh?" Glen raised his voice the trifle his genteel persona allowed. "You've never spoken of being spoken for!"

"Education! I serve the goddess of education!" Not wanting to compromise Monika or admit affection for her, John covered quickly.

Glen appeared to accept this. "Oh," he said serenely, "a *religion* of sorts." But John suspected his friend of hiding amusement.

"While on the subject of noticing things," John decided best concealment lay in counter-questioning, "*Wendy* has *her* eye on *you.*"

"Yes, but, I'd never *dream* of paying court to a married lady." He thought for a moment. "She must find it trying to have her husband away at sea."

Glen took to visiting on Saturdays. Those Saturdays started with breakfast. "It's a good thing, Andrew," he tapped the baby's nose, "you're up early. You're my breakfast guarantee."

"He woke at four," Wendy looked tired. "I hope we didn't wake you, John."

"Didn't hear a sound, never do," John replied. "Wouldn't mind if I did." Picking up Andrew, he swayed from side to side.

"You'd make a good father," Wendy commented sleepily. "But," she turned to Glen, "where does John go on Saturday nights? *That's* what *I* want to know!" She removed an empty plate before setting down flapjacks covered in syrup, a jug of very hot chocolate and four mugs.

"What an array!" Glen complimented Wendy. "But, yes, I agree. John here," he took up the subject, a twinkle in his eye, "our civilised friend, is reliable, a studious bachelor, never utters a word out of place." He took a flapjack. "Yet there's a mystery." Syrup dripped as he bit into the flapjack. "He's not to be found after six on Saturdays. He disappears *just* when we're all off to the tavern. And ……. remains absent the following Sunday. Where *on earth* does he go?" He turned to John.

"Where do you go, Romeo? Is it time to tell?"

"He probably doesn't go far," Wendy guessed, "because his motor-cycle stays here."

"Yes," Sonia joined in, "you're *so good*, John. Quiet. Never do *anything* wrong. You're never even tipsy, let alone drunk. For a boy you're *amazingly* tidy. But you don't sleep here on Saturday nights! *And* you return *late* on Sundays. Often very late. Are you leading a double life John? Is there something you're not telling us?" All present looked at John.

Forced into revelation, John did his best to sound matter-of-fact. "I meet with my aunt." He shifted position slightly and, glad of the diversion, put his finger to his lips and pointed at Andrew falling asleep in his arms.

"You've an aunt who lives in Exeter!" Sonia exclaimed. "I didn't know!"

"Shhhh……" John gestured at Andrew.

"And you meet her on Saturday nights?" Wendy whispered agog. "Why've you never mentioned her?"

"Well now. I hope you'll not think of going to live with her," Sonia whispered. "We like having you here, you know. Not to mention we need the money."

"Bloody money," Wendy grinned.

"Don't swear, love," Sonia whispered. "I don't want Andrew learning bad language."

"He's *asleep*, mum!" Wendy whispered emphatically. "Won't hear *a thing* and wouldn't understand if he did."….. "So, John, we're waiting. Tell us about your aunt. Is she *very* young and *very* pretty?" Engaging in one of her lengthy bouts of eyelash fluttering, she smiled provocatively.

"She doesn't live locally," John whispered. "She visits Exeter regularly and we meet."

"She must be *special* if you spend your weekends with her," Wendy teased. "Lots of people love their aunts but ….. are you sure she's actually an *aunt?*"

"It is rather *novel,*" Glen whispered, looking closely at his friend.

"She's always been my friend," John breathed. "After mother died her home became my real home. I spent my time with her."

"Oh, my *poor* love," Sonia sensed John's reluctance. "I'm sorry. You did once tell me. Losing a mother is terrible."

"Yes," John whispered, "…….. it was terrible."

"Your aunt lives in Wimbledon?" Glen asked.

"Yes."

"What's her name?" Wendy asked.

"Monika."

"Don't worry my love," Sonia reacted to John's diffidence, "we won't ask more questions. It must be difficult to talk about."

"Life deals many a difficult hand," Glen sympathised. *"But ...."* brightening, he deliberately changed the subject, "after sausages and bacon, superb flapjacks, and not forgetting Sunny Jim, the sun's come out. Let's," he looked with mock gravity from one to another, "take our pork for a walk. Are we still agreed on Exminster? John can carry Andrew! Afternoon tea's on me as usual. That place we saw near Exminster station does scones and clotted cream. Paul Lundy might join us. We'll catch the train back to Exeter Central. It's *all* on me, train fares, *everything*."

Several days later, cold from the walk home, John stopped in surprise when he entered his room. He found a fire crackling merrily in his fireplace. Everything had been tidied. Fresh towels, perfectly arranged, hung on the towel rack.

"Hallo dear," Sonia carried in a tray of hot chocolate. "I've done your linen and made up the fire. It's been *so* cold today."

"Oh, thank you," John would have preferred solitude. "That fire's welcome. I'm freezing."

She placed the tray on the table.

"I want to say I'm sorry we pried about your aunt," Sonia was genuinely concerned. "I didn't mean to intrude, dear."

"That's thoughtful of you," John responded, "mother and aunt were close friends."

The front door knocker sounded. "I'll see you at supper," Sonia said and left.

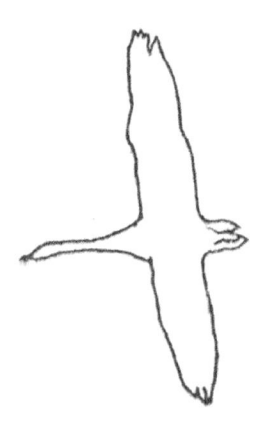

"Three years!" John protested, "I don't know where the time's gone." Hands clasped behind heads, they lay on the floor staring at the ceiling. "I can't believe it's my final year."

"There's a lot going on in your head this morning, boy," Monika turned to look at him.

"I wish," he sighed, "things could stay exactly as they are. We have *everything*, don't we? But ……. change is coming. One day soon, I'll have to earn a living. Somewhere. I wonder where *'somewhere'* will be?"

Concern crept into Monika's voice. "At present," she agreed, "life is mild and pleasant."

"It's *much* better than 'mild.'"

"Our normality *is* mild," Monika maintained. "I never take normality for granted. Being mild makes it a form of perfection. Too often I've watched perfection recede. It slips away ethereally. People don't notice it leaving them. Only realise when its gone." She looked at him. "Earning a living might be a shock after university life. Dull routine instead of academic pioneering. Speaking of routine, I'm glad I gave up the idea of different hotels every visit. The Imperial's perfect isn't it? It's……mild…. and… we've not encountered any slurs, have we? No comments, no suspicions, no glances. Nothing."

"None!" John replied, "People accept us as aunt and nephew. It's been a golden time and it'll be a golden memory. The Imperial became *our* place."

"Being the older woman who declined children," Monika involuntarily released a sliver of regret, "the memory will be poignant. You and I contend with rarity."

"Being declined is miserable, you know."

"I know my love." Monika understood. "*Kind* women minimise such hurt. *To you* I gave reasons."

"Your *'reasons'* didn't alleviate *anything*. Wake up Monika! You can *still* change your mind. It's *still* a proposal."

She studied him. "One day you *must* have children. You *want* them. But *I* cannot be their mother. I'm *too old* a flower-bed to yield flowers."

"'Lady,' John quoted, "you are the cruellest she alive if you would take these graces to the grave and leave the world no copy.'"

"*John!* You need a *young strong* bride. Don't fret! I'll be around. Your wife will know me as your mother's friend. I'll be great-godmother to as many children as you like! Fortunately I owe this world *nothing*. Have no need to replace myself. Don't worry. I *know* what I'm doing. We'll *both* gain. My *platonic* way will sustain us. We won't lose one another as the married often do. Because we'll be *old* friends. We'll be one another's reserves. I'll love you forever, even if …. sometimes …. remotely. You and I'll never be nostalgic because we'll be always in the present. As friends are. Not as spouses are."

John's brow crinkled. "Great-godmother?"

"Yes, great-godmother."

A set of returning memories made John stare.

"Monika, are you my *godmother?*"

"I am. Had you forgotten? I often wonder how much you remember."

"I don't think I ever really knew," he said slowly. "But a series of impressions is surfacing. *Great Scotland!* My *godmother!*"

"That's me," Monika repeated.

"Why was there never any talk of it?"

"Oh, there used to be a lot. When you were very young I took you to church, taught you about Christmas and Easter, observed the Anglican calendar, discussed God, did godmother things."

"But godmothering must have ended," John pondered. "It hasn't been mentioned …. for years."

"Yes. That's because …… your father's views changed. By 1916 he'd become an angry sceptic. It wasn't difficult to see why. Hospitals overflowed. Everywhere you looked there were wounded soldiers, bandages, slings, crutches, amputees……. and we *knew* ….. we knew we were seeing only the visible casualties, more were invisible. At that time my lover was *missing*. Your parents knew him. We were all friends. So ….. in deference to and in agreement with Eric, your mother and I became silent about religion. I lived in dread, waiting for resolution of the word, 'missing.' Which came. Harshly. We felt anger at the all-knowing deity, 'The Omnipotent.' I doubted all belief and faith."

Monika quoted,

"'God The Omnipotent
Thou Who Ordainest,
Great Winds Thy Clarions,
The Lightnings Thy Sword,
Show Forth Thy Pity
On High Where Thou Reignest,
Give To Us Peace
In Our Time
Oh Lord.'

God's Pity was absent. As was Peace. Scepticism took over. When your father came home on leave we didn't speak of our misgivings. They were understood. Although your mother never recanted her beliefs. Being your mother. And your father never opposed her. Instead he paid lip service. The scepticism didn't narrow friendship. Rather the opposite. But godmothering faded. Newspapers appalled us. There was urgency to re-think everything. Absolutely everything."

"Ugh!" John swore in undertone. "Nietzsche was right. God *did* die. But Nietzsche didn't foresee how *The Marne and The Somme* would be God's deathbed. For many. And yet. When I look at you, Monika, I think God survived."

"Mass killing derides certainty."

"Life couldn't go on as before."

"The present peace," Monika mused, "deserves immaculate use. In honour of the dead."

"It's *so* odd! A dynastic tiff caused a *cataclysm!* Ordinary men *volunteered* to kill one another by the million. Fighting for a king is odder than fighting for a religion. It's *all* balderdash! And … *what* turned the fair sex into distributors of white feathers? Madness….. sheer madness. If it's bad for us, it's worse for the losers. Worst of all for those left without a homeland. Being both a victim of gas warfare and a holder of the iron cross, Adolf will know what to do. He'll protect culture. The absolutes of the past are no more."

"War," Monika said soberly, "causes loss of comfortable familiarities. I *hope* you're not wrong about your Mister Hitler. From what I've read, he's violent. War revealed faultless beatitudes like the importance of contentment and the value of normal routine. Logic directs us to *work,* like Jews, rather than to fight."

She was quiet for a while.

Deutsches Reich
20
Milliarden
20 000000000 M

Deutsches Reich
50
Milliarden
50 000000000 M

"Conscription! Being forced to go abroad and kill people!" John ignored Monika's attempt to be at peace. "It's *outrageous!* I still think our way to escape European madness," he touched on a recurring subject, "is to migrate. We'll learn to live without government. Beyond the state. Who needs highly organised stupidity?"

"On that subject," he continued, "I still wonder about the Transvaal. Life might be exotic there, you know. I read of a British woman in the days before the Boer War who drove around Johannesburg in a carriage pulled by a team of zebra. Who could imagine such a thing?"

"I don't know," Monika said doubtfully, "It's *such* a long way away…….. the other end of Africa."

"Three weeks on an ocean liner followed by a long train journey," he agreed.

"But also………," Monika reflected, "Can we *really* leave England?" She looked enquiringly at him. "To live in a *jungle*? What if we discover the place of our dream is actually hostile? I've read of primitive clans in Africa who've no houses, no clothes, no money, no possessions and they know no history. They cannot read or write. So their only history is that which happened in living memory. They're cruel and will watch another human being die out of interest rather than with any pity or sympathy. I can't see myself living with *that!*"

"It isn't jungle," he said running his fingertips over her finely pointed knuckles, "Its grassland."

"England," she meditated, "especially London, is all we know. In Africa, everything will be different. We'd miss things we love. The city, the buses and the restaurants and shops and markets and the libraries and the art galleries and the concert halls. And what about 'Clear Sky' ….. and our garden and our ……. just our lives."

"Yes, but we'd escape European militarism. Which will return, one year soon. *Inconceivable* as that may be. I *won't* be part of yet another impressed legion sent to kill Germans as they rebuild. Everyone's been at it for centuries, The Romans, The Turks, both Napoleons, The French Republic, The Russians, The British, The Italians. They all found reason to attack Germania. It's time to leave it all behind. Inconsequential African difficulties will be easy by comparison. So much water off a swan's back."

"Think carefully," Monika cautioned. "Colonial militarism is intrusive. The Transvaal has *big* gold mines. Gold mines *never* bring peace. They caused The Boer War. To realise our dream of living beyond formal jurisdiction, we'd need to find 'unexplored territory' as mapmakers describe large parts of Africa. And… somehow…… we'd *have* to disappear from records. ….. The trouble is, unlike you, I think human beings need at least *some* government."

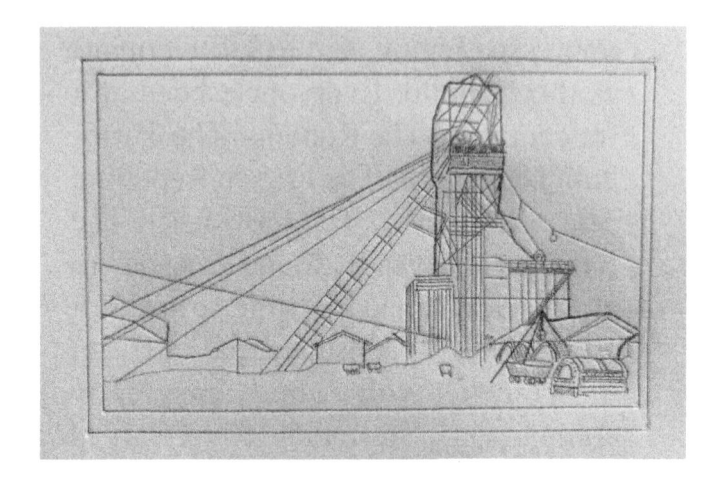

"Maybe you're right," John pondered. "But I hope internal politics will keep South Africa out of future European wars. Memories of The Boer War and a pro-German population make for South African neutrality. Unlike the other dominions."

THE TRANSVAAL WAR
ELANDSLAAGTE
KIMBERLEY
PAARDEBERG
LADYSMITH
BLOEMFONTEIN
MAFEKING
PRETORIA
THE ILLUSTRATED
LONDON NEWS

"Should we be thinking of the USA?" Monika asked.

"The USA has a militarism all its own. Don't be fooled by isolationism. We *have* to find 'some strip of herbage strown that just divides the desert from the sown.'

"Yes …. Well …. Who knows? Anyway. You must complete your education before decisions are possible. And ….. a period working in England wouldn't harm your record. Meanwhile, *vive, valeque!*"

"It needn't mean a complete break with England. Some colonists spend every summer in England."

"*Chook* chook chook chook, *Chook* chook chook chook," Andrew made steam engine sounds.

Sonia watched her grandson pull a long piece of string around the breakfast room, threading his way between pieces of furniture. "John taught him that," she said. "Simple things…... A piece of string is his train! Keeps him occupied for hours."

"WooWooo," Andrew pulled his string-train through the French windows out onto the lawn into the crisp spring sunshine.

John and Sonia followed him. "Wendy, be a love," Sonia called, "watch the flapjacks while we watch Andrew."

"Where'll you go next year?" Wendy asked Glen when the others were out of earshot.

I don't know," Glen grew cautious. "Much'll depend on the exams. I'm not thinking about it yet."

"Would you like to live in Exeter?"

"It depends ……… I'll have to go where there's work."

Wendy brushed past him to check the flapjacks. "I *have* to get used to this new-fangled electric oven," she said. She drew out the baking tray and rested it on the oven surface. "Do you think they've been in long enough?" She looked doubtfully at the tray.

Glen walked over. He held a hand over the rising heat. "They look good," he said, "but still too hot to try."

"Bit like you then," she moved closer.

Surprised by proximity, Glen took a moment to react. "Wendy, you're lovely, *but* … you're *married*." He embraced her briefly and drew back.

Seemingly unperturbed, Wendy went to the French window. "Mum," she called, "Glen says the flapjacks are ready."

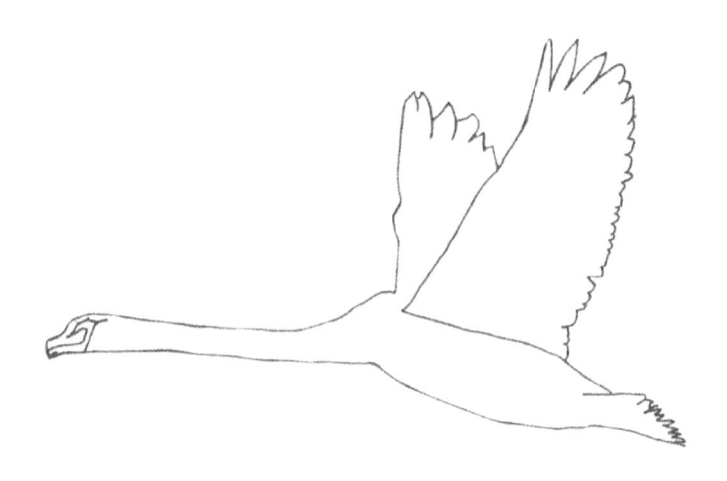

Two days later, at breakfast, Sonia appeared red-eyed and tearful.

"What's up?" John asked.

"In a few weeks you'll leave us. I can't *believe* it."

John, his mind full of civil engineering studies, patted her shoulder. "Don't worry. We'll stay in touch. Must go," he said. "I'm late. Let's talk this evening."

"I met your brother in the street this week," Monika said over breakfast at The Imperial. "He's talking of going to live in Canada."

"Oh! *Is* he?" John said. "Isn't life strange? I haven't seen him in more than two years and we've not exchanged a single word or letter all that time. Not even a postcard. I don't think its procrastination."

Monika made a face. "Brotherly love ….. Did you know he's living and working in Croydon?"

"No, I didn't," John replied. "Oddly, I'm not disinterested."

"He lodges near his work. I can't say I understand what he does although he described it. Something to do with aircraft. Wants to be a pilot. He seems happy. Loves the aerodrome and having aeroplanes buzzing around all the time."

"Goodness! I've heard *nothing* of it. From anyone. It shows how families drift apart. No doubt when *we* leave my family will be too busy to notice we've gone."

Monika nodded. "*Brothers*, often drift apart. Worse, I notice you've more or less lost touch with your father. And ….. talking of drifting, I've *more* news. Someone has moved in with your father and Eileen."

"What?" John exclaimed.

"Well, not moved in exactly. Your brother told me Eileen's father comes for long visits and uses your bedroom. He's in poor health. His family's spread out between Danzig and Konigsberg. He himself is continuously on the move. Instead of a permanent home he lives on trains and ships and in limousines. Often puts up in hotels. By having no fixed address he avoids paying tax. In recent years he's employed a full-time *chauffeur* who also stays in the hotels. Neil says there are agencies and direct interests throughout Europe. And in the USA and South America. Now the old man's too weak to manage it all, he's handing over to Eileen. She's working harder than ever and must be doing well because the interior decorations grow more extravagant each day."

"Another invader," John groaned. "What's his name?"

"Heinz Mandelsonn, Jewish I think."

"Now you mention it," John thought aloud, "I've a *distant* memory of mother saying the neighbours had connections with East Prussia …….. It was all foreign and odd…………" He stared at nothing. "God, I'm glad I have you, Monika, you're better than *all* of them."

"And …….." he changed the subject, "I've a small piece of news for you, godmother. I won a prize for best student design of the year."

Monika clasped her hands and beamed. "How *wonderful!* I *knew* you'd do well! *What* did you design?"

"A diving-board tower which could be built at lidos. It has an internal stairway leading to diving boards at different heights….. Apparently the judges thought it practical and unusual and liked the art deco lines."

"I didn't know you were interested in swimming," she said, surprised.

"I'm not. In fact I can't swim."

Monika leaned forward on an elbow. "You won a *prize* for *designing,*" she was intensely amused, "something to be used in *a sport* in which you have *no experience*?"

"Yes."

They laughed.

"Goodness!" she said, "it *delights* my curiosity. For me its all the more impressive because *you're* the designer! ...... Fact really *is* more interesting than fiction!"

Monika leaned back savouring John's achievement.

"Let's not linger today," she continued, dreamily. "Let's go out and *look* at the world. Let's Live!"

"Yes. Let's," he agreed. "But," he added, "I need a few minutes before we go. There's something which 'it is meet I should set down in my tables'."

"Oh, *no*," she protested, "this is no time to be writing in 'My Tables' *or* to be designing another diving board. I want you to engage with *me* today."

"In a way I *am* engaging with you because it's a poem about *you*. If I don't write it down*, this minute,* it'll be lost because it'll never return to me in exactly the way I'm thinking of it now."

"Oh, okay then," she agreed, "I'll be patient."

He moved crockery and cutlery aside and brushed away crumbs. From a pocket he extracted his notebook and began writing.

"I like watching you write," she said.

John did not comment. Opening 'My Tables' he turned to a new page.

DAYS AND NIGHTS

Denied the mystery of her nights
Shunning facile sleep
I keep all hours for Monika.

Monika my Musicke,
Monika my Verse,
Monika my hopes,
Monika my nights unrequited.

Never underestimate
The Damage
women and men
Do one another.

He finished writing and closed the notebook.

"May I read it?" she asked. "After all, if it's about me, in a way it's mine."

Doubtfully he opened the notebook to the page he had just finished and handed it to her. She read.

"Oh! ...." she said resignedly, "I cannot do better than my best."

"Nietzsche," John replied, "was right to expect The West would discard the false and unnecessary. Including dogma surrounding love and marriage. But what *you and I* have is *not* false. It's *real*. It's not some myth. Even if the world found some reason to criticise us, I believe in what we have."

John reached for the notebook but as she handed it back it opened at another page. "Let me *see!*" she said looking with interest and withholding the book.

"*Hey!*" John protested, those are 'My Tables.' The contents are private."

"*Oh no!*" Monika retorted, holding the notebook behind her back. "We have *no* secrets!"

"Oh," John conceded, "Okay then."

Monika turned to the page that had caught her attention and studied it. Amused, she began reading aloud.

"EXTRACTS FROM DEBATES OF THE VOLKSRAAD.

(Note: The Volksraad was the parliament of a Boer republic called The South African Republic. This land later became the Transvaal Colony. Now it is a province of the Union of South Africa.)

8 May 1889.

On the application of the Sheba G. M. Co. for permission to erect an aerial tram from the mine to the mill,

MR GROBLAAR asked whether an aerial tram was a balloon or whether it could fly through the air.

The only objection that the Chairman had to urge against granting the tram was that the Company had an English name, and that was not acceptable with so many Dutch ones available.

MR TALJAARD objected to the word 'participeeren' (participate) as not being Dutch, and to him unintelligible. 'I can't believe the word is Dutch; why have I never come across it in the Bible if it is?'

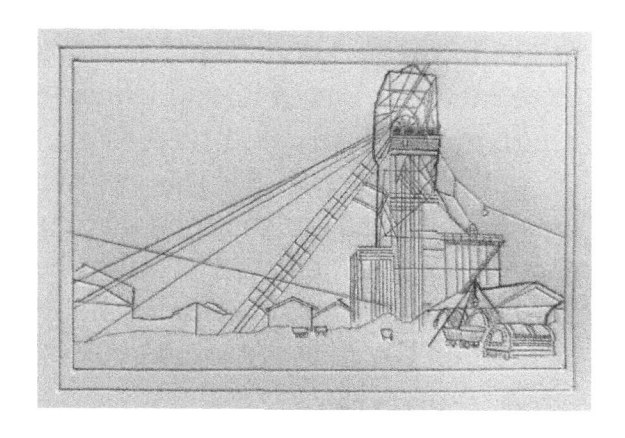

18 June 1889

On the application for a concession to treat tailings, (the residue after gold has been extracted from ore,)

MR TALJAARD wished to know if the words 'pyrites' and 'concentrates' could be translated into the Dutch language. He could not understand what it meant. He had gone to night-school as long as he had been in Pretoria, and even now he could not explain everything to his burghers. He thought it a shame that big hills should be made on the ground under which there might be big reefs, and which in future might be required for a market or outspan. He would support the recommendation on condition that the name of the quartz should be translated into Dutch, as there might be more in this than some imagined.

5 August 1891

CLAUSE TWENTY-THREE OF THE GOLD LAW.

THE PRESIDENT said that owners of properties had quite sufficient privileges already, and he did not want to give them more.

MR LOMBAARD said the Gold Fields wanted too much. The revenue from The Gold Fields was already less than the expenditure. He was of the opinion that the best course would be to let the Gold Fields go to the devil and look after themselves."

Monika looked in amusement at John as she turned another page. She continued to read aloud.

FIRST BRITISH OCCUPATION

"6 May 1892

Protracted discussion arose on the Postal Report, the Conservatives being opposed to erecting pillar-boxes in Pretoria on the ground that they were extravagant and effeminate.

OOM DYLE (MR TALJAARD) (Oom is Afrikaans for uncle.) said that he could not see why people wanted always to be writing letters. He wrote none himself."

Monika giggled. With an effort she silenced herself. She stole a glance at John hoping not to catch his eye. But he was laughing. Doing her best to ignore him she steeled herself and continued reading.

"In the days of his youth," Monika read on, "he had written a letter, and had not been afraid to travel fifty miles and more on horseback and by wagon to post it; and now people complained if they had to go one mile."

Monika broke off her reading. "And *this* is where you want *us* to *live*?"

"Yes," John replied. "We've agreed *ineffectual* government is *always* a good thing. I imagine we'd have little difficulty side-stepping such a government. In distant countries the administrations often have little control over their remote regions. Although……of course …. there's been an awful lot of water under the bridge since those minutes were taken. Anyway…the place sounds more interesting than England, don't you think? Still untamed. Quite wild actually."

"A far-off land," Monika mused, "which might become home?"

John took her up. "Yes. A land where the powers that be have learned the cost of war …. and discovered some enemies turn out to be nice people… The victor may write the history," he added, "but history cannot destroy the reasoning of the defeated. It can only hide that reasoning …… for a

while….. I wonder......" John's voice

trailed off.

Monika studied the youth. "I have to admit, having agreed, advocated even, migration to any place beyond the reach of the next European war, it would be silly of me to be surprised at fetching up in some outlandish place."

"We shall undertake our own Copernican Revolution," John said.

"From a European midden to an African mire ….. it's a step in the right direction, I suppose," Monika admitted.

"Maybe we should 'go far with little.' Maybe we should resign British citizenship and become citizens of some banana republic. That might work. Although …….. I'm not sure."

"A *banana* republic? I doubt it. Why a banana republic?" Monika asked. "The banana republics of South America aren't exactly *inviting* places, are they? They're kakistocracies. Actually, throughout history, most states have been mere banana republics by another name. Whether it was Hamlet's Denmark or Macbeth's Scotland or Orsino's Illyria. Or even Juliet's 'fair Verona'. The norm in such places is internal stranglehold and frontier war. Who wants to live like that?"

John frowned, "To be free, we must move to a country where government control is minimal. That rules out most of the civilised world. The intelligent response to industrialised warfare is to disappear. The individual must be not simply absent, but *completely unknown* to any national roll-call. I've long wondered whether it might be possible to develop a bureaucratic counter-balance to state control. Anyway, for the time being, probably the best way to exit a system is to ease out gradually, rather than make a big splash about leaving. It'll require steady effort to become less and less visible. Eventually officialdom will lose track of us. It might be achieved by a series of migrations through several banana republics rather than by one long-distance move."

Monika's forehead wrinkled. "Where would we keep *the money?* I'm having difficulty seeing how we'd *ever* put your plan into action."

"So am I," John admitted. "However, sometimes one has to do insane things to remain sane."

"For myself," Monika conjectured, "I begin to foresee perpetual summer. Like some rich Indian, I might find myself spending the English winters with you in some 'sunny clime', wherever you are, and returning to England for the joys of every English summer…… and to confirm my English residency. Sadly," she predicted, "periods of separation may be inevitable. Perhaps you might accept it's the one you can never fully have that remains always in your heart?"

"*You've said such things before*," John emphatically dismissed her thought. "But I believe we have the intelligence to *create* our happiness."

"Oh, I *can't* configure it all," Monika groaned. "Not at the moment." She returned to reading from John's 'Tables.'

"13 June 1892," she read.

"THE PRESIDENT said the reason why he did not subsidize some papers by giving them advertisements was that they did not defend the government. It was the rule everywhere to give advertisements to papers which supported the government."

"What's a kakistocracy?" John asked.

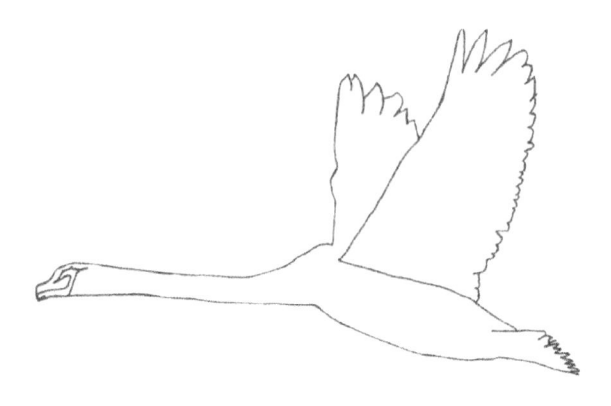

"Oh, my love," Monika closed the notebook, "Governments *do* what you don't want and *don't do* what you do want. I wish to be clear of their nonsense well before the sighs of old age engulf me. But, *for you,* when I think about *your* future, I know you must seek both the country and the work you find most inspiring. And *then,* you must travel there and start your work. And I shall follow where I can. But. In the meantime I have a request. Please keep collecting and writing down these pearls."

Tense groups of final-year students gathered in the familiar wood-panelled lobby. The last exam would begin in a few minutes. "Once more into the breach, dear friends," Paul Lundy voiced the fatigue and anxiety. "Oh, it's too late for that, boys," he added as John and Glen peered at a diagram in a technical book. "Put the book away. Let's talk about something else. It'll be better for our nerves and our results."

Glen shut the book. "You're right," he agreed. "What shall we talk about? It's hard to believe our student days are almost over. Everything's about to change. Who *knows* where each of us will be, a year from now."

"Probably at opposite ends of the earth," Paul said glumly.

"In my case, probably waiting right here," John said, "to re-sit this exam."

"For a prize-winner, you're one hell of a pessimist," Paul disagreed. "You *know* you'll do better than most of us."

"Maybe," John said, "but the money isn't in the bank yet. .... So, Glen," he changed the subject, "has it been a good three years?"

"Yes it has," Glen said wistfully. "I'm going to miss it, the learning and the logic, the challenges of the academic world. And the friends. *Especially* the friends. The Saturday nights and Sundays without John. Trying not to fall asleep in geology lectures. I really *don't* want to leave this place. But, strange to say," he opened out uncharacteristically, "do you know what I'll miss *most?* I'll miss breakfasting at Sonia's the most. And the walks we all took. The long summer picnics. The sublime company. Leaf and grass. Stone and stream. Sparkling waters."

John stared at Glen. "It's never been mentioned," he said, "but the affinity between you and Wendy is obvious. It's palpable."

"Has anyone ever even *seen* her husband?" Glen's frustration shot to the surface. "We've known her *three whole years*, watched Andrew grow from a baby to a small boy. We've breakfasted together, lunched together, taken train-rides, rambled.

It's been wonderful. Pastoral! We've been friends, a group of close friends, we speak about things *friends* speak about. Yet……. there's a veil, a realm into which I cannot see …… all that time I've not *once* seen Andrew's father nor has the matter of his existence ever come up in conversation. But. I think about it, because," he hesitated, "because … I'd never touch a married woman."

"How do you know she's married?" John asked.

"Because she has *a child*," Glen answered directly. He stared at John. "She *is married* isn't she?"

"I honestly don't know. She doesn't wear a ring."

"Poor Glen," Paul said softly. "When I was one of the gathering, I also noticed the bond. *Very* close …….

Maybe," he added slowly, "and I speak from some experience, we should've stuck with looking at text books rather than raising *this* subject just before the last exam."

"No …… I'm okay," Glen assured him. "But what do you think, John? Have you ever *seen* Wendy's husband? Has she spoken of him? *You're* there much of the time. What's going on? *How* can a man stay away from such a child and *such* a woman? Does he not *see* the perfection of which he is a part? Is he *blind?*"

"Perhaps he suffers a different blindness," John spoke in a flat voice. "I've no certainty, know little more than you. It's a closed book. Not ours to read. Andrew might be a love-child. Perhaps class distinction's at work? Perhaps it's class war blindness? Perhaps it's a supreme irony? …. A few years ago millions were denied children by The Great War. They *still* mourn their lost fertility. Yet now.

Today. Here's someone who was given the chance. But he wants no part."

John reflected for a moment.

"*Often* men who *long* for children are denied the privilege. .... Fate is *outrageous.*"

A double door opened. An invigilator wearing an academic cloak appeared.

"You may take your places for the examination," he called.

"So far as I know," John added, "in the time I've been there, the father hasn't been anywhere near. And I rather suspect they don't expect to see him again. He's never mentioned. I sense it's *not* a good idea to raise the subject. There's a photograph of a marine officer. In an album. Could've been

P&O perhaps. Of high rank, judging by the uniform."

"We'd better go in," Paul said, nodding towards the door.

"Time is *up!* Stop writing *now!*" the invigilator demanded in a strident voice. "Leave your answer papers on your desks. Ensure your name appears on *every* page of your answers. You may take the question paper with you. You must now *leave* the examination hall." The invigilator cast a beady eye on Paul and went up to his desk to insist by standing in front of the desk and looking down at Paul that he stop writing. "*Cease writing!*" he repeated.

Minutes later several clusters of students had gathered in the wide corridor leading to the lobby. In an intense hubbub they discussed the questions and compared their answers.

"Oh, I forgot *that*," one said in dismay.

"No but that was the answer expected for question four, *not question five*," insisted another.

"How did it go?" John asked Paul and Glen.

"Probably okay," Glen's reply was measured. "But ... let's not have a post-mortem."

"I only answered half the last question," Paul said gloomily. "And then that invigilator with the monocle made me stop writing."

"Did you manage to jot down a summary of what you still wanted to say?" Glen asked.

"More or less," Paul replied doubtfully.

"Oh, you'll be okay." Glen reasoned. "Examiners prefer quality to quantity. Gives them less to read. Sometimes they can see where you were going."

"Nothing to do now but wait and see," John accepted their fate. "I thought it a difficult paper, though." He paused. "Well boys, this is the end. The very end. Except for one last thing."

"And that is?" Paul asked.

"I told my aunt you'd both be in Exeter for a day or two before you went home, so she asked whether you'd like to join us at The Imperial for dinner tomorrow night?" John watched his friends closely for their reaction.

"*Good Heavens*, are we going to meet your mystical aunt at last?" Paul asked. "We can't miss *this*, Glen, can we?"

"We definitely *can't!*" Glen agreed, his vitality instantly relegating the stress of the exam room. "Golly, I look forward to *finally* meeting this lady who's taken up so much of your time!"

"Good, I'll see you both at The Imperial at six. Meet you in the foyer. And………Glen………."

"Yes?" Glen wondered what more was coming.

"I mentioned how Wendy dotes on you and so my aunt invited Wendy, Andrew and Sonia as well."

"Ah! ..... I wondered why," one of Glen's anxieties diminished, "Wendy seemed hesitant about one last breakfast together tomorrow ...... but I thought it was for .... other .... reasons."

"It *was*, as you say, for 'other reasons,'" John confirmed. "But The Imperial might be neutral ground for farewells."

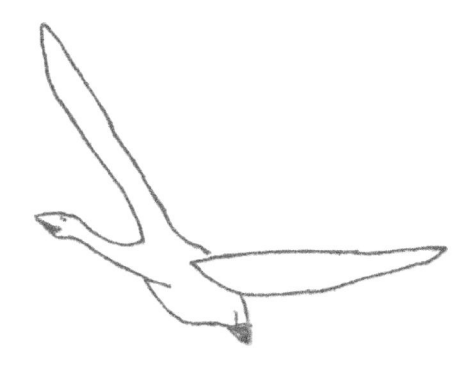

"Read to me again from 'My Tables'" Monika asked. It was the afternoon before the last supper.

John took out the notebook. "One day," he said as he paged through his writing, "I'm going to write a novel in which there are no heroes. Just a few good people mixed in with humanity."

"This is quite good," he handed Monika the notebook. "You do the reading. It's The Volksraad again."

In taking the notebook, Monika lost the page John had suggested.

"Heavens," she looked for the page again, "this notebook is almost *full* already. Even though your writing is *tiny*. It was only *a quarter* full last week." She squinted at the minute writing.

She found the page and began reading.

"21 July 1892.

MR ROOS said locusts were a plague, as in the days of King Pharoah, sent by God, and the country would assuredly be loaded with shame and obloquy if it tried to raise its hand against the mighty hand of the Almighty.

MESSRS DECLERQ and STEENKAMP spoke in the same train, quoting largely from the Scriptures.

THE CHAIRMAN related a true story of a man whose farm was always spared by the locusts, until one day he caused some to be killed. His farm was then devastated.

MR STOOP conjured the members not to constitute themselves terrestrial gods and oppose the Almighty.

MR LUCAS MEYER raised a storm by ridiculing the arguments of the former speakers, and comparing the locusts to beasts of prey which they destroyed.

MR LABUSCHAGNE was violent. He said the locusts were quite different from beasts of prey. They were a special plague sent by God for their sinfulness."

"Thank you," Monika returned the notebook. "Our life is bewilderingly different from theirs. We don't get plagues of locusts at Clear Sky. Or religion."

"We are quintessentially English," he agreed. "But what was once The South African Republic is now a self-ruling dominion. If we lived there we'd no longer be 'Uitlanders'. *And*, we'd be a long, *long* way from The Somme and Passchendale. Of course I realise officialdom can overcome geographical distances. But, we'll keep a few jumps ahead."

"What are Uitlanders?" she asked.
"'Outlanders,'" John translated. "In other words, foreigners."

"But I thought ….. I more or less understood ….. the aim to be the avoidance of *any* citizenship?" she questioned.

"Moving to South Africa would only be our first step towards nomadic life. By not belonging to any state, we'd belong to the world."

"But ….. *what* about *the money?*" Monika asked doubtfully.

John did not answer.

"In 'Seven Pillars of Wisdom'" Monika said softly, Lawrence described England as 'a land so long delivered that national freedom had become like water in our mouths, tasteless.' Quite a view, considering his viewpoint."

She returned to reading.

"26 July 1892.

MR DE BEER attacking the railways said they were already beginning to eat the bitter fruits of them. He was thinking of trekking to Damaraland, and his children would trek still further into the wilderness out of the reach of the iron horse."

Monika reflected for a moment. "Do the Boers find railways more acceptable these days, I wonder?"

"I've also wondered that. I gather the railways have gone from being an instrument of defeat during The Boer War to an organisation providing defeated Boers with employment."

"Where is Damaraland?" Monika asked.

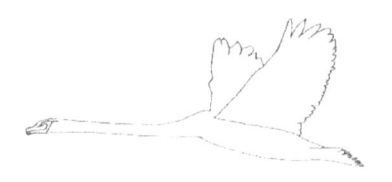

The middle-aged woman did not look her years. She held out an elegant hand.

"Very pleased to meet you," Paul said concealing his surprise at Monika's vivacity.

Sonia, Wendy and Andrew appeared. Andrew ran straight to John, clung to his leg, and demanded to be picked up.

"Andrew, meet Aunt Monika," John lifted the child for the introduction. Andrew half-buried his head in John's neck and peeped at Monika. Monika winked at him. He hid his head again. But when next he peeped, to everyone's surprise he held out his arms to Monika. Monika took the child with easy confidence. For the moment Andrew ignored his mother and grandmother. Proper introductions began. "So," Sonia gazed at John, "this is your aunt!"

"*And* godmother," Monika answered, obviously prepared for any turn in the conversation. "Let's have a drink before we eat." Easily the most striking person in the busy foyer, she led the way to the lounge.

"If," Paul whispered to Glen, "God hadn't made apples round, they wouldn't roll on the grass."

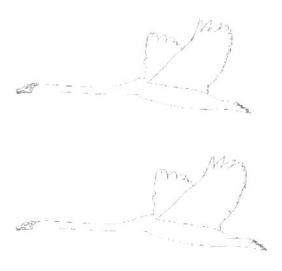

John studied Monika. It was their last breakfast at The Imperial. "You're *absolutely* sure you don't want a child?" he asked.

"*It will never be!* my boy!" she spoke with assurance. "But," her voice softened, "I'm glad you asked. Yet again. It proves your constancy. I promise I'll be your *platonic* friend. We'll share *much*. Whatever happens."

"You," he quoted, "'Render death and forever with each breathing.' You defeat mortality, refuse the unacceptable."

"Love, like pain," Monika replied, "is immeasurable. A friend is not necessarily an everyday person. Things you long for *will* come to you."

At the house of Mrs Sonia Snow, words now trivial, Glen consumed the flapjacks. Drinking chocolate wordlessly placed, was silently consumed. Andrew, receptive to the mood, played on the carpet, making woo-woo sounds for Glen's farewell gift, a toy steam engine. The steam engine, made of wood and painted sky-blue, was, if anything, bigger than its new owner.

Eventually, Glen pushed back his chair, went to the child, kissed the auburn curls, embraced Sonia quickly, embraced Wendy momentarily longer, said, "Thank you," and left.

"What shall I say?" John asked.

"There is nothing to say," Wendy stormed. She swept Andrew up and went to her room. Hearing her raised voice, Glen paused on his way down the path and half-turned. It was only a momentary pause. Soon he was out of sight. John stood up. He looked at the rucksack leaning against the doorframe. It bulged with his few belongings, ready to be shouldered. The Triumph Ricardo, prepared for the journey to Wimbledon, stood at the garden gate.

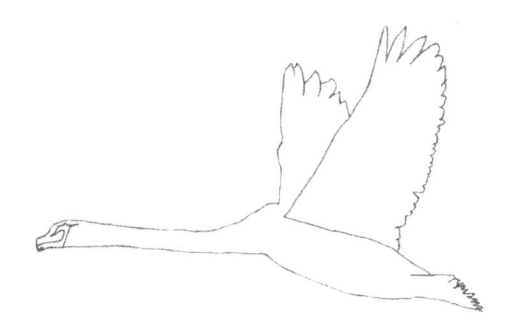

TO BE CONTINUED...

Printed in Great Britain
by Amazon